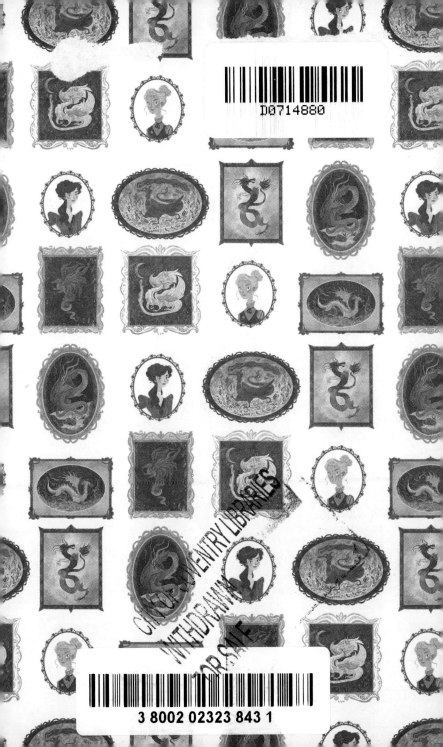

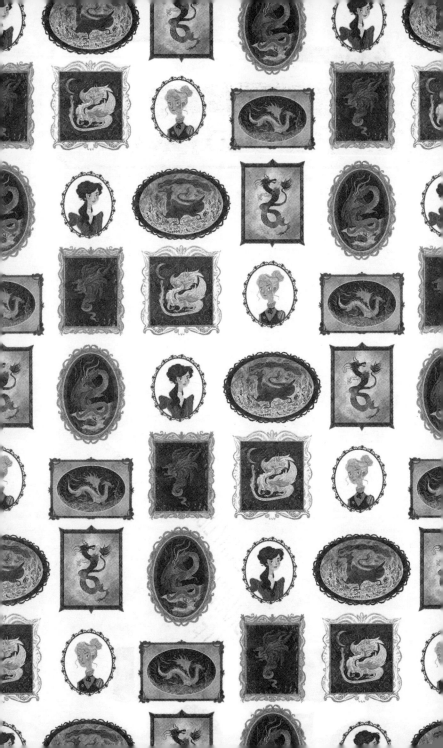

The Sinclair's Mysteries

THE PAINTED DRAGON

Also by Katherine Woodfine

The Sinclair's Mysteries

THE PAINTED DRAGON

KATHERINE WOODFINE

EGMONT

EGMONT
We bring stories to life

First published in Great Britain 2017
by Egmont UK Limited
The Yellow Building, 1 Nicholas Road, London W11 4AN

Copyright © Katherine Woodfine, 2017
Illustrations copyright © Karl James Mountford, 2017

ISBN 978 1 4052 8289 5

www.egmont.co.uk

A CIP catalogue record for this title is available from the British Library

Typeset by Avon DataSet Ltd, Bidford on Avon, Warwickshire
Printed and bound in Great Britain by the CPI Group

63961/1

For Jackie and Zoe,
for all the mysteries
and adventures

£1000 REWARD

STOLEN: Between 9.30 p.m. 29th and 7 a.m. 30th July, from the Picture Gallery, No. 5c Old Bond Street, the celebrated painting by Casselli, *The White Dragon*.

Size 22 inches by 14 inches, painted on board. The central image of the painting is a white dragon against a dark blue background patterned with ornate devices and crescent moon and star decorations in gold leaf.

*The above reward will be paid by **Messrs Doyle & Sons, 5c Old Bond Street**, to any person giving such information as will lead to the apprehension and conviction of the thief or thieves, and recovery of the painting.*

Information to Detective Inspector Worth, Criminal Investigation Department, New Scotland Yard, London S.W.

PART I
White Dragon

Visitors to London's Bond Street galleries should not miss works such as Casselli's The White Dragon, *currently on display at the Doyle Gallery. This exquisite example of Italian painting has a fascinating history, having been owned by many of the crowned heads of Europe, including Philip II of Spain and Catherine the Great . . .*

From Chapter IV of *A Traveller's Guide to London with 4 Maps and 15 Plans* by the Reverend Charles Blenkinsop, 1906 (from the library at Winter Hall)

CHAPTER ONE

October 1909

She wasn't sure exactly when she realised that someone was following her. The interview with Detective Worth had taken longer than she had expected, and when she stepped out on to the street, it was already dark. The daytime crowds had vanished and Piccadilly seemed unnaturally quiet, with only a few figures hurrying by in the rain, their faces hidden beneath their umbrellas.

In a different mood, she might have thought that the way the yellow light from the street lamps shimmered on the wet road was beautiful. She might have wondered about how she could paint the hazy reflections in the shop windows, or the headlamps glowing in the dark. But for once, she was not thinking about painting. She was too distracted by her conversation with Detective Worth to pay attention to anything around her.

The evening air was cold and dank: she found herself

shivering in spite of her good coat. She thought longingly of tea and a warm fire, but she dared not hurry home too quickly – the pavement was slick with water, and slippery with damp leaves. Instead, she slowly picked her way towards the underground railway station.

When she became aware of the man walking behind her, she had the feeling that he must have been there for some time. Lost in her thoughts, sounds muffled by the rain, she had not noticed his presence. Now, she glanced up into a darkened shop window and saw his reflection for a split second: a shadowy shape with square shoulders and the outline of a bowler hat. He was a few yards behind, keeping pace with her – she could hear the regular rhythm of his footsteps. All at once, she felt the creeping sensation that there were eyes fixed upon her back.

She shook herself. She was being stupid, she squashed down the impulse to turn around and look. He was probably just some ordinary man leaving his office late after a long day. To prove it to herself, she made up her mind to cross the road, feeling sure that he would not follow. *There*, she told herself triumphantly, as she made her way across the street, and on to the opposite pavement. She knew she had been imagining things. The interview with Detective Worth had rattled her, that was all.

For a few yards, she walked more easily. But a moment or two later, she heard it behind her again: the steady beat of footsteps. A chill swept over her. The man was still there.

She couldn't help glancing over her shoulder now, but in the darkness all she could see was the silhouette of the bowler hat moving towards her. Alarmed, she turned and crossed the street again: a minute later, the man followed. Her heart had begun to thump painfully in her chest, and her breaths were quick and sharp. She hurried on, as quickly as she dared, but the footsteps just seemed to grow louder. She went faster, panic rising, sure of nothing except that she must get away.

As she drew closer to the station, the street became busier, and she saw to her relief that a little crowd of people had gathered outside a brightly lit concert hall. The evening performance was about to start: there were motor cars and hansom cabs outside, and the sound of voices and music. She made her way into the crowd, weaving her way through the mass of people, and then out again, on to the street beyond, red-cheeked and panting – but alone.

Just around the corner was the entrance to the underground station. She hurried thankfully down the steps and out of the rain, her heart still bumping, fumbling for her ticket with shaking fingers. She made her way along the empty tiled passageway, moving more slowly now. The sudden quiet was a relief.

There was no one to be seen on the station platform –

not even a guard on duty. She stood alone at the edge of the platform, staring up at the big clock, watching the second hand flick forwards. Here, everything seemed ordinary again. The ticking of the clock, the tattered advertisements for Bird's Custard and Fry's Milk Chocolate, the colourful poster instructing her to 'Take the Two-Penny Tube and Avoid All Anxiety!' were soothing. Her breathing began to slow. She almost began to wonder if she had imagined the man in the bowler hat was following her, after all.

She felt more tired than ever now, and she stared down the tunnel into the darkness beyond, willing a train to appear. But even as she did so, she heard it again: the heavy, hollow thud of footsteps approaching along the empty platform.

There was no time to turn around; no time to think; no time even to scream. The man was behind her; she felt the scratch of his rough coat sleeve, the cold leather of his gloved hand, pressed hard and shiny across her mouth, silencing her before she could make a sound.

Even as she tried to twist away, she knew it was hopeless. The leather glove covering her mouth was scarlet: the bold cadmium red of her paintbox. It was the last thing she saw clearly before he pushed her. There was a clatter and a gasp, and she was falling through the air for a moment, landing on the train tracks with a sickening thump – then everything was still.

She groaned. Her eyelids fluttered. She was sprawled painfully across the tracks: she could feel the hard metal rail pressed against her side. Before her, the dark mouth of the railway tunnel yawned open, vast and pitch black. Then came a flicker of light ahead – and the scream of a train, rushing out of the tunnel towards her.

CHAPTER TWO

Three months earlier – July 1909

The letter was lying on the silver tray on the hall table when she came down to breakfast. A narrow white envelope with her name, *Miss Leonora Fitzgerald*, typed at the top. The sight of it made her mouth suddenly dry, and her chest squeeze tight. She knew there was only one thing it could be.

She reached for the envelope, but before she could take it, Vincent came swaggering into the hall, still doing up the studs on his collar. She snapped her hand back at once, but it was too late.

'What's this? A letter – for *you*?' He grabbed for it, but Leo shot out her hand and snatched it up first. She might not be very fast on her feet, but she had learned to be quick in other ways.

'That's mine,' she said. She began to back away, but Vincent stepped forwards and seized her wrist.

'I know what that is,' he said, his voice triumphant. 'That's a letter from your little art school, isn't it? Let me guess what it says: *Dear Miss Fitzgerald, We are terribly sorry but we can't accommodate talentless lady daubers at our establishment.*' He twisted her wrist hard and Leo gasped, but she kept clutching the letter. 'Shall we have a look and see?'

To her enormous relief, just then, she heard the jingling of the housekeeper's keys: Mrs Dawes was coming along the corridor towards them. Scowling, Vincent let go of her wrist, and Leo shoved the letter into the pocket of her frock, darting down the passage and away.

Breakfast didn't matter. She was too excited to eat anyway, and it wasn't as though her absence would bother anyone. Most days Father barely grunted at her from behind the newspaper; and as for Mother, she always took her breakfast in bed, then spent the morning relaxing in her room. The main thing was to get as far away from Vincent as fast as she could, so she could open her letter in peace.

She slipped around a corner where an old tapestry hung on the wall, woven with a design of lions and unicorns. Glancing quickly around her to be sure that Vincent hadn't followed, she lifted up one corner, revealing a small door in the wooden panelling. A moment later, she was through the door and into the narrow, stone-flagged passageway that lay beyond, letting the tapestry fall back across the door behind her.

Winter Hall was an enormous old mansion, rich in secret stairways, forgotten cubbyholes and concealed corridors that no one seemed to know or care about, except for Leo herself. These hidden passageways had fascinated her for as long as she could remember – but what's more, they came in useful. This wasn't the first time they'd helped her escape from her family.

Now, she made her way carefully along the crooked passage, and then up a skinny staircase. There was a hidden room tucked away at the top that was one of her favourite corners, which she had furnished with an old chair and an oil lamp. She kept her sketchbooks there, away from Vincent's prying eyes, as well as a collection of objects that were interesting to draw, but that Nanny would certainly say were 'nasty old rubbish': some pieces of wood twisted into interesting shapes; a couple of small animal skulls that she had picked up on her walks in the grounds; an abandoned bird's nest.

Safe at last, she felt able to take out her letter – a little crumpled from being stuffed into her pocket, but no less precious for that. She held it for a moment, weighing it in her hands, and then she ripped it open, drawing out the thin sheet of typed paper inside.

Dear Miss Fitzgerald,

I am writing on behalf of The Spencer Institute of Fine Art to offer you a place for the academic year commencing September 1909. As a first-year student

The rest of the words swam in front of Leo's eyes: she couldn't take them in. She sank into the chair, the letter fluttering down into her lap. She had actually done it. She had been accepted to the best art school in London!

It still seemed incredible that she had been allowed to apply to the Spencer at all. She had been begging Father and Mother to let her go to art school for more than a year, but they had barely listened, while Vincent had scoffed and jeered. Even Nanny had said 'nonsense' and that such places weren't for young ladies. If it hadn't been for Lady Tremayne, she doubted that any of them would ever have taken her seriously.

Lady Tremayne was Leo's godmother. She was an old friend of Mother's, a wealthy widow who lived in London, and who seemed to Leo to be unimaginably sophisticated. She always wore wonderful clothes: gracefully draped dresses in jewel colours; embroidered silk shawls; gorgeously feathered hats. She talked of the writers and musicians she knew; the art galleries and concert halls she visited; the new books she had read.

Lady Tremayne was the only one who cared about Leo's passion for drawing. Mother just said 'very nice, dear' in a bored voice; while Nanny grumbled that the charcoal marks on her muslin frock were dreadful to get out, and suggested she might like to learn some nice embroidery stitches instead. But Lady Tremayne was different. On her all-too-rare visits to Winter Hall, she always asked to see Leo's sketchbooks; and sometimes she even brought her presents – pencils, a new drawing book with lovely paper inside, once a little set of watercolour paints in a neat leather case.

It was to Lady Tremayne that Leo had been able to pour out her dream of going to a London art school. She longed to learn from proper teachers; to work in a real artist's studio; and perhaps most of all, to see London and explore its wonderful galleries and museums. She had told all this to her godmother, who had promised she would try to help.

Leo was not supposed to have heard Lady Tremayne's conversation with Mother, but it had been an easy thing to listen in from the secret passage with its discreet 'peephole' that ran behind the boudoir sitting room. Leo knew that she ought not to eavesdrop on other people's conversations, but any sense of guilt she might have felt was swept away, as she realised what her mother was saying in her high, whining voice.

'The truth is that I haven't the slightest idea *what* to do with her. She's so sulky and difficult. I never had any of these troubles with Helen!'

'Leo's growing up,' came Lady Tremayne's voice, clearer and deeper. 'She needs something to occupy her. Don't forget, at her age, Helen was busy planning her coming-out ball, and getting ready for her first Season.'

'But whatever am I to occupy her *with*?' Leo's mother demanded, sounding even more petulant than usual. 'A London Season is quite out of the question for her. If she was a different sort of girl, I suppose I might have taken her abroad with me this autumn, but Horace doesn't like her to be *on show*. She doesn't care for society, and she doesn't take any interest in anything except fiddling around with pencils and paint – and this preposterous idea of going to a London art school.'

'It's more than just fiddling, Lucy. Leo has a real talent – I've always thought so. Are you so sure that art school is out of the question for her?'

'Really, Viola! *Art school*! She couldn't possibly – what

13

would people think? We couldn't allow her just to racket about London, all by herself!'

Mother's voice was shocked, but Lady Tremayne laughed. When she spoke, her voice was warm and amused: 'Oh, Lucy, don't be so old-fashioned! She'd be far too busy for any racketing. Why, at the Spencer Institute they have drawing classes every day, and then there are lectures and museum visits. It would be good for Leo to have that sort of occupation, and to meet other young people who share her interests. Far better than moping around here, with only her old nanny for company.'

Mother sighed heavily. 'I suppose you're right. Something ought to be arranged. Perhaps a good finishing school might help to rub off her corners?'

Leo's heart sank to her stomach, but Lady Tremayne had not given up. 'Finishing school?' she repeated. 'I hardly think dancing and deportment are going to be of any use to Leo! Art school would be a much better use of her time. They are perfectly respectable places these days – after all, the Duke of Roehampton's sister went to the Spencer, you know.'

Leo smiled to herself in the dark. Her mother's sudden little sound of interest and approval did not surprise her in the least. 'Oh! Did she really? I had no idea!'

Evidently aware she had an advantage, Lady Tremayne continued: 'So, you see, it couldn't possibly do Leo any harm. Perhaps she may become a little more *unconventional*, but that doesn't really matter, does it? After, all, it's not as if . . .'

Her godmother's voice trailed away, but Leo could have finished the sentence for her. *It's not as if she will marry.* Suddenly feeling that she didn't want to hear any more, Leo turned away from the peephole.

Marriage was something that girls from a good family were supposed to do. It was all that was expected of them – to look pretty, to be charming, and then to eventually marry a 'suitable young man' and produce lots of children, exactly like her perfect older sister Helen had done.

But Leo knew that no 'suitable young man' would ever want to marry her. For one thing, she was not in the least bit pretty. Pretty girls had curls and rosy cheeks and dimples; Leo was thin and pale, and her hair hung straight and smooth, refusing to curl in spite of Nanny's best efforts. Pretty girls dressed in dainty gowns with ribbons and lace trimmings. Leo preferred plain things: as a child she had always looked enviously at Vincent's clothes, admiring the smart cut of his velvet jackets, the shiny leather of his riding boots. Mother had been horrified when she had asked why she couldn't dress like her brother, and Nanny had told her to 'hold her tongue' and to 'act like a little lady'.

What's more, she knew she wasn't charming. She had always spent so much time alone that she never seemed to know what to say to people. Then, just before her eighth birthday, she had been ill, and that had changed everything. The long illness had confined her to bed for months. One of her legs had been badly affected; they had thought she might never walk again but she had been determined, and at last she had been able to manage with the help of a crutch. It was this, of course, that Lady Tremayne was referring to. Far more important than being pretty, marriageable young ladies were expected to be perfectly healthy: as glossy and energetic as prize racehorses. They could not possibly have what Mother referred to, in a hushed voice, as an *affliction*.

But it had been when she was ill in bed that Leo's drawing had really begun. She had spent hours drawing anything and everything she could see: Nanny, the medicine bottles by the window, the view of leafless trees outside. When she had at last been able to hobble about the house, she had amused herself by exploring the long passageways, opening doors on neglected rooms and drawing what she found there. She spent hours contemplating strange old oil paintings, sketching the shapes of Chinese vases and marble statuettes, copying the intricate patterns of old carpets, and later painting her own careful imitations of the portraits of her Fitzgerald ancestors.

'Of course, the Spencer is very competitive,' Leo heard Lady Tremayne say, as she turned back to the peephole.

'It's the finest school in the country – they take only the very best.'

'She probably wouldn't even be able to win a place,' said Mother, more comfortably. 'I suppose I'll speak to Horace about it – perhaps he may consent to her writing to them. But really, Viola, that's quite enough about the matter. I'm longing to hear about your trip to Vienna – is the opera as splendid as they say?'

Now, remembering this, Leo felt hot inside. She knew that Mother had never believed she stood even the slightest chance of winning a place at the Spencer – but she had been accepted. *The Spencer Institute of Fine Art*, she read again, tracing her fingers along the shape of the letterhead, and murmuring the words to herself as though they were a magic spell. She couldn't wait to write to Lady Tremayne to tell her the news.

But first, she had work to do. She grabbed her crutch and pulled herself to her feet. She was going to the Spencer, and she would not let Mother or Father or anyone else stand in her way. Moving quickly, she made her way along the secret passageway, and back out into the corridor. So much for Mother's relaxing breakfast in bed, she thought grimly. She pushed open the door to Mother's bedroom. 'Mother!' she announced. 'The Spencer Institute have written – and I've got in!'

CHAPTER THREE

September 1909

It was a wet afternoon in London, and on Piccadilly Circus the windows of Sinclair's seemed to shimmer. The city's most famous department store spilled out golden light on to the dull grey street. The people hurrying by under their umbrellas were unable to resist pausing for a moment to look at the glittering displays of glorious autumn fashions in the store window, or to peep through the grand entrance, at the throng of elegant shoppers within.

Up the steps and through the great doors, the store was warm and inviting, delicious with the fragrance of chocolate and warm caramel that drifted from the Confectionery Department. Customers were dawdling in the Book Department, flicking through the latest novels, or dallying in Ladies' Fashions, taking their time to choose exactly the right fur tippet, or silk umbrella. Meanwhile, others simply luxuriated in the thick softness of the carpets and the glitter of the chandeliers, watching the people go by. There was always something – or someone – to watch, at Sinclair's.

No one knew that better than Sophie Taylor. But that afternoon, she was walking swiftly past the store windows, without even a glance at the brightness within. Today, she was quite unrecognisable as a smart salesgirl from the Millinery Department. Her fair hair was windblown; her frock was streaked with mud; her buttoned boots were dirty; and her thin coat did little to keep off the rain. In fact, she was so bedraggled that one or two people looked askance as she came through the door of Lyons Corner House. Holding her head high, and ignoring their curious glances, she dripped over to a corner table for two, spread with a white cloth and laid for tea. She dropped down into a chair with relief.

'Tea, miss?' asked the waitress hovering at her elbow.

Sophie looked up at her with a rueful smile as she peeled off her sodden gloves. 'Yes please,' she said. 'Tea would be heavenly.'

The pot was almost empty when the door opened again, and a young lady hurried in. She was tall and striking, snug in a smart blue coat with a velvet trim. A matching hat with a crest of feathers was pinned at a dashing angle upon her shiny dark hair. She was not dressed expensively, nor in the very latest fashion, yet there was something about her appearance that made the tea-shop customers sit up straighter in their chairs. Suddenly, an ordinary wet afternoon seemed tinged with a sparkle of glamour.

One lady nudged her friend, and nodded in the newcomer's direction. Surely she was the young actress whose photograph they had seen in the *Daily Picture*? A young man who considered himself quite an expert on the theatre whispered to his companions: 'That's Lilian Rose! She plays Arabella in *The Inheritance*. Last week's *Theatrical News* called her a rising star!'

The only one who did not look at all taken aback was the girl sipping tea by herself at the corner table. The other customers exchanged surprised glances as the young actress hurried straight over to Sophie.

'Oh, Sophie – I'm so sorry that I didn't make it to Mrs Long's!' exclaimed Lil, as she flopped down into the chair opposite her friend. 'My dress fitting took an *age*!'

'That's the third appointment you've missed this week, you know,' said Sophie, decidedly unimpressed.

'I say – it isn't really, is it?' Lil looked stricken with guilt. 'Gosh! I really am most awfully sorry. Let me buy you some cake to make it up to you. Excuse me, waitress!'

After ordering more tea and a quantity of cake that would have fed a large family, Lil turned back to her friend and looked so beseechingly at her across the table that Sophie couldn't help smiling. It was impossible to be annoyed with Lil for long.

'Tell me all about what happened at Mrs Long's. Did you find the stolen cat?' Lil took in Sophie's appearance for the first time. 'I say, you do look rather . . . er . . . *damp*.'

Sophie laughed. 'I hadn't noticed,' she joked. 'I found the cat all right. It hadn't been stolen at all! It was stuck up a tree at the bottom of Mrs Long's garden. I had a terrible job getting it down.' She pushed up the sleeve of her blouse to reveal several long, angry-looking red scratches.

'Golly!' exclaimed Lil. 'But I suppose Mrs Long was awfully grateful?'

'For about two minutes. Then she gave me a long lecture about how, in *her* day, girls didn't clamber about in trees like monkeys, and it wasn't really *ladylike behaviour*.'

'Oh, I say!' exclaimed Lil. 'That's a bit much! I'm surprised you didn't ask her if she'd rather you left her silly old cat up there for good!'

The cakes arrived just then, as well as a plate of hot buttered toast. The girls were both hungry and helped themselves before Sophie carried on: 'Then there was the matter of the bill. Since it turned out that Snowy hadn't actually been stolen after all, Mrs Long thought this would suffice.' She drew a sixpence out of her pocket and put it on the table, where it made a sad clinking sound against the milk jug.

'*Sixpence!*' exploded Lil. 'What awful cheek!'

'Well, I suppose it will pay for the tea,' said Sophie. 'Though perhaps not my laundry bill.'

'We certainly shan't be taking on any more cases from *her* in future. We're worth a whole lot more than sixpence,' said Lil indignantly. Then she giggled too. 'The Sixpenny Detectives. Gosh, that sounds rather like the title of a tale in one of Billy's story-papers!'

It was true that since they had solved the mystery of the famous Mr Sinclair's stolen jewels – and then exposed one of London's most dangerous criminals in the strange affair of the Jewelled Moth – Sophie and Lil had gained something of a reputation for their detective skills. Barely a week now went by without someone turning up with a new 'case' for them to solve. At first, they had been rather astonished that so many people wanted their help – but they had soon grown used to these enquiries.

To begin with, it had been thrilling. Sophie had felt full of pride when they helped people, even when the mysteries they solved were as small and ordinary as helping to find an old watch that had been a family heirloom, or reuniting a young lady with a long-lost grandmama. The small fees they had earned had helped to supplement the slim wages she earned as a salesgirl at Sinclair's, but more than that, there had been the fun of teaming up with Lil – and often with their friends, Billy and Joe, too – to pit their wits against each new puzzle.

Just recently though, she had begun to feel a little less excited by their 'cases'. It had been a while since they had had a really interesting mystery to solve – getting lost cats out of trees didn't pose the same kind of challenge. And since winning a role in a fashionable new play in a West End theatre, Lil had far less time for detective work. She was always very busy flitting from rehearsals to dress fittings to appointments with photographers, and Sophie missed her. Solving mysteries without Lil was harder work – but what mattered more, it wasn't nearly as much fun.

'I'm just glad I didn't see anyone from Sinclair's while I was going down the street like this,' she said now. 'I was dreading bumping into Mrs Milton – I'm rather in her bad books at the moment,' she went on, referring to the Head Buyer of the Millinery Department.

'Nonsense!' exclaimed Lil. 'I don't believe that for a second. Mrs Milton thinks you're wonderful.'

Sophie shrugged. Perhaps that had been true a few months ago, but recently she knew that she had been distracted, and her standards had slipped. The truth was that being a salesgirl wasn't always very interesting, and there was rarely much chance for her to use her brain. She knew she ought to be grateful to have work at all, never mind a job somewhere as marvellous as Sinclair's, but after everything that had happened to her over the past few months, it was difficult to go back to simply selling hats.

But it wasn't as though she had any other options. Sophie was all alone in the world, and she had to work to support herself. She might sometimes have fanciful thoughts about becoming a professional detective, but she knew they were just that – fancies.

She opened her mouth to begin to try and explain some of this to Lil, but before she had said anything, she noticed that her friend was staring over her shoulder at someone who had just come through the door of the tea shop.

'Lil? Are you all right?'

But Lil didn't seem to hear her. Her mouth had fallen open as though she had seen a ghost.

'What on earth are you doing here?'

CHAPTER FOUR

Sophie turned around to see that a tall, dark-haired young man was striding energetically over to their table. To her surprise, she realised that he looked slightly familiar.

'What do you *think* I'm doing here?' asked the newcomer in a cheerful voice. 'I'm looking for you, of course! I went to the theatre to find you and the fellow at the stage door said you'd be here.'

Lil's expression shifted from shocked to delighted. 'Well, I like that!' she exclaimed, as the young man gave her a hearty hug – much to the interest of the people sitting around them, who all began whispering and nudging each other. 'I hope he doesn't go giving out my whereabouts to any old Stage Door Johnny!'

'Ah, but I'm hardly any old Stage Door Johnny now, am I? Don't pretend you aren't pleased to see me!' Releasing Lil, the young man turned to Sophie and held out a hand. 'How do you do? Awfully sorry to barge in like this. I'm Lil's brother – Jonathan Rose. Most people call me Jack.'

'Jack, this is my dearest friend, Sophie Taylor!' exclaimed Lil. 'You remember – I've told you simply heaps about her.'

Jack grinned at her, and Sophie found herself smiling back. It would be hard not to, she thought. His resemblance to Lil was obvious – and it wasn't only that they looked alike, but he had exactly the same kind of bouncy confidence. She found herself blushing as she shook his hand, and rather wishing she didn't look so very muddy and bedraggled.

'I'm delighted to meet you,' he said heartily. 'I say – do you mind if I join you?'

A moment later, he had conjured a chair for himself seemingly out of nowhere, and was sitting down beside them, while a waitress hurried over with an extra cup. 'But whatever are you doing here?' Lil was saying, pushing the plate of cakes towards her brother. 'I thought you were back in Oxford. Isn't term about to start?'

Jack leaned back in his chair. For the first time since his arrival, Sophie detected that he was suddenly a little less sure of himself. 'Well . . .' he began, in a rather-too-casual voice. 'The thing is that I've given it up. Quite a lark, don't you think?'

'*Given it up* . . . ?' Lil's voice was incredulous. 'Whatever do you mean?'

'I'm not going back.'

'*What?* But . . . but . . . you can't!'

Jack's voice was impatient now. 'Of course I can! You

know that Oxford isn't for me. Oh, I had a jolly enough time there last year – and I met some decent fellows – but it was just like school all over again. I don't want to study law and spend all my days in a stuffy office, like Father – any more than you want to stay at home and go to tea parties with Mother. You *know* what I want to do.'

Lil nodded. 'You want to go to art school and be a painter. But you know Father's never going to agree to that He's always talking about what a wonderful asset you'll be to the firm. Jack, do be serious. You can't leave Oxford – he'll never allow it.'

'Too late, I'm afraid. It's already done.'

Lil looked astounded. 'But . . . how? What will you do now?' she demanded.

'That's the good part,' Jack said, all at once looking more cheerful. 'I've got myself a place at the Spencer Institute. It's one of the top art schools in London. All the best painters have studied there. I met a couple of the professors in the spring and showed them some of my work – and the long and short of it is, they offered me a scholarship, so here I am! Classes there began this week.'

'Well – that's marvellous, of course, but you never said a word about *any* of this,' said Lil, still staring at him, her cake quite forgotten now. 'Where are you staying? What about Mother and Father? Have you told them?'

'No, and I don't plan to,' said Jack, rather more stiffly.

'There's a fellow at my college in Oxford who is going to forward on my mail to my new digs – I've found a studio in Bloomsbury not too far from the art school that I can afford on my allowance. There's no sense in telling the Aged Parents – it would only upset them. If I can get myself established and get my work noticed – *then* I'll tell them. They'll see I'm serious and that this is going to work.'

'Oh golly,' said Lil, her eyes round. 'Father will have forty fits! He still hasn't got over me leaving home to go on the stage – and now you'll be throwing away all their plans for you too. And you *know* what they think of artists. Why, they're practically worse than actresses!'

Jack gave a rueful grin. 'I know. Awful bohemians who live in dirty attics and lead scandalous lives. Sounds rather fun to me. But that's exactly why I'm not going to tell them. Do say you'll keep the secret.'

'You *know* I will,' said Lil. 'But I do think this is all a ghastly mess. Don't blame me when it all blows up in your face.'

Jack relaxed in his chair. 'Thank you,' he said. Then he turned to Sophie. 'I say, I'm sorry to have interrupted your tea with all this family business, Miss Taylor.'

'Don't be so prim and proper, Jack. Her name's Sophie,' said Lil.

'And what do you do, Sophie?' he asked. 'Are you an actress too?'

28

'Oh no,' said Sophie hurriedly. 'I work at Sinclair's – I'm a salesgirl.'

'Yes, but much more importantly than that, she solves mysteries,' chimed in Lil. 'We both do. But Sophie is an awfully good detective. Fearfully brainy. You *know* that. I wrote to you and told you all about our adventures.'

Jack laughed. 'Oh yes, I remember. Stolen jewels – and criminal gangs – and being chased over rooftops. It all sounded awfully exciting!' He sounded as if he hadn't believed a word of it, Sophie thought; although she supposed she couldn't really blame him. After all, some of the things that had happened to them over the last few months had seemed almost too extraordinary to be real.

'I do hope you won't mind if I tag along on a few of your adventures, now that I'm in town,' Jack continued. 'In fact, what are you both doing this evening? I'm heading to the Café Royal – why don't you come too?'

'The Café Royal? You mean that place on Regent Street?' asked Lil.

'That's right – it's where all the artists spend their evenings. It's awfully good fun. You can spot all sorts of famous painters there. It's exactly the sort of place that the Aged Parents would loathe and despise.'

'Oh, I wish I could – but we've got a show tonight,' said Lil, her eyes gleaming at this description.

'Sophie? What about you?'

'I can't tonight,' said Sophie hurriedly. 'Maybe another time.' Enticing as the idea of spending an evening with Lil's charming – and she had to admit, rather handsome – older brother might be, staying up late was hardly an option. She was working at Sinclair's first thing the next morning, and she knew she had to be there early if she was going to get back into Mrs Milton's good graces.

'I'll hold you to that,' said Jack, flashing her a grin.

He and Lil left soon after that. Sophie watched them as they headed down the street arm in arm, their dark heads close together as they chattered. She turned away in the direction of her lodgings, pulling her coat close around her, feeling very cold and tired now. It had been fun to meet Lil's brother, but she couldn't help feeling disappointed that his appearance had meant that her rare tête-à-tête with her friend had been over almost before it had begun.

As she passed the newsboy on the corner, she handed him a penny in exchange for a copy of the evening paper. 'Good evening to you, miss,' he said, touching his cap just as he did every day. Reading the newspaper each morning and evening had become part of Sophie's daily routine. She told the others that it was because it was useful for their detective work, but the real reason was that she was looking for news of the man called 'the Baron'.

The Baron was never very far from Sophie's thoughts. She and Lil and the others had tangled with him twice now, and she found herself thinking back, as she often did, to the last moments she had seen him, on the edge of the docks in the East End, just before he had made his escape. *I daresay we'll meet again*, he had said. *For now, adieu.*

Lil and the others believed that the Baron was gone, and wouldn't come back. Mr McDermott had told them that Scotland Yard believed he had fled the country. But Sophie knew that his photograph had been sent to police detectives across Europe, and as far afield as America – and as yet, no one had seen so much as a glimpse of him. She couldn't feel so confident that they had really seen the last of the Baron, and that he was really gone from their lives for good. She knew he wouldn't forget that they had been the ones to blow apart his false identity.

Now, she let herself into the lodging house, and trudged up the staircase to her room. Once inside, she took off her muddy boots and hung up her wet things, then settled down in the easy chair, spreading the newspaper across her lap.

Across from where she sat, on the wall above her dressing table, she had carefully pinned up the few pieces of information she had managed to gather so far about the Baron, including several newspaper cuttings from his time posing in the guise of Lord Beaucastle. In the very centre was the mysterious photograph that Mr McDermott had given to her after it had been taken from Beaucastle's study.

It showed Sophie's parents standing either side of the Baron, with the words *Cairo, 1890* inscribed on the back.

This had been her most unexpected – and disconcerting – discovery of all. She had learned that the Baron had known her parents, and that they had perhaps once even been friends.

Now, as usual, she carefully combed the evening paper for anything that might be relevant. A jeweller's shop in Knightsbridge had been robbed, but only a few cheap trinkets had been taken, and the burglar's methods were much too crude for the Baron. She flicked to the society pages where, for a brief moment, she paused to grin at a photograph of some friends who had helped them in their last adventure. Two smart young men and a young lady were sitting in an expensive new motor car, the picture captioned: *Young gentlemen-about-town Mr Devereaux and Mr Pendleton take the Honourable Phyllis Woodhouse out for a spin!* But there was no mention anywhere of Lord Beaucastle. The summer's scandal was all but forgotten.

But if London society had moved on, Sophie had not. The photograph of her parents still niggled at her. She had to know the truth – how had her parents known the Baron? And worse still, could he really have had some part to play in her papa's sudden death? She had spent hours searching through what little she had left that had belonged to her papa – a few letters and papers, a couple of postcards, but nothing that indicated even the smallest connection with the Baron, or with Cairo. If she hadn't had the photograph, she would never have believed it could be true.

She had stopped talking to the others about the Baron. She knew that they were tired of hearing about him. 'He's *gone*, Sophie,' Lil had said to her in frustration. 'I understand why you keep coming back to him, I do. But not everything is always going to be about him. Besides, I don't know about anyone else, but I'm jolly well ready to forget all about the Baron. That horrible man wanted to blow up Sinclair's with us in it – he would have killed us if he had had the chance – and he made life a misery for all those people in the East End. But the Baron's Boys are safely under lock and key in prison, and the Baron is gone, and I'm grateful for that.'

Now, Sophie gazed for the hundredth time at her collection of cuttings and photographs, trying to make sense of them. As she did so, she twisted her necklace between her fingers. It was a string of green beads, one of the very few things she possessed that had belonged to her Mama. She might have stopped talking about the Baron to Lil and the others, but she knew she would never stop thinking about him. She was determined to find out the truth – even if that was a secret she would have to keep to herself.

She opened her drawer and took out a sheet of writing paper and her pen and ink. There was still one person she

33

could try contacting who might just know something about her papa being stationed in Egypt – her old governess. She knew that Miss Pennyfeather had gone to India to work as a governess for an English family out there. A letter would take a long time to reach her, but it had to be worth a try. *Dear Miss Pennyfeather . . .* she began to write.

CHAPTER FIVE

Leo stared at the paper in front of her, trying to concentrate on the whisper of soft pencil, the scratch of charcoal. Around her, the hum of voices began to blur and fade. Here in the Antiques Room there was always such a clamour of noise. It made her realise how accustomed she had become to quiet and stillness.

The students and their easels were ringed around the edge of the big airy space, scattered among the plaster casts of classical statues that gave the Antiques Room its name. The first years spent most of each day drawing here, and would continue to do so until they were considered to have mastered the basics of line and form.

Today, Leo had chosen to draw the figure of a nymph with a garland of evergreen: it reminded her a little of one of the statues in the Long Passage at Winter Hall that she had drawn many times before. The familiarity was comforting. The action of her pencil against the paper, outlining the figure's shape in smooth strokes, felt soothing.

Nothing else felt familiar in the least. Everything here seemed so strange. The big room was stark and bare as a blank canvas: the white-painted walls, the white shapes of the plaster casts, the white shirtsleeves of the young man drawing next to her. She sensed her chest tightening as she looked around at the circle of strangers. After a week, she was beginning to recognise a few of their faces: the young man with the carefully waxed moustache; the tall girl with the habit of chewing the ends of her pencils; the red-haired, freckled boy with the Northern accent. While she drew, she stole glances at them under her eyelashes. She liked looking at their clothes: that young lady's flowing Liberty-print smock; that young man's paisley-patterned scarf.

Most often, her eyes were drawn to the girl who wore the most striking and unusual outfits, usually including brightly coloured stockings and odd shoes – today one was red and the other blue. She had a wild tangle of curls and a pouting mouth, and Leo had heard the boy next to her call her Connie. Leo would have liked to draw her. Now, as Leo glanced over at her again, Connie noticed her watching and frowned. Blushing, Leo let her eyes fall back to her work.

Behind her, she sensed the presence of the drawing master – the professor, she should call him. He paused, glancing over her shoulder, and she froze for a moment. Even she knew that Professor Jarvis was legendary here at the Spencer. She had already seen the way he spoke to some of the students – firing out sarcastic criticisms: 'Is that the best you can do?' 'And you say you want to be an *artist?*' Or sometimes, worst of all, merely a short snort of contempt. Now, he was standing right behind her, so close that she caught a whiff of his tobacco. Not knowing what to do, she kept on drawing, taking refuge in the familiarity of the pencil between her fingers. A moment later, she realised that he had moved on.

'I say, you got off lightly!' said the young man next to her. 'Didn't you hear what he said to me yesterday?'

She had – it had not been very complimentary – but the young man's good humour did not appear to have been dented. 'They say he's like that all the time,' he went on cheerfully. 'He must think you're good if you escaped a tongue-lashing.'

Leo kept on drawing, not knowing what to say. She had noticed the young man before: the way he drew, in bold, assertive strokes, pausing to stand back and survey his work every now and again. The way he swept back his dark hair and tossed a charming smile to the giggling girls across the room, before turning to make a friendly aside to his neighbour. She had never seen anyone so sure of himself in her life.

'Gosh, you are good, aren't you?' he went on, coming closer to look at her drawing. 'I wish I could draw half as well as you.'

Suddenly, she felt annoyed. 'Well, maybe you should spend more time concentrating on your own work instead of looking at mine,' she said. But as soon as the words were out of her mouth, she wished them back again. This was exactly the sort of thing that made Mother say that she was *awkward* and *difficult*. Why couldn't she just be friendly, like everyone else?

To her surprise, the young man didn't seem at all offended. Instead he laughed – a cheerful, hooting laugh, as though she had made a particularly good joke. 'Yes I suppose you're right there!' he exclaimed. 'Probably if I did, old Jarvis wouldn't have told me yesterday that my fellow's arms looked more like strings of sausages. I can see you're going to be a good influence on me.' He stuck out a hand, and Leo stared at it in surprise. 'I'm Jonathan Rose, but everyone calls me Jack. What's your name?'

She managed to shake his hand, and mumble her own name, her face still burning with embarrassment at her own rudeness.

'Leo – I say, that's quite a name. Short for Leonora? Oh, I see. Well, Leo it is. You're new too, aren't you?'

She nodded, surprised to discover that he was one of the first-year students. He seemed so comfortable, it was like he'd been at the Spencer for years.

'Seen him?' asked Jack, gesturing over to the corner of the room with his pencil, where Leo now noticed an older gentleman, with a sweep of iron-grey hair, deep in conversation with Professor Jarvis. He was elegantly dressed in a smart, tailored suit, in contrast to the professor, who was rather shabby in tweeds. Leo noticed that the gentleman's silk waistcoat was finely patterned, his shoes were polished to a gleaming shine and he wore a gold lapel pin and an elaborate fob watch and chain.

'Who is he?' she found herself asking.

'That's Randolph Lyle,' explained Jack in a low voice. 'He's one of the most important art collectors in London. But, more than that, he likes to support young artists while they're getting started. They say he comes here every year looking for new talent.'

Leo looked over at Mr Lyle, intrigued.

'Maybe that's what he's doing here now,' suggested Jack, but before he could say anything else, Professor Jarvis began to speak, and the lively chatter around them fell silent. 'This is Mr Randolph Lyle,' he said in his usual brusque tone. 'As I hope at least some of you are aware, Mr Lyle is a leading expert on fine art. He has come to speak to you today about an important opportunity. Mr Lyle.'

Mr Lyle gave a small bow. 'Thank you, Professor. I am delighted to be here to speak to you all this morning. I am honoured to be a supporter of this wonderful institution. I have the greatest interest in our next generation of artists – and am proud to say that in my own small way, I have been able to help some of them on their path to success.' He spoke with an elaborate politeness that contrasted starkly with the professor's short, sardonic way of speaking. He looked – and sounded – very much like one of the guests that Leo might have encountered in her mother's drawing room. 'Today, as you have heard, I am here to talk to you about one such opportunity. I am currently working on a new exhibition, which will be opening in London in a few weeks' time.

'This exhibition is to be unlike any other: a combination of the very best new works and some of the masterpieces that have helped to inspire them. I have been lucky enough to have the chance to bring together a selection of old masters, including some works from my own collection, but also some treasures which have been most generously lent to me by a number of London's museums, galleries and private collections.

'The venue for this exhibition will also be rather unusual: it will take place at Sinclair's, the department store on Piccadilly. As some of you may be aware, I have a passionate interest in bringing our best works of art to what we may call "the masses" – and Mr Sinclair happily shares that enthusiasm. Together, we are mounting what I hope will be one of the most exciting exhibitions of this year, in the store's beautiful Exhibition Hall. Admission will be free to the general public, and we hope that many hundreds will attend.

'Today, I am here to seek out some volunteers to assist me with putting together the exhibition. We will require a considerable commitment of time from our volunteers over the next few weeks, but in return I can promise a most interesting, instructive, and I hope also enjoyable experience.'

He smiled around the room again, and Professor Jarvis stepped in. 'If you'd like to take part, come and see me this afternoon. And now, carry on with your work.'

The room instantly came to life again, with a rustle of papers and a hubbub of voices.

'Well, I'm definitely volunteering,' Leo heard Connie say decidedly. 'I don't care how much work it is – you'd be mad to miss the chance to get to know Randolph Lyle!'

'It would be splendid to see all those paintings up close,' said the freckled boy beside her enthusiastically.

Connie snorted. 'That's not the half of it. Lyle can make or break artists' careers, you know. He's terribly well connected.'

'Well, I don't know about that, but I reckon this exhibition sounds a lark,' said the boy in a good-natured voice. He turned around. 'What about you, Jack?'

'I'm all for it,' said Jack. 'Let's go and put our names down on Jarvis's list. Coming, Leo?'

Leo glanced back over at Mr Lyle, who was already moving through the room, looking keenly over students' shoulders to see their drawings. The exhibition sounded interesting, but all the same, she thought it would be a mistake to get involved. It was enough just getting used to being here in London without anything else to think about. Most of all, she wanted to *work* – and helping with this exhibition would mean time away from that.

'No thank you,' she said awkwardly. 'I don't think so.'

'Well, it's your funeral,' said Connie, shrugging. She grabbed Jack's sleeve. 'Come on, let's go before all the places are filled.'

Leo turned back to her drawing as they all hurried across the room, putting the exhibition out of her mind. She was so absorbed in her work that she barely noticed anything else until the session ended, and she became conscious that the others were beginning to pack up, chattering in little groups as they tidied drawings into portfolios.

'Time to go,' said Jack, with a grin, as he shrugged on his jacket. 'I say, a few of us are off to the Café Royal later – want to come along?'

Leo looked up, uncertainly. Beyond, she could see that Connie and the other boy were waiting for Jack expectantly, their satchels slung over their shoulders.

'Don't tell me you've never heard of the Café Royal?' Jack asked in surprise. 'It's where all the artists go!'

'Oh, do come on, Jack,' said Connie, impatiently.

'She doesn't even know what the Café Royal *is* – of course she doesn't want to come.'

Leo felt her face flush redder, and she shrugged and shook her head. But Jack was still smiling at her. 'Well, if you change your mind, you'll know where we are,' he said, before he was swept away, at the centre of a gabbling crowd of art students.

Leo was left alone to slowly pack up her things. She always seemed to be lagging behind the other students: she was used to being the last to leave, but today, as she made her way towards the door, Professor Jarvis stopped her.

'Miss Fitzgerald – you haven't put your name down to help with the exhibition.'

Leo shook her head. He stared at her for a moment, and she explained: 'I just want to focus on my work for now, Professor.'

Professor Jarvis gave her a searching look. 'Mr Lyle has seen your work, and he has requested you particularly for the exhibition, Miss Fitzgerald,' he said in his dry voice. 'If he takes an interest in your career, it could be very beneficial for you. I'd suggest you take him up on his offer.'

CHAPTER SIX

On London's bustling Piccadilly Circus, Mr Randolph Lyle's new exhibition was also creating plenty of conversation. In the Sinclair's offices, high above the shop, it was time for an afternoon tea break, and the clerks were all discussing the news of the exhibition, while Billy Parker, the office boy, poured out tea from the big pot.

Billy felt that he was quite a different fellow to the one he had been just six months ago, when he had first started working at Sinclair's. He had grown up a lot. For one thing, he was taller now: his mum had been complaining about how often she had to let down the sleeves of his jackets, and the legs of his trousers. The Billy of six months ago wouldn't have cared very much if his trousers were too short or not – nor would he have taken such satisfaction in doing each little job carefully, whether it was preparing the clerks' afternoon tea, or filing Miss Atwood's papers. But, perhaps the biggest change of all was that these days, just like his uncle Sid, who was the Head Doorman,

Billy felt proud to say that he worked for London's finest department store.

Working for Miss Atwood, Mr Sinclair's own private secretary, suited him in a way that being a shop porter never had. He enjoyed the company of the other clerks and the lively bustle of the offices. He liked seeing all the people who came and went – Miss Atwood, Mr Betteredge the store manager, and of course, the great Mr Sinclair, 'the Captain' himself. He liked being the person responsible for delivering the Captain's own messages, in their special yellow envelopes, to staff around the store – tipping his hat to the salesgirls and waving a greeting to his old friends the porters as he went. He liked being able to answer the telephone, saying in his most important-sounding voice: 'Good afternoon, Miss Atwood's office, this is Parker speaking, how may I assist you?'

One of his favourite tasks was taking Mr Sinclair's pug, Lucky, on her daily outing to the park. The little dog had become almost as much of a London celebrity as the Captain himself, and attracted a good deal of attention on these walks, especially on cold days, when she was wearing the little blue jacket with the gold Sinclair's livery that had been specially made for her.

Most of all though, what Billy loved about being an office boy was being among the first to hear all the latest news. Billy loved a good story – and there always seemed to be something exciting to talk about at Sinclair's. Today was no exception.

'Some of those paintings are worth a mint. Proper famous, they are,' reported O'Donnell, as he helped himself to another biscuit.

'When do they arrive?' asked Billy.

'Next week,' said Crawley. 'Mr Lyle is going to oversee the hanging of them himself. Very particular, he is. He's bringing some art students to help him.'

'Well, he'll not have much help from the Captain, that's for sure,' contributed Davies. 'He'll be away for another fortnight yet – that's what Betteredge says.'

'But he's been gone weeks already! Whatever's he up to?'

'He's out in the country. Buying himself a new house, or so I hear. Some great big country pile.'

'That's right,' said Crawley, nodding authoritatively. 'He's setting himself up as a proper English gent. His valet told me he's getting kitted out with tweeds and shooting outfits and the like.'

'It'll take more than a bit of tweed to make the Captain into an Englishman,' said O'Donnell. 'He's a Yankee through and through!'

'I heard that's why he's so keen to pal up with this Mr Lyle. He thinks Lyle might be able to recommend him for membership of Wyvern House,' offered Davies.

'Wyvern House! He'll be lucky,' said O'Donnell sagely.

'What's Wyvern House?' asked Billy at once.

'One of the oldest gentlemen's clubs in London. It's in the City, near the Bank of England. Very exclusive. You have to be invited to join, and they only take people from the best old families – lords and so forth,' explained Crawley.

'As a matter of fact, I had a great-uncle that was a member there once,' announced O'Donnell.

'Ha! You had a great-uncle who cleaned the boots there once, more like!' spluttered Davies.

A bit of good-natured bickering broke out, until Miss Atwood stepped out of her office, and said in her clipped voice: 'Back to work, if you please, gentlemen!'

Reluctantly, they put down their cups and headed back to their desks. But O'Donnell paused to throw the latest edition of the paper in Billy's direction: 'Here, you can read a bit more about the exhibition in there, if you like.'

'What on earth's a "Living Painting?"' asked Joe, as Billy broke off to turn the page.

It was the end of another day at Sinclair's, and the four of them were sitting cosily in the hayloft, the rain pattering gently on the roof above them. Until recently they had spent many lunches and tea breaks in this way, and had often met here after the store had closed to

SINCLAIR AND LYLE BRING FINE ART TO LONDON'S SHOPPERS

TWO OF LONDON'S MOST PRE-EMINENT GENTLEMEN HAVE JOINED FORCES FOR AN IMPRESSIVE NEW EXHIBITION OF FINE ART AT SINCLAIR'S DEPARTMENT STORE. *Arranged by Mr Randolph Lyle, the exhibition will bring together works by famed old masters as well as those of some of today's most admired painters.*

Visitors will be excited by a rare opportunity to view such works as *The Green Dragon* by Casselli, loaned to the exhibition from the Royal Collection, with the permission of His Majesty the King.

Other notable paintings include *The Duchess* by Gainsborough, loaned by the Duke of Roehampton, and a new portrait of Lady Hamilton by the Russian artist Max Kamensky, inspired by this famous work.

The exhibition will open with a gala evening at Sinclair's, which London's most eminent artists are expected to attend. Mr Sinclair will also be marking the exhibition with an extraordinary new spectacle in the windows of the store – a series of 'Living Paintings' featuring Sinclair's famous mannequins . . .

Story continued on page 6

 ## SUFFRAGETTES AT WESTMINSTER

– Mrs St James leads a march on Parliament – Page 8

discuss whatever mystery they were solving. Billy had even taken to referring to it as 'Detective HQ'.

In the past weeks though, these gatherings had become rather less regular. The others always seemed to be so busy, Sophie thought now. Lil was occupied with her new play; Miss Atwood kept Billy busy in the office; and even Joe was immersed in life at the stable-yard. More than once, Sophie had found herself spending her tea breaks here alone, with only the day's newspaper for company.

But today was different – they were all together again, crunching apples and passing around a bag of toffees that Sophie had bought with some of her hard-earned sixpence from Mrs Long. Sophie felt delighted to see the others. It was quite like old times.

'The Living Paintings are Mr Sinclair's latest big idea,' explained Lil now. 'A sort of stunt to help advertise the exhibition. Claudine is going to recreate a series of famous paintings in the store windows, and we the mannequins – are going to pose there, just as if we were the people in the paintings.'

'I thought you weren't working as a mannequin very much now, because of the play,' said Billy in surprise.

'I'm not really, but I couldn't resist this. It sounds like such splendid fun – and Mr Mountville at the theatre thinks it might be good publicity too. I'm to be a painting by Fragonard, and I wear a marvellous frilly pink dress, and

I sit on a swing surrounded by flowers.'

Winking at the other two, Joe said in a very serious voice: 'Blimey, Lil. You're awful grand these days. I'm surprised you think we're fit to associate with someone so fancy.'

Lil gave a little squeak of indignation, and threw the bag of toffees at him, spilling sweets everywhere. Joe coolly picked one up, unwrapped it and popped it into his mouth, making them all laugh.

Sophie laughed too. She sometimes found it hard to believe that the Joe they knew today – still rather quiet, but with a very definite sense of humour – was the same down-and-out vagabond she had once seen begging outside Sinclair's. Now, he was respected for his skill with the horses, and well liked by all the stable boys. Since the summer, he had been spending more time with Lil: indeed, the girls in the Millinery Department had all been asking Sophie if it was true that they were 'walking out' together.

Sophie had just shrugged and smiled. 'They're friends. We all are.'

'Well, you wouldn't catch me stepping out with a groom,' said assistant buyer, Edith, in a superior tone. 'I like a man with *prospects*.'

'Didn't that Joe used to be some kind of a *criminal?*' chimed in Ellie.

'Ooh, he never did!' squeaked Minnie, delighted by this titbit of scandal.

Sophie had given her short shrift, but now she found herself wondering what Jack would make of his sister spending time with a young man who, it was true, had once been part of the Baron's gang. Joe was her friend and she trusted him as much as she would trust anyone in the world. But how might someone who didn't know him feel about his history?

It was Joe who asked now: 'When do we get to meet this famous brother of yours?'

Lil smiled at him, and shrugged. 'I haven't the faintest,' she said. 'He was awfully keen to meet you all when he arrived – wasn't he, Sophie? But I haven't heard a peep out of him for days. I suppose he must be busy at the art school.'

Outside, a clock began to strike the hour. 'I think I'd better go,' said Billy, getting to his feet reluctantly. 'Uncle Sid's coming round for tea tonight and Mum wanted me to stop at the grocer's on the way home.'

'Me too,' said Joe. 'The Gaffer'll be wondering where I've got to.'

'And I have to get to the theatre,' added Lil. 'Why don't you walk with me?' she suggested to Sophie. 'It's on your way home anyway.'

Sophie was only too glad to agree. She didn't want their

jolly afternoon to be over just yet – and besides, Jack's sudden arrival meant that she and Lil hadn't had as much chance to talk over tea as she had hoped. But as they walked towards the theatre, she soon found that her brother was the only thing that Lil wanted to talk about.

'I still can't believe Jack has left Oxford! He's always been such a goody two shoes. You know, top of the class at school, captain of the cricket team and all that sort of rot.' She paused for a moment. 'But then, in another way, I suppose I'm not exactly surprised. He's always had a way of managing to do exactly what he wants.'

As they approached the theatre, she was still talking: 'I am awfully glad he's here though. It will be fun to have him in London – just as long as he isn't going to start trying to boss me around. I just hope he likes Joe – and Billy, of course – and that they like him.' She looked over at Sophie slyly. 'He liked *you* awfully, you know.'

'Oh don't be silly.'

'He did! He told me so on the way home.'

By now they had come to the stage door, and it was time to say goodbye. Sophie turned away from the bright lights of the theatre, and headed back towards her lodgings. For once though, she didn't stop to collect the evening paper. She wasn't thinking about the Baron – instead, she found herself turning over the memory of meeting Jack Rose. Surely he couldn't *really* have told Lil that he liked her awfully? In spite of her long day in the Millinery Department, she found that she was, after all, feeling rather cheerful.

PART II
Green Dragon

Painted in approximately 1455, this rare surviving painting from Casselli's 'Dragon Sequence' was given as a wedding gift to Her Majesty Queen Victoria by her husband, Prince Albert of Saxe-Coburg and Gotha . . .

Randolph Lyle, *A Short History of the Royal Art Collection*, 1901 (from the Spencer Institute Library)

CHAPTER SEVEN

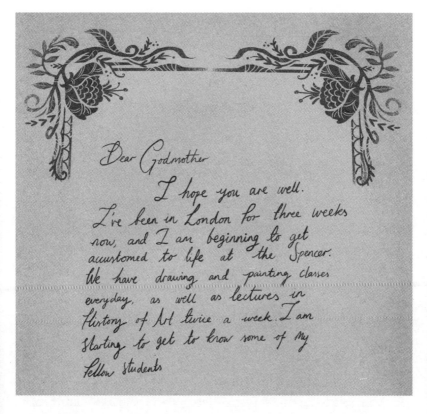

Dear Godmother

I hope you are well.
I've been in London for three weeks
now, and I am beginning to get
accustomed to life at the Spencer.
We have drawing and painting classes
everyday, as well as lectures in
History of Art twice a week. I am
starting to get to know some of my
fellow students

Leo paused for a moment, tapping her pen against the
paper, unsure what else to say. She had never been very
good at putting her feelings into words. What's more, it was

difficult to express just how different her life was here in London to life at Winter Hall. There, the fields and woods would be golden now and the air would smell of smoke and moss. Father and Vincent would be preparing for their autumn shooting parties; Mother would be packing for her European trip.

But autumn meant something else to Leo now. It meant rain on the windows of the Antiques Room in the morning; afternoons spent walking through the grand spaces of London's museums and galleries; or sitting on the rug before the fire in her room, reading art history books. It meant a jumble of raincoats and umbrellas on the underground railway in the morning; the steamed-up windows of the little tea shop around the corner from the Spencer, where all the art students went to eat buns and drink endless cups of coffee.

Most of all, it meant long hours working in the studio. Professor Jarvis was working them all hard, but no matter how much effort she put in, Leo had found she could not entirely avoid the sharp edge of his tongue. His criticisms rattled her confidence – and she knew she was not the only one. A couple of the other first-year students had left, unable to handle Professor Jarvis's acid remarks – but Leo kept on, refusing to allow herself to be discouraged.

When she was not at the Spencer, she was usually at Sinclair's. Working on Mr Lyle's exhibition had turned out to be more enjoyable than she had expected. It was fun spending time at the beautiful department store, but most of all, she had been surprised by how much she had enjoyed the chance to get to know the other students who were helping with the exhibition – particularly Jack Rose and the red-haired, freckled boy, Tom Smith, who everyone called 'Smitty' – though she was still a little intimidated by their outspoken friend, Connie.

Now, as she sat in her room, hesitating over how to say all this in her letter to Lady Tremayne, she found herself thinking back to that afternoon, when Mr Lyle had gathered the students together to see the unwrapping of one of the most important works in the exhibition. It had arrived earlier that day in a large motor van painted with the Royal crest, and two men had personally delivered it into Mr Lyle's own hands. Usually Mr Lyle allowed the students to unwrap the paintings, wearing white cotton gloves and following his careful instructions, but this particular painting was so precious that he was handling it himself. The students had gathered in a semi-circle around him to watch.

'This is one of the finest pieces in our exhibition,' he had said, as he gently removed the painting from its wrappings, and stared at it reverently. 'I am honoured to say that His Majesty the King himself has lent us this magnificent piece.'

Leo gazed at the painting. It was much smaller than the other paintings in the exhibition, but it at once drew the eye towards it. It was clear that it was extremely old, and yet its colours were lush and intense. The central image was of a dragon, with a twisting, serpent-like body, magnificent wings and a coiling tail. It was painted in a rich emerald green that almost seemed to glow. The background was elaborately patterned with gold leaf in ornate symbols and tiny stars. Mr Lyle stared at it for a long moment before he spoke.

'Is anyone familiar with this painting?' he asked. 'Yes – Miss Clifton?'

'It's part of the Casselli Dragon sequence,' offered Connie.

'Very good,' said Mr Lyle. 'That is quite right. This is in fact one of only two surviving paintings from the sequence thought to have been painted by the artist Benedetto Casselli in Venice in 1455. Miss Clifton, do you know how many paintings we believe there were originally?'

'Was it seven?' said Connie, a little less confidently this time.

'Oh *excellent*, Miss Clifton,' said Mr Lyle, and Connie looked pleased. 'Yes. Seven paintings, each one depicting a dragon. This is known as *The Green Dragon*. I am sorry to tell you that the other surviving painting, *The White Dragon*, was most unfortunately stolen from Mr Doyle's gallery on

Bond Street earlier this year.'

'That's right – I read about it in the paper!' exclaimed Smitty. 'Wasn't it supposed to be worth a whole lot of money?'

Lyle looked troubled. 'The loss of such a treasure is a genuine tragedy. I only hope that the thieves have the sense to take proper care of the painting, and that it will find its way back into the hands of a museum or a reputable collector before long.

'Now, as Mr Smith rightly points out, both *The White Dragon* and *The Green Dragon* are of great value. They are particularly special because of their unusual subject matter. There has been much speculation about why the artist chose the dragon as his subject, though of course it is unlikely we will ever know for sure. But the painting is a fine example of the craftsmanship of the time. I urge you to study it closely.

'Moving onwards, I am very pleased to say that I have another special painting to show you today, painted by Gainsborough around 1780. This is on loan from a dear friend of mine, the Duke of Roehampton, and it also has a remarkable history. Mr Rose, if you could perhaps assist me? This one is large and rather heavy . . . thank you . . .'

The others crowded around the new picture eagerly, but Leo found that she couldn't stop staring at the painted dragon. The dragon's expression was inscrutable: at first glance it appeared proud and regal; in another light, cruel and fierce. But the more Leo looked at it, the more she began to feel that it looked in fact a little sad. How was it possible that a painter so many hundreds of years before had managed to capture so many shades of feeling in just a few blobs of paint?

She was still contemplating it when Mr Lyle's little lecture on Gainsborough came to an end, and the students dispersed. After a moment, he came over to her, and she started back, afraid that he was going to accuse her of not paying attention to what he had been saying. But then she saw to her surprise that he was smiling. Up close, she was struck all over again by his exquisite clothing: the fine silk of his necktie, the immaculate kid gloves, the richly spiced scent of the unusual cologne he wore, the gleaming gold pin at his lapel.

'It's Miss Fitzgerald, isn't it? Professor Jarvis was kind enough to show me a little of your work. I was particularly impressed by some of the copies you had made of one or two very fine pieces – I believe I recognised them from the collection at Winter Hall.'

Leo looked up, astonished. 'You've been there?' she blurted out.

'Oh, not for a few years. But I remember some of the paintings well. Let me see – I believe it was your grandfather,

Lord Charles, who was the keen collector?'

Leo was suddenly embarrassed. She should have known that a man like Mr Lyle was bound to know her family.

But Mr Lyle was still talking: 'I wonder if perhaps growing up surrounded by such a collection has helped to set you on this path,' he said thoughtfully. 'Your copies of some of those pictures are very skilful. Your version of that little Watteau portrait, for example – an ambitious choice, but cleverly done. I have a soft spot for Watteau, myself, I must confess. You have a real gift, Miss Fitzgerald.'

Leo looked back at him, surprised and pleased. None of the guests in her mother's drawing room – with the exception, of course, of Lady Tremayne – had ever spoken to her like this. 'I don't know if I should spend so much time copying other people's work,' she managed to stammer out. 'Professor Jarvis says it's important that I find my own style, instead of imitating others.'

'My goodness, my dear, no!' Mr Lyle looked so horrified that Leo almost wanted to laugh in spite of herself. 'There is no finer way to learn than to apprentice yourself to the masters. Professor Jarvis is quite right, of course – all artists need to find their own style eventually, but for now, I would encourage you to keep on this path.'

Leo felt a sudden sense of relief. She knew that she did not have the same bold, definite style as some of the other students. Smitty, for example, painted enormous scenes of jagged abstract industrial landscapes; while Connie's taste seemed to be for large portraits in odd colours, which exposed every blemish of her subjects' faces. Leo knew that she did not want to do work like that herself, but what exactly she did want to paint, she was not quite sure.

'Why not see what you can do with *The Green Dragon*?' said Mr Lyle now, gesturing to the painting before them. 'It won't be easy, but it would be a good challenge for you.'

Leo gaped at him. 'But . . . I could never recreate that! It's so old, and I don't have any of the materials. All that gold leaf . . .'

Lyle waved a gloved hand, as if to say all that was nothing. 'Oh, I can supply you with the materials you would need. Think of it as a little commission. Perhaps, if it turns out well, I might buy it as a memento of this exhibition? I'd rather like to be able to say I purchased your first piece.'

She had still been stumbling over her thanks as he had strolled away to talk to Connie about the Gainsborough. Now, remembering this, Leo set aside the letter to her godmother. Instead, she took out one of her art history books, which she felt quite sure contained a picture of *The Green Dragon*.

Back at Sinclair's, there were preparations of a different kind under way for Mr Lyle's new exhibition. In their dressing room, some of the mannequins had gathered to try on their costumes for the Living Paintings display, and to practise their poses. As Sophie made her way along the passage, carrying a couple of hat-boxes, she could hear the voice of Claudine, the window-dresser, emanating loudly from within:

'Rosa! You're supposed to be a painting – you ought to be *still*. Don't twitch like that! And Millie – you're meant to be Joan of Arc. A *saint* – a *heroine* – not a music-hall dancer!'

Sophie grinned to herself as she went on her way down the stairs into the Entrance Hall. At the foot of the stairs, she was rather surprised to see none other than Mr McDermott standing waiting, accompanied by a large dog. Mr McDermott was the private detective who worked for Mr Sinclair – and sometimes, Sophie knew, with Scotland Yard too. The thin, grey-haired man might not look much like it, but she knew he was a clever detective – and someone that she could rely on. She suspected that he might be one of the only people to understand how she felt about the Baron, although they had never really talked about it.

'Miss Taylor – good afternoon,' he said, tipping his hat

to her as she approached.

Sophie smiled back a greeting, and stopped to give the big Alsatian a pat. 'He's lovely – is he yours?'

'He's a she – and as a matter of fact, she belongs to Sinclair's department store,' explained the detective. Sophie frowned, confused, and McDermott went on: 'She's a guard dog. Trained by Scotland Yard's experts.'

'A guard dog?' repeated Sophie in surprise, looking down at the dog who was currently licking her hand in an extremely affectionate manner.

'Oh she's friendly as anything now, but when she's on duty, it's a different matter. Mr Sinclair has asked me to put some additional security measures in place while the exhibition is here,' McDermott explained.

'Is that because of the burglary that happened before, when the Clockwork Sparrow was stolen?' Sophie asked. She knew that Mr McDermott had already helped to improve the store's security after the last break-in. The windows of the Exhibition Hall had been specially reinforced, and there was always a nightwatchman patrolling the store after closing time.

'It's just an extra precaution,' said McDermott in a neutral voice. 'Mr Sinclair didn't want anyone to be concerned about the safety of the paintings.'

Just then, the Head Porter Sid Parker appeared, accompanied, rather unexpectedly, by Joe.

'This the dog, then, is it?' asked Sid briskly.

'Her name's Daisy,' said Mr McDermott. Daisy yawned, lolling out a long pink tongue.

'*Daisy?*' repeated Sid. 'What kind of a name is that?'

McDermott laughed. 'It doesn't matter what her name is – she's an excellent guard dog. She'll bark the place down if she gets so much as a sniff of an intruder.'

Sid grunted. 'Well, Joe here is going to take charge of her for the time being. He'll look after her at the stables, and then we'll station her on guard with the nightwatchman outside the Hall each night.'

'Just the man for the job,' said McDermott, nodding approvingly. 'Make sure you introduce her to the nightwatchman, and anyone else who might be in the store at night. Otherwise she'll bark if she hears them coming.'

As he said this, the detective reached out to hand over Daisy's lead, but before Joe could take a firm hold of it, Billy appeared through the main door, leading Lucky. As usual, several passing customers turned at once to coo and fuss over the adorable little creature.

Lucky, however, had other ideas. Glimpsing Daisy across the Entrance Hall, she made up her mind that here was a new friend. To everyone's astonishment, she shot suddenly away, jerking her lead right out of Billy's hand. As Lucky bounded towards Daisy, she leapt forwards too, barking joyously, obviously quite delighted by this new game.

Several customers turned to stare at the commotion.

'Good heavens!' sniffed a fashionable lady.

'Bless my soul!' exclaimed a gentleman in a top hat.

'Oh blimey,' said Uncle Sid. 'Joe – Billy – get after them – *quickly!*'

Joe and Billy chased after the two dogs, who were now racing up the main staircase – and Mr McDermott and Sid hurried along behind. After a moment's pause, Sophie followed too. She knew she had already been far too long delivering the hat-boxes, but she simply couldn't resist seeing what would happen next.

The two dogs bounded up the stairs, darting between customers, upsetting a porter with a stack of boxes, and knocking over a small boy in a sailor suit, who began to wail. One lady screamed as the big Alsatian rushed past her, but luckily Uncle Sid was there in the nick of time, with a steadying arm. 'I do apologise most sincerely for this unseemly disturbance, madam,' Sophie heard him saying in his politest voice.

Upstairs, the dogs had dashed along the gallery and through the Stationery Department, sending sheets of writing paper and envelopes fluttering up into the air, and upsetting several bottles of coloured ink. They paid no heed to the chaos left behind them, or the angry salesman shaking his fist as they raced on, with Billy and Joe hot on their heels. They careened past the door to the Library, where a very serious-looking lady looked over her spectacles in great disapproval. Finally, they shot through the door into the mannequins' dressing room: for a moment, the two boys hesitated on the threshold, and looked at each other.

'We're not allowed to go in *there!*' hissed Billy.

A cacophony of shrieks and yells were heard from within, followed by the distinct sound of tearing fabric, and then Claudine screaming something very angry in French.

'I think we better had,' said Joe, and dived through the door, Billy following close behind him.

Some more yells were heard, but a few moments later, the two boys emerged, each leading a dog, and looking rather red in the face. Daisy had the remains of what looked like a long white glove in her mouth. Lucky, meanwhile, was dragging a chewed feather boa behind her, wriggling her little tail in pride and delight.

Sophie couldn't help laughing. McDermott was grinning too. Behind them, Uncle Sid panted along the passageway, having safely delivered the swooning lady to the Ladies' Lounge, smoothed down the rumpled feelings of the salesman in the Stationery Department, and extended all due apologies to the lady in the library.

Now, he wiped his forehead with his handkerchief, shaking his head.

'Crikey,' he gasped. 'I reckon this art business is a whole lot more trouble than it's worth.'

CHAPTER EIGHT

For the next two weeks, Leo thought of nothing but *The Green Dragon*. When they were working on the exhibition at Sinclair's, she often found herself neglecting what she was supposed to be doing to come back to examine the original picture. Before long she felt as though she knew each individual brush mark.

'There are *other* paintings in this exhibition, you know,' said Connie, rolling her eyes.

'Never mind her,' whispered Smitty to Leo. 'She's just annoyed because Lyle hasn't offered to buy any of *her* paintings.'

But Leo didn't mind what Connie said. She was happy to have a project of her own, and she poured her whole heart into it. She spent hours in the Spencer Library researching the artist, Benedetto Casselli, and worked until late in the studio, experimenting with the materials that Mr Lyle had provided.

I am beginning to enjoy London, she wrote in one of her

letters to Lady Tremayne. She was beginning to enjoy the Spencer too. It wasn't that being there had got easier, exactly, but she was starting to feel more comfortable at the art school. She liked the way that the other students seemed to take each other exactly as they were – it didn't matter in the least if you walked with a crutch, like Leo, or spoke with a northern accent, like Smitty. Girls could cut their hair short, or wear rainbow-coloured outfits and mismatched shoes like Connie; boys could grow their hair long, like Richard Nicholls, one of the third-year students, who Leo thought dressed rather like an elegant pirate.

Most of the other students didn't have a great deal of money, but that didn't seem to matter much either. There was a great deal of good-natured pooling of pennies to buy cakes for tea, or loaning each other a shilling or two for the rent. Most of them lived in tiny shabby attic studios or basement rooms in Bloomsbury or Chelsea, existing on soup and boiled eggs, and spending what little they had on books and art supplies and evenings at the Café Royal. Leo herself felt very lucky to have a good allowance, and the pleasant rooms that Lady Tremayne had arranged for her.

Something else that was different was that everyone at the Spencer seemed to have very strong ideas about things. The art studios were always buzzing with debate and discussion – whether it was about a new exhibition, or the political issues of the day. Leo rarely joined in, but she listened a

72

great deal – whether it was to Jack arguing in favour of socialism, or Connie speaking up for votes for women. She had learned that Connie was a passionate supporter of the Suffragettes, and regularly attended their meetings. Leo had never even heard of the Suffragettes until she had come to the Spencer, but Connie had shown her copies of their newspaper *The Suffragette*, as well as the enamel badge she always wore on the lapel of her coat – reading 'Votes for Women' in the Suffragette colours – purple, white and green. 'You really ought to come with me and see Mrs St James speak, some time,' she enthused to Leo. 'She's one of the leaders, and she really is the most marvellous person.'

Leo also learned that Jack thought some of the Suffragettes' tactics – like chaining themselves to railings and breaking windows, or even setting buildings on fire – were too extreme. He and Connie had some heated discussions on the subject, but it didn't stop them being good friends. Leo listened and marvelled, trying to imagine how Father or Vincent might have reacted to the idea that women should be able to vote, or that a young girl could have the slightest idea about politics. Here, everyone paid attention to what Connie had to say.

Best of all, though, what Leo liked about the Spencer was that no one cared where you came from, or who your family were. In the drawing room at Winter Hall, class and pedigree were the only thing that mattered – but here, they did not count for a jot. Your home could be a butcher's shop in the East End, like one of the most talented of the third-year students, or a country house like Leo's, and there was no difference in the way anyone treated you. It was your work that really mattered.

And Leo had thrown herself into her work wholeheartedly. She was spending almost every spare minute on her painting of *The Green Dragon.*

She was staring at the original again one afternoon at Sinclair's, when Mr Lyle came over to talk to her. At first, she was so engrossed in her thoughts that she didn't even notice he was there.

'It's compelling, isn't it?' came Lyle's voice from behind her. 'It draws you back. I find myself fascinated by what could have been in the artist's mind. What was his intention?' He was speaking in his special 'lecturing' voice now, as he went on: 'A dragon is a mythical beast, but also a symbol. In some cultures, dragons mean wisdom; in others power, or prosperity, or luck. For some, they represent an all-seeing eye; for others, they can even signify evil.' He smiled at her. 'How are you progressing with your version?'

'I believe I'm almost finished,' said Leo shyly. 'I just hope it does justice to the original.'

'Well, I can certainly see that you've taken the challenge seriously. Good work, Miss Fitzgerald. I very much look forward to seeing it when I visit the Spencer tomorrow morning.'

He made as if to walk away, but emboldened by his words, Leo spoke up. She wanted to ask him something. 'I've noticed this,' she began, pointing to the top left-hand corner of the painting, just beside the dragon's proud head. 'There's a place just there where the texture is different. It looks as though something might have been overpainted.'

Lyle followed her gaze. 'Yes, that's quite likely,' he said, nodding. 'Many paintings as old as this one have been altered over the centuries.'

'When you look closely, you can still see some of the marks underneath,' Leo went on, growing more excited. 'It looks like a word – or maybe even a signature? Perhaps it would prove for certain that the painting is a Casselli!'

Lyle frowned contemplatively. 'Well, it's possible, I suppose – although I think unlikely. I think it's most likely that the painting was simply amended later by another artist, who didn't have Casselli's skill.'

'I thought I'd mention it to Professor Jarvis and see what he thinks. He gave us an awfully interesting art history lecture the other day, all about –'

But Mr Lyle shook his head. 'Oh, no need for that, my dear. This painting has been examined by many experts, you know – and they wouldn't have missed something like that. There's no need to trouble Professor Jarvis about it.'

Leo felt rather crestfallen, but Lyle was smiling now. 'But it was very well spotted – you are becoming quite the art historian.' He turned to her portfolio, which was lying close to them on a table. 'Now, is this yours? Why don't you show me what else you have been working on lately?'

A few hours later, as they finished their final tasks for the day, Leo couldn't help smiling. Mr Lyle had spent a good half an hour with her, and he had promised to come and look at her painting the next day. Having his input on her work had made her confidence soar.

'I say, Leo,' said Jack, coming over to her as he shrugged on his jacket. 'Why don't you come with us tonight? Connie's taking us to hear the great Mrs St James – she's giving a lecture at the University of London.'

'Well . . .' Leo hesitated, wondering if she ought to spend the evening working on the dragon painting.

'You really ought to come. She's supposed to be a tremendous speaker.'

Smitty followed him. 'Come on, Leo,' he said cheerfully. 'Have a night off for once. It's obvious that Lyle's picked you out as his rising star – and quite right too. The old fellow's got taste. But you can't think about painting all the time.'

'Yes, do come,' added Connie, rather to Leo's surprise. 'It'll be worth hearing – I promise you that.'

'All right,' she said, a little shyly. 'I will.'

Outside, the rain had finally stopped, and they went along the street in a noisy, colourful group. Leo found herself rather enjoying being at the centre of their little band. People turned to look at them, but, for once, it wasn't Leo's crutch that they were staring at.

They soon arrived at the lecture hall. Leo wasn't sure what she had expected from a gathering of Suffragettes, but it certainly wasn't in the least like this. The big room was buzzy with people: giggling girls in white frocks; sober-faced women who had brightened their shabby hats with bright bows of purple and green ribbons; society ladies, in gowns as fashionable as her own mother's. There were lots of men there too, she realised in surprise – from gentlemen in silk top hats to young students like Jack and Smitty.

The noise fell away at once into a respectful hush as Mrs St James came up to the lectern. Leo watched her: a tall, elegant woman with a commanding presence, stylishly dressed in a big feathered hat that could easily have come from one of the window displays at Sinclair's.

'We have heard a great deal from politicians about why women should continue to be denied the right to vote,' she began. 'But what is of far more interest to me is the many reasons why women *should* be given the vote – reasons that I believe to be obvious to any fair-minded person. It is those that I shall be discussing here today.'

As she listened, Leo found herself watching the faces in the audience: a series of perfect portraits. She would have liked to draw them all, she thought. That girl's hopeful face, her cheeks curved like a china doll's; that older lady, with her tired eyes and a few wisps of hair straggling out from underneath her felt hat; even Jack beside her, frowning with concentration as he listened. Almost without thinking about it, she felt for a pencil in her satchel, and found herself sketching faces on the back of the lecture-bill.

Every now and again, something that Mrs St James said chimed out clearly like a bell, almost as though she were speaking directly to Leo:

'Today's young women have more opportunities than ever before – but to gain these opportunities, they must *fight*, they must *struggle* against the expectations of our society.'

'Is it fair that one half of the human race should have no say in the matters of education, housing or employment? How can we accept that we are merely to be represented by our fathers, brothers and husbands, as if our thoughts and beliefs have no value of their own?'

'I have learned for myself the strength, the integrity, the independence and the wisdom of today's young women. How could anyone doubt their capability to stand aside men – and to express their opinions at the ballot box?'

When the lecture ended, Leo felt dazed. She found

herself on her feet with dozens of others, all clapping and cheering.

'Leo, were you even paying attention?' scolded Connie, shaking her head at Leo's page of drawings.

'Of course I was!' Leo protested. She wanted to explain that somehow drawing the faces of the listeners had made what Mrs St James said mean *more*, not less, but she couldn't find the words.

On the way out, young women were handing out little bits of ribbon in the Suffragette colours. Leo took one and pinned it to her collar. The others were still talking about Mrs St James's lecture as they hustled out of the crowded hall, and back out into the dark street, fastening their coats against the cold.

'Oh, I can't bear to go home just yet!' exclaimed Connie. 'I know – let's go and have coffee at the Café Royal!'

The others agreed at once, and Leo found herself nodding too. Somehow she didn't want the evening to be over yet either.

It was not far to the Café Royal on Regent Street. Once inside, Leo stared around, trying to take it all in: the rich crimson plush of the seats, the snow-white tablecloths; the twirling gold devices that twined across the ceiling. She could hear the faint tinkling of a piano melody, but rising above it was the hum of voices and laughter. The candles on each table lit up another series of small portraits: here a woman with a red rose in her hair; there, a waiter in a white apron, carrying a silver tray; there a bearded man leaning forwards to whisper something to a lady in a wine-dark brocade jacket. The air smelled of spices. All at once, Leo understood why the others seemed to enjoy coming to this place so much. It was fascinating and grown-up and exotic – everything that she had imagined that London might be.

She felt rather small and young, but Jack and the others seemed quite confident here, and found themselves a table towards the back of the room. They ordered coffee because it was the cheapest thing on the menu. It came served in tall glasses with a silver jug of cream, and they all declared they would sip it very slowly to make it last as long as possible.

Leo barely noticed her coffee. She was too busy wondering how she could paint this scene: the glare of red and gold, the way the light smeared and blurred; the shadowy forms of the people, illuminated here and there by the light cast from the candle flames. Meanwhile, the others were pointing out important people to each other, and speculating in low voices about the conversations that might be going on at the different tables.

'I say,' said Jack excitedly in her ear. 'Isn't that Max Kamensky, the painter?'

Recognising his name from the exhibition, Leo stared over at a little white-haired man with a pointed beard.

He seemed to be at the centre of a large group of people, all talking vociferously.

'Yes, and look – that's Lady Hamilton with him,' added Connie, nodding in the direction of the fashionable lady who was leaning forwards across the table to speak to him. 'She's the one who modelled for his painting in Mr Lyle's exhibition. I've seen her at the Suffragette meetings too.'

At that moment, they caught a glimpse of none other than Mr Lyle himself making his way through the crowd. Leo felt rather astonished to see him. She hadn't somehow expected to find him in a place like the Café Royal.

'What's Mr Lyle doing here?' she asked.

'Oh, he's always here,' said Jack with a grin. 'Every night, more or less. He's a real regular.'

They all watched as Lyle paused to say a few words to a small group of artists sitting at another table, and then went over to a table in a private corner, followed by a waiter with a bottle of red wine and two glasses. Leo glimpsed someone else sitting there already, partially hidden by shadows – a lady in a velvet hat, facing away from them. As she turned her head to greet Mr Lyle, Leo frowned for a moment. If she hadn't known better, she would almost have thought from that brief glimpse that it was Lady Tremayne. She knew it couldn't possibly be: she'd had a letter from her godmother only yesterday, saying that she now wouldn't be back from the South of France for another fortnight.

Connie grabbed her elbow. 'Look – Kamensky's going over to him!'

'He looks like he's in a proper temper about something,' exclaimed Smitty, leaning forwards to get a better view.

They all watched in fascination as Kamensky stopped beside Lyle, said a few inaudible but clearly very angry words, then turned on his heel and stormed out, leaving Lyle spluttering behind him.

'What do you think that was all about?' asked Leo curiously.

'Well, they can't stand each other, can they?' said Connie. The others looked at her in surprise. 'Oh yes – it's true. They had a fearful row – years ago. I had assumed they must have patched it up, since Mr Kamensky has a picture in Mr Lyle's exhibition, but I suppose they haven't.'

'Blimey – there's always some sort of a squabble going on here, isn't there?' said Smitty, looking intrigued. 'Remember when we saw Nicholls smash all those glasses in a fit of temper? Apparently he got himself banned from the place for a month.'

'I can well believe that of Nicholls,' said Jack with a grin. 'I say – here he comes now.'

Leo looked up to see Richard Nicholls coming towards them. He had a reputation for being very talented – his work had already been included in some important shows

– but also for his wild behaviour. He was continually in some kind of trouble: it was rumoured that last year he had even been arrested.

Now, he came strolling up to their table. 'Come to see the fun, first-year minnows?' he drawled, pushing back his long hair. 'Did you see Kamensky giving Lyle a piece of his mind?'

'We couldn't exactly miss it,' said Jack.

'What was he so cross about?' asked Connie.

Nicholls shrugged. 'Take your pick. I must say I'd rather like to yell in his face myself.' Seeing their surprised faces, he went on in a bitter voice: 'Oh, you haven't heard? Thanks to dear old Mr Randolph Lyle, I've been given the boot. Expelled from the Spencer. He doesn't think much of my "moral character", you see.'

'Expelled?' repeated Smitty, shocked.

'Yes – jolly kind of him, wasn't it?' said Nicholls in the same sardonic voice. 'Such a nice fellow. Well, he'll get what's coming to him eventually. I just hope his ridiculous exhibition is a flop. Oh, I know you little minnows are helping him with that – and who can blame you? But if you ask me, I don't know what things are coming to if we're exhibiting paintings in a *shop*.' He slammed his fist on the table, making Leo jump. 'You know, shopping is a sickness. Frills and fancies, fashionable frocks. Who cares about such trivial nonsense? It's Art that matters! Shopkeepers are parasites. I can't think how *he* even dares to show his face around here!'

'Who – Lyle?' asked Jack.

'No – Edward Sinclair, of course. The King of Shopping himself! He's trying to keep a low profile – I daresay he knows he isn't welcome here – but don't say you haven't noticed him, over there by Lady Hamilton?'

They all looked over, and to their surprise, they glimpsed a smartly dressed man who was instantly recognisable to anyone who read the newspaper as Mr Edward Sinclair.

'He may be frequenting the Café Royal, but if he thinks *he* can understand Art, then he's very much mistaken,' announced Nicholls, as he strolled away from them towards another group of students. '*Shopping* is artifice!' they could still hear him muttering. 'Art – Truth – Life! That's what really matters.'

'What a lot of rot,' sniffed Connie.

'Fancy him being expelled from the Spencer!' exclaimed Smitty. 'D'you really think it was Lyle who got them to give him the boot?'

But Leo was watching Mr Sinclair. Her eye had been caught by the simple elegance of his black and white tails, creating a stark contrast with the vivid splashes of colour around him. It would make the perfect focal point for a painting, she thought, as she watched him lean forwards to say something in a low voice to Lady Hamilton. After a moment, she gave a brief nod, and then Sinclair slid away into the crowd.

Across the room, Leo saw that Mr Lyle did not seem to have noticed Mr Sinclair's brief appearance. He was alone now; his companion had vanished; and he looked ruffled and out of sorts after his run-in with Mr Kamensky. As Leo glanced over at him, he looked up and saw her watching. She smiled, but rather to her surprise he merely frowned slightly and looked away.

'Enjoying yourself?' asked Jack, beside her. 'I told you the Café Royal was worth seeing. It's quite a circus, but by golly it's entertaining.'

'It certainly is that,' said Smitty. 'This is the life, all right. Let's drink a toast. What was it Nicholls said? "Art, Truth and Life"!'

'Actually *I* think we ought to drink to "Votes for Women!"' argued Connie.

'Why not both?' said Jack with a grin, and they all clinked their glasses together, before turning back to watch the next part of the fun.

CHAPTER NINE

Under different circumstances, Leo might have been feeling sleepy as she made her way up the steps outside the Spencer Institute the next morning. It had been a late night, and as she came into the Antiques Room, she could see that Smitty had dark shadows under his eyes, and that Connie was trying to hide her yawns behind her hand.

But Leo didn't feel in the least bit tired. Mrs St James's words had been running through her thoughts all night long. Now, she felt filled with excitement about everything – the exhibition opening to the public the very next day, and most especially, Mr Lyle's visit to the studio, where she would be showing him her version of *The Green Dragon* for the first time.

Of course, Leo knew she would never be able to replicate the intricate detail of a painting created by a master hundreds of years ago, but her tribute – for that was what it felt like – seemed to have taken on a new life of its own. She'd decided that instead of replicating the painting's ornate devices, she would adapt them. Now, her dragon seemed to glow on the canvas, richly green and gold: both different and similar to the original. Best of all, she liked the expression in her dragon's eyes: not cruel or sad this time, but clear and strong.

'It's good,' said Connie, briskly, looking over her shoulder at the painting in the studio later. 'Really good. Maybe the best thing you've done.'

Leo looked up at her in surprise. Connie was never one to fawn over other people's work: praise from her felt doubly special.

'Never mind good – it's brilliant!' exclaimed Smitty.

'Mr Lyle is going to be impressed,' agreed Jack, from across the studio, where he was daubing oil paint energetically on a canvas.

In spite of what they had said, Leo still felt nervous when Lyle appeared, as immaculate as ever in an elegantly cut suit and pearl-grey gloves. As always, he wore his gold watch and lapel pin and smelled richly of his expensive spiced cologne. He went first to spend some time looking at work that one of the second years had been doing, and then paused by Connie's easel, before at last making his way over to Leo.

Now, he stood before her easel frowning as he contemplated her painting. She waited excitedly, her stomach twisting itself into knots. Would he like what she had done? Was she about to have one of her paintings bought by a real art collector?

After what felt like hours, Mr Lyle finally spoke up. 'What is this?' he said, pointing to some of Leo's decorations and devices.

'I adapted the designs,' she explained eagerly. 'I wanted to add something more contemporary. I took inspiration from an exhibition of ceramics, and from some new textile work I saw at the Victoria and Albert Museum.'

Lyle stared at her for a few moments. 'You wanted to add something more *contemporary*?' he repeated, his voice disbelieving.

'Yes. Professor Jarvis said I should put my own stamp on my work, so I've tried to blend the ancient with the modern, just like in the exhibition,' Leo stammered. She was beginning to realise that Mr Lyle was angry.

'This is not what I expected, Miss Fitzgerald,' he said shortly. 'It's childish – crude. It's no good to me – no good at all. I have to say, I am disappointed. You are not the artist I thought you were.'

He walked away without saying anything more, but Leo stayed where she was, not daring to look up. She knew the others were watching, and could not bear the sensation of their sympathetic eyes upon her. Instead, she stared fiercely at the dragon. It looked back at her, its eyes flat and empty now – not bold and strong as she had thought. Its expression seemed blank – *crude*, she thought, remembering what Lyle had said. She seemed to hear Vincent's voice, taunting her. *Pride comes before a fall*, said Nanny in her head.

Suddenly she couldn't bear to be in the studio for a single moment more. Without stopping to think about what she was doing, she seized the painting and flung it into the wastepaper basket. Then she grabbed her coat and hat, and hurried out and away.

'Up she goes!' exclaimed Claudine, flinging her hands in the air with a dramatic gesture.

Lil held tightly to the swing, as Sid Parker obediently heaved on the rope, and she found herself hauled slowly upwards. Behind her, a canvas backdrop had been artistically swirled with a suggestion of blue sky, fluffy clouds and green leaves. Several branches of artificial foliage had been arranged around her, along with sprays of pink silk flowers. Completing the scene were plaster statues of cherubs, painted to look like stone. Claudine had done a splendid job, thought Lil.

'Are you sure this contraption's safe?' asked Sid anxiously, down below her.

'Safe? Of course it's safe! I designed it myself!' exclaimed Claudine, puffing out her chest indignantly.

This did not make Sid look any less anxious. If anything, he looked more nervous than before, as Lil rose a little higher.

But Lil didn't feel anxious at all. She was not so very high, and she rather liked the view. It was oddly peaceful up here, peeping out at the street outside. Even though Claudine's window display had been carefully concealed from the street by blue silk curtains, she could see out through a narrow gap between them. It was going to be quite a lark, sitting up here tomorrow afternoon, watching the world go by.

As she watched, she saw Jack and some of the other art students coming along the street, probably to do some more work on the exhibition. It was frightfully funny that he had ended up working at Sinclair's! Not that she had seen much of him here, but at least he was finally coming to see her play that evening – and bringing some of his new art student friends with him.

'Try swinging back and forth,' came Claudine's voice from below.

'But *carefully*!' added Sid.

Lil began to swing, watching the street as she did so. There seemed to be a little group of women lingering by the store entrance, talking to each other intently. Every now and again, one of them looked up at the store windows, or pointed in her direction. She wondered what they could be discussing so earnestly. Could they already be speculating about the new window displays?

'Kick one leg up in the air, like the girl in the painting,' called Claudine. 'No, not like that – be *ladylike*!'

Lil did as she was told, still watching. The group was joined by a tall, well-dressed woman in a large hat. Lil thought her face looked familiar. Surely she had seen her somewhere before – in a photograph in the theatre papers, perhaps?

Now she saw Mr Lyle – the curator of the exhibition himself – coming along the street too. With his elegant suit, and the leather portfolio that always seemed to be tucked under his arm, he was now almost as familiar a figure at Sinclair's as the Captain himself. As he approached, the group of women seemed to scatter away. She watched as the tall lady's hat bobbed off along the street, before being lost in a crowd of shoppers.

'Stop craning your neck like a giraffe!' Claudine was shouting. 'Sit back on the swing. *Point* your toe. Like a dancer! Now swing a little higher!'

'Not too high!' protested Sid, but the words were barely out of his mouth before there was a snapping sound. The rope had broken, and Lil found herself plummeting downwards in a flurry of pink frills, scattering artificial flowers everywhere.

'Look out!' yelled Sid, and flung himself forwards,

his arms outstretched as Lil dropped right into them. He tottered under her weight, but by some miracle managed to stay upright.

'Gosh, that was lucky,' said Lil, bouncing out of Sid's arms and down to the ground. 'Awfully good job you were there, Sid. Oh don't worry, I'm not in the least hurt. I say, Claudine – I rather think your mechanism needs a little more work.'

Claudine was already examining the ropes and pulleys, muttering crossly to herself.

'Good grief,' groaned Sid, massaging his back. 'This exhibition is going to be the death of me.'

Back in the Exhibition Hall, the students were all trying to make Leo feel better about what had happened that morning.

'Your painting really is good, you know,' said Smitty. 'Whatever Lyle said, you should be proud of it.'

'Come out tonight, and forget about it,' suggested Jack. 'We're going to the theatre to see my sister's play. It'll take your mind off things.'

But Leo shook her head and said nothing. She couldn't bring herself to talk about what had happened. *Least said, soonest mended*, said Nanny, in her head.

'Lyle's an old stuffed shirt,' declared Smitty. 'Anyone with eyes could see that your painting was top-notch.'

'*Hush!*' whispered Connie, elbowing him. 'Here he comes now!'

They were busy putting the final touches to the exhibition. The last picture had been hung, and they were now adding labels bearing the title of each painting and the artist's name. Under normal circumstances, it would have been exciting to see the exhibition finished, but Leo felt that she could no longer take much pleasure in it. Across the room, she felt as if the eyes of the green dragon were watching her.

Now, Mr Lyle bustled back into the room. 'Very good,' he announced, looking around with a pleased expression on his face. He was behaving exactly as normal, Leo thought unhappily, just as if that morning had never happened. 'We're almost there – excellent work, everyone! I must leave you now – I have some appointments this afternoon – but you may go home just as soon as those last labels are up. Just put the covers over the paintings first – *carefully*, very carefully, I implore you, Mr Smith – and make sure you inform Mr Parker when you leave so that he can lock up. Then you should all be back here first thing tomorrow morning so we can prepare for the opening.'

The other students grinned at each other excitedly. The grand opening would take place the next day, and they had all been talking about what they would wear and the celebrated artists that would be in attendance. But Leo could not join in with their enthusiasm. The last thing she wanted to do was go to a party.

She was relieved when Mr Lyle left, and more relieved still when the others began preparing to go too. 'Good thing Lyle said we could leave early,' said Jack. 'We'll have time to get some supper before we go to the theatre.'

'Leo, do change your mind and come with us,' said Smitty.

'It's too late now – I don't have a ticket,' she said stubbornly.

'Don't be silly – we can easily get you one.'

'We're all going backstage afterwards to meet Jack's sister, and then we might go on to the Café Royal,' said Connie, trying to persuade her.

But today, the thought of the Café Royal was not at all appealing. 'No – I'll stay here and finish this off. You go and have supper.'

'I'll stay and help you,' volunteered Smitty, but Leo shook her head.

'It'll only take me another ten minutes to finish this. You go on.'

Seeing that she could not be persuaded, they left in a buzz of chatter. Leo was relieved to be by herself at last. Yet, for the first time, the lofty room seemed unfriendly, and her echoing footsteps sounded hollow as she went along the row of paintings, fixing the last labels into place, and carefully hanging dust sheets over the ornate picture frames. The room looked strange with each painting shrouded in its white cover – like a roomful of ghosts, she thought, with a sudden shiver.

She wasn't sorry when the work was complete and it was time to go. She checked over everything one final time, and then closed the doors carefully behind her, looking around for Mr Parker.

'Hello . . . ?' she called out tentatively, into the darkness of the Entrance Hall. The store always felt odd at this time in the evening, when the shoppers had gone. The Entrance Hall was deserted now, but she could still hear the sound of the fountain playing – and there was a peculiarly rich spicy scent in the air. She heard soft footsteps in the gallery above her head, and for a moment she stopped still, feeling a prickle of fear – but then Mr Parker came jogging down the big staircase towards her, jingling his keys.

'All finished now, miss? I'll lock up, shall I?'

Outside, she found it was raining again. It was hard going, trying to juggle both an umbrella and her portfolio, and a cold dribble of rain slid miserably down her neck as she made her way towards the underground railway station. She found herself thinking of the others who would be sitting around a tea table somewhere, chattering and laughing. She began to wish she had joined them after all. Her mind felt jumbled up with thoughts of Mr Lyle and the dragon painting, and she tried hard to think of something – *anything* – else, as she walked on towards the station, alone in the small circle of her umbrella.

Night drew in, and the rain fell on. It fell in silver curtains against the windows of Sinclair's, where Claudine was putting the very last touches to the Living Paintings display. It fell on as Sid Parker and Mr Betteredge finished the long task of closing the store for the night, locking the doors and turning out the lights one by one.

The rain fell as Jack and his friends emerged from the theatre, talking excitedly about the play and their visit backstage. It fell upon the windows of Leo's bedroom, where she lay awake and miserable late into the night. It drummed upon the roof of the lodging house, where Sophie lay deep in sleep, lost in an odd dream of searching for the Baron through an endless mountain of hat-boxes. It gurgled in the gutters outside Lil's bedroom window, as she wiped the last traces of greasepaint from her face and clambered into bed.

On Piccadilly, everything was dark. The bright lights of the Sinclair's windows had long since been extinguished. In the room above the stables, where the grooms slept, Joe lay with his head stuck under the pillow as usual, because the stable boy who slept in the bed next to him had a tendency to snore. But tonight, even he was silent.

Inside the store, there was no one left but the nightwatchman. He padded softly up the thickly carpeted stairways and down the empty passageways, keeping a careful watch all through the night. Daisy the guard dog was alert and watchful too, her eyes gleaming in the shadows. Not a mouse stirred. And yet, behind the locked door of the Exhibition Hall, something was different. The painted dragon had gone.

PART III
Red Dragon

Of all the lost paintings in this sequence, one of the best-known is perhaps The Red Dragon *... After a tumultuous history in which it changed hands numerous times, it was sent as a gift to the Governor of the Bahamas in 1720. However it never reached its destination: the painting was destroyed when the British government ship upon which it was carried was set upon by renowned pirate 'Black Bart' and went down with all hands ...*

Dr Septimus Beagle, *The Life & Work of Benedetto Casselli*, 1889 (from the Spencer Institute Library)

CHAPTER TEN

The sunlight glittered on the wet road, as Billy hastened down the street towards Sinclair's. If he didn't get a move on, he was going to be late, and Miss Atwood would not be impressed. On his way, he had passed a news stand, where the papers were full of the Suffragettes' recent demonstration at the House of Commons, as well as the news of Mr Lyle's exhibition, which was due to open at Sinclair's that very day. He had at once noticed a new edition of his favourite story-paper, *Boys of Empire*, which he knew contained the first instalment of a new serial about the brave boy detective, Montgomery Baxter: 'The Locked Room Mystery'. He hadn't been able to resist buying it and having a quick, tantalising read of the first few sentences, before he realised the time and hurried on his way.

But it was very difficult to hurry on such a fine morning. The rain had finally stopped; and for the first time in what seemed like weeks, the sun was actually shining. The coloured flags on the roof of Sinclair's were fluttering against a blue sky; the city streets seemed to have been washed clean by the rain; and the air smelled faintly of bonfires.

He ducked into the stable-yard, darting around the puddles. In the distance, he could see Joe whistling as he led a horse out of one of the stables, the new guard dog Daisy following close at his heels. He knew he was too late to stop and say hello, but instead he waved a hasty greeting and then rushed in through the side door.

'Aha – the very fellow I need,' said Mr Betteredge immediately as he came in. 'We're getting everything ready for the opening of the exhibition and it's all hands on deck. Help me with these flowers?'

'But Miss Atwood's expecting me upstairs,' said Billy.

'Never mind that – Miss Atwood will understand. Hurry up, Parker, shake a leg. We've a lot to do this morning.'

Billy didn't need telling twice. If he helped Mr Betteredge, Miss Atwood would never know he had been running late – and besides, he was pleased by the idea of seeing the new exhibition before anyone else. He grabbed the large floral arrangement that Mr Betteredge had indicated, and followed the store manager out on to the shop floor.

At this hour of the morning, the store was not yet open; but there was already quite a crowd waiting outside the Exhibition Hall. Uncle Sid unlocked the door, while

Mr Lyle stood close by, twitching from one foot to another as if he could hardly wait to get inside. Beside him were the art students who had been helping with the exhibition, all chattering excitedly. One girl stood a little apart from the rest, and as he glanced at her, he realised that he'd noticed her here before. She had a pale, interesting face, and she obviously had something the matter with one of her legs – she walked slowly and awkwardly, using a big wooden crutch to help her. Now, she stood frowning at the floor – almost, he thought, as though she didn't want to be there at all.

As Uncle Sid swung the doors open, Mr Lyle and his gaggle of students rushed in, followed rather more sedately by Mr Betteredge, then Billy himself with the flowers and two porters struggling with a large table. Last of all was Uncle Sid, who had first made sure that the large sign reading 'Exhibition Opens This Evening' was firmly in place outside.

'Table over there in that corner,' instructed Mr Betteredge. 'We don't want the refreshments getting in the way. Put those flowers over there too,' he added to Billy.

Billy did as he was told, all the while craning his neck to try and see the paintings. There were lots of them, either hung upon the panelled walls, or carefully displayed upon grand carved easels, but each was covered by a piece of white cloth. As he watched, Mr Lyle and the students began to remove these coverings from each of the paintings – and having set the flowers in place, he lingered for a moment, hoping to get a good look.

One by one, the pictures appeared: a hazy sunset over a river; a lady in a green dress holding a lapdog; a lush garden; a banquet scene. Some were huge, painted in rich, sombre colours; others were tiny and glittering as jewels.

Beside him, the girl he had noticed on the way into the Hall removed a cover from a painting and made a little strangled sound of astonishment. Billy glanced over in surprise, and one of the other students noticed too.

'What's the matter?' she asked loudly.

Everyone else turned around to look now, and Billy heard a couple of gasps – though at first, he couldn't see why. Beneath the cover was a small painting of a twisting green dragon, set against an ornate background, shimmering gold.

'But that's not *The Green Dragon*!' exclaimed the other student. 'That – why that's *your* painting, Leo! But – but – whatever can it be doing here?'

Mr Lyle strode over to them. 'What is the meaning of this?' he demanded, gaping at the painting. 'Miss Fitzgerald . . . ?' he said hoarsely, turning to the other girl who was still gazing at the painting herself.

'Is something the matter, sir?' asked Betteredge, leaving the two porters struggling with the refreshment table and hurrying over.

'The painting – *The Green Dragon* – where is it? What has happened to it? I demand to know at once!'

Betteredge stared at the wall, at Mr Lyle, and then back at the wall again. 'Why – it's there, sir. Right in front of you,' he said gently. 'The label says so – *The Green Dragon* by – er – Benedetto Casselli,' he added, stumbling a little over the Italian name.

'But that painting is *not* Casselli's *The Green Dragon*,' said Lyle, his face growing redder and redder. 'It has been switched! That is merely a crude copy! Where is the original?'

Betteredge stared back at him, confused.

'It was here yesterday – someone has been meddling!' Lyle went on. 'Who has done this? Was it one of you?' He turned to the girl next to him, and frowned at her. 'Is this some sort of prank?'

The girl shook her head, mutely. She looked terrified, and Billy noticed a dark-haired young man who looked somehow familiar, stride over and stand at her side.

'Of course it isn't!' he retorted. 'None of us would dream of larking about with a painting like that!'

'It was here last night when the door was locked – I know it was,' said the girl, in a voice barely louder than a whisper. She was still gaping at the painting, as if she could hardly believe this was real.

'But – are you *sure* this isn't the right painting?' asked

Betteredge again, still frowning in confusion.

'Sure? *Sure?* Of course I'm sure!' exploded Lyle. '*The Green Dragon* is one of a kind – it's centuries old! It's priceless, irreplaceable! This is just a copy – a mere *child* could tell the difference.'

'I do beg your pardon, sir – it's just that – well, as I say, I can't rightly see when this could have happened. If the painting was here when Parker locked up last night – well, no one has been in or out of here since then, and the door was still locked fast this morning.'

'That's right,' spoke up Uncle Sid. 'No one's been in here. Everything's exactly as it should be – no broken windows, nor anything of the kind.'

'Look here, why don't we search the room?' suggested Mr Betteredge. 'Perhaps the painting has simply . . . er . . . been moved by mistake.'

Everyone began to search – but even when every covering had been removed, and every corner checked and double-checked, it was quite clear that the missing painting was nowhere to be found.

'It's like it's disappeared into thin air,' said Uncle Sid.

'It's been stolen – I know it!' croaked Lyle. 'And on loan from His Majesty's own collection too.' He gave a desperate gasp. 'Someone has done this to spite me! My reputation – it will be ruined!'

'Now, now, sir,' said Mr Betteredge, trying to keep him calm.

'We'll get to the bottom of this soon enough. Why don't you sit down?' As he guided the white-faced Lyle over to a chair, he turned and hissed over his shoulder to Uncle Sid: 'Make sure no one else comes in here – we have to keep this quiet. Put through an urgent telephone call to McDermott.' He glanced at Mr Lyle, who now had his head in his hands. 'You'd better fetch some brandy,' he added to Billy. 'Mr Lyle has had a shock.'

Billy ran off to the Gentlemen's Club Room, his heart bumping. But when he returned with the glass of brandy, he found that Mr Lyle had progressed from shock to fury.

'This is utterly unacceptable!' he began to storm, even as Billy tentatively tried to offer him the brandy glass. He glared darkly around at the art students and the Sinclair's staff. 'How could this be allowed to happen?'

At that moment the door opened, and McDermott came in, his expression serious. Betteredge looked relieved. 'Look, sir here is Mr McDermott, Mr Sinclair's private inquiry agent. He will launch an investigation at once,' he said.

But Mr Lyle looked angrier than ever. He gestured furiously to McDermott. '*Him*? This is all *his* fault in the first place! Why, Sinclair assured me that *he* would put proper security measures in place to ensure the paintings were safe! But it's obvious that the security here is a joke! That idiot guard dog is as good as useless. It's nothing but a

Scotland Yard reject – just like *him*. Seeing McDermott look rather astonished at this, he went on in a low, angry voice: 'Oh yes, I know all about your history, and I tell you, I won't have the likes of *you* anywhere near this investigation. You've done more than enough already. I'm telephoning Scotland Yard. I'll speak to the Commissioner himself and have his top man sent down here immediately. Take me to the telephone!'

Looking rather helpless in the face of this outburst, Mr Betteredge led Mr Lyle away in the direction of the office, while Mr McDermott looked around at the little crowd of people left in the Exhibition Hall – Uncle Sid, Billy, the group of art students, and the two porters. Meanwhile, Billy looked after Mr Lyle, confused and intrigued. What could he possibly have meant about Mr McDermott?

'Don't touch anything,' was all Mr McDermott said, in a calm voice. 'Scotland Yard will need to see the scene exactly as it is when they get here. This exhibition won't be opening today, so I think you would all be well advised to go about your usual business. But I wouldn't stray too far.' He looked particularly at the group of art students as he said this. 'I am sure that the police will want to speak to you all very soon.'

He turned on his heel abruptly, and walked away. Billy stared after him, open-mouthed.

'Stop gawping, lad,' hissed Uncle Sid in his ear. Then he

stood straight and coughed in an important sort of manner. 'Right then, everyone. You heard Mr McDermott. Staff, get back to work. Leave that table. And no gossiping about this, you hear, or you'll have me to answer to.' He turned back to the students. 'As for the rest of you, well I think you'd best leave me your names and addresses, and then be on your way. We'll be in touch when the police want to talk to you.'

Billy took one final glance at the false painting of the green dragon, still hanging on the wall, then followed the others, as Uncle Sid chivvied them all out of the room.

CHAPTER ELEVEN

Uncle Sid might well have said 'no gossiping' but this was Sinclair's, and soon rumours were flying around like wildfire. Everyone had heard about the oldest and most precious painting in Mr Lyle's exhibition being stolen – apparently out of a locked room.

There was much speculation about how it could have happened.

'There's only one way through a locked door – and that's with a key,' said Edith, authoritatively. 'Someone must have stolen the master keys out of the safe – that's the only explanation.'

'But how could they?' asked Ellie. 'No one knows the combination except for Mr Betteredge – and Mr Sinclair himself!'

'Perhaps it was a *skeleton key*,' said Violet, her eyes widening. 'I've heard about those – criminals have them – special keys that can open any door.'

'But even if they did have one of those skeleton thingies,

how could they have got past the nightwatchman – and the guard dog?' asked Minnie.

The girls all looked rather expectantly at Sophie. They all knew about her reputation as a detective. She was the one who had found out what had happened to Mr Sinclair's stolen jewels, wasn't she? She was the one that people came to, when they wanted help. Surely she would have some interesting theories about what had happened.

But to their disappointment, Sophie said nothing, and kept on arranging fur-trimmed hats for a new display of winter millinery. Inside, though, her thoughts were racing. Another robbery at Sinclair's – in spite of all Mr McDermott's careful preparations! The store was all agog with it; the Exhibition Hall had been sealed off by the police; the launch of the exhibition and the display of Living Paintings had been cancelled. Mr Sinclair had been telephoned – he was coming back from the country; and the store was swarming with journalists, all desperate for the scoop on the day's big story.

'I heard it was one of those art students,' said Edith now. 'They look like a peculiar bunch. They were the last ones to see the painting – I'll bet it was one of them who took it.'

'No, no – I heard it was a *cat burglar*,' said Jim from Sporting Goods, who had come through to deliver a note to Mrs Milton and was lingering to discuss the latest.

'One of the clerks told me. He came in the night and climbed in through a ventilation shaft. Nobody even knew he was there!'

Sophie knew better than to believe any of these rumours, but she felt very eager to hear about what had really happened. She wondered if Mr McDermott was here, carrying out an investigation – maybe he would tell her the details? In the meantime, she kept a sharp eye out for Billy, hoping that he might come past with some real news.

But Billy's day had taken an even more unexpected turn. After he'd been dismissed by Uncle Sid from the Exhibition Hall, he had gone straight up to the office, where he had enjoyed relaying all the details of what he had seen to the other clerks. Then Miss Atwood had sent him with a message down to the stable-yard, and he had shared a few snippets with some of the porters and drivers. But on his return to his desk, Davies had called out to him:

'Parker! Miss Atwood wants to see you in her office, right away.'

Billy felt suddenly alarmed. 'Why?' he asked anxiously.

The older clerk shrugged and grinned. Billy felt rather queasy. He supposed he had been gossiping, exactly as Uncle Sid had told him not to. Suppose Miss Atwood had found out, and was going to haul him over the coals? He hurried over to her office door, trying hard not to look as nervous as he felt. He knocked and went inside.

Inside the office, he found to his surprise that Miss Atwood was not alone. She was sitting at her desk, making her way through a pile of paperwork, while a tall, fair-haired man with a neat moustache stood beside the window with his hands in his pockets. He turned and looked Billy up and down.

'This the lad you were talking about?' he demanded, before either Miss Atwood or Billy had a chance to say anything. 'Can he write shorthand? Is he quick? I'll be putting him through his paces, you know. No chance of slacking or shirking.'

Miss Atwood looked at him in a haughty manner over the rims of her spectacles. 'This is Sinclair's Department Store, Inspector. We are not in the habit of employing either *slackers* or *shirkers* here.'

'I'm quite sure that's the case, madam,' said the strange man, gravely. 'But this is no ordinary clerking job, you understand? I need someone sharp and reliable.'

Miss Atwood drew herself up even taller than usual, and looked the man straight in the eye. 'This boy is very bright and *extremely* reliable, Inspector. You may trust him as you could trust myself.'

Billy's cheeks flamed scarlet and for a moment, he didn't quite know where to look. Miss Atwood never praised anyone! He barely heard her as she made the introduction, in her usual crisp fashion: 'Parker, this is Detective Inspector Worth from Scotland Yard. He is here to investigate the missing painting, which I believe you have heard about. His sergeant has come down with a bad cold rather suddenly, and he needs a clerk with him to make notes, during his interviews.'

'That dashed idiot Potts,' muttered Worth, half to himself. 'Didn't even have the sense to put on a raincoat and a muffler when he was out on duty. A trifling cold would never have bothered me when I was a lad!'

Miss Atwood ignored him. 'You will give Detective Inspector Worth every assistance, Parker,' she said sternly.

Billy stared at her, realising what she meant. 'But . . . but . . . what about those letters you wanted me to do?' he stammered. 'And the filing – it isn't finished yet!'

'One of the other clerks can deal with that. This takes precedence above your other work for as long as Detective Inspector Worth requires your services.' She turned to the detective. 'An office on this floor has been set up for you to use for your interviews. Parker will take you there, and see that you have everything you require.'

Detective Worth nodded and headed for the door. 'Don't let me down, Parker,' said Miss Atwood in a low voice, as Billy followed along behind him.

CHAPTER TWELVE

'I don't understand it,' said Jack, frowning as he paced to and fro in the studio. 'Who would do something like that? I don't just mean stealing the picture, but putting Leo's painting in its place.'

Smitty leaned forwards. 'Do you suppose that whoever did it might've believed that Leo's painting would fool people?' he suggested. 'Maybe the thief thought that no one would notice that the paintings had been switched?'

'They mustn't have known the first thing about art, then,' said Jack. 'No one who did would ever believe that Leo's painting could really be mistaken for the original.'

After leaving Sinclair's that morning, the students had returned to the Spencer, where they were in the studio, supposedly working. In fact, they had all given up even pretending to do that. Leo could hardly bear to touch her pencils and paints; and the others were keyed up too, knowing that they could be called back to Sinclair's at any time to talk to the police as part of the investigation.

Meanwhile, Jack and Smitty couldn't stop speculating about what might have happened to the painting.

'Do you suppose that there might have been something in what Mr Lyle said about the whole stunt being done out of spite?' Jack was asking now.

'You mean, someone is trying to embarrass him?' suggested Smitty. 'Or damage his reputation?'

There was silence for a few moments, and then Connie, who had been rather quiet until now, suddenly spoke up: 'I say, Leo – I don't suppose *you* might have . . .'

'*Connie!*' interrupted Smitty, shocked.

'I'm just *asking*,' said Connie, defensively, shaking back her curls. 'It was Leo's painting, after all!'

'Of course Leo had nothing to do with this!' exclaimed Jack.

'I know, I know,' said Connie, sounding ruffled. 'I just wondered – you *were* awfully upset about what Mr Lyle said, you know, Leo. And you did insist on staying behind all by yourself.'

Leo stared at her. 'Yes, I was upset – and angry too – but that doesn't mean I'd ever do something like this!' She blew out a long breath and then tried to go on, struggling to explain. 'I never wanted to see my painting again, you know. You all saw me throw it away. It was like something from a bad dream, seeing it up on the wall in the exhibition like that.'

Ever since then she had been filled with an unreal, nightmarish feeling – a sickness rising up from the pit of her stomach. She knew that her friends – even Connie – didn't really believe that she had anything to do with the theft, but what would other people think, when they heard what had happened? Might Mr Lyle suspect she had something to do with the robbery? Would the police? Most of all, why would someone decide to take her painting and hang it up in the Exhibition Hall? There was something about it that seemed so cruel – as though they were taunting her with her own failure.

Now, Connie had restlessly wandered over to the window. She looked almost as rattled as Leo felt herself. 'So that's it – it's all off!' she burst out. 'This was supposed to be the most marvellous opportunity for all of us – and now there's no exhibition, no launch party, no chance of meeting any famous artists! I had the perfect frock to wear too, with red and orange poppies embroidered on it. And new Turkish slippers, silver ones.'

'They've cancelled the Living Paintings display as well – Lil will be jolly disappointed.' Jack turned to Leo to explain. 'My sister works for Sinclair's sometimes, as a mannequin, and she was supposed to be part of the display. She told us about it last night when we went to see her.'

But Leo didn't care a farthing for Jack's sister, or the Living Paintings display, or the launch party, or Connie's new frock. All she could think about was the dragon painting. The sick feeling grew deeper still when the door opened suddenly, and the Spencer secretary came into the studio.

'Telephone message for you, Miss Fitzgerald. You're needed at Sinclair's. A Detective Inspector Worth from Scotland Yard has called you in for an interview.'

'Just Leo – but what about the rest of us?' said Jack, frowning.

'I don't know, Mr Rose – the message was simply Miss Leonora Fitzgerald, at once.'

The secretary turned on her heel and left the room. With an uneasy glance at the others, Leo followed her – leaving them staring after her, in silence.

Leo hastily put on her outdoor things and grabbed her portfolio, but just as she was about to go out of the door, the secretary called her back.

'Oh – Miss Fitzgerald – in all the upset, I almost forgot. This was delivered for you earlier.'

She handed Leo an envelope with her name written across it. No one had ever sent Leo a letter at the Spencer before, and under normal circumstances, she would have been curious, but now she just mumbled her thanks to the secretary and hurried away.

A moment or two later, she was walking through the quad towards the busy street beyond. It was late afternoon and students were beginning to leave for the day, hurrying out of classes carrying armfuls of books. She stopped for a moment, putting down her portfolio to rip open the little envelope, her gloved fingers making her clumsy.

Inside, she saw a small slip of paper, containing only a short message, written all in capitals. There was no signature. Leo stared at the words in shock.

IF YOU WANT YOU
AND YOUR FRENDS
TO STAY SAFE KEEP
YOUR MOUTH SHUT
ABOUT THE PAINTED
DRAGON

Her mouth shaped the words as she read them. What could it even mean? She stood still, trying to make sense of it, a fingertip tracing the misspelled word 'friends'. But, as she gazed at the note, a group of students pushed noisily past her. The note slipped from between her gloved fingers, fluttering down into a puddle on the path at her feet.

Anxiously, she bent down to pluck it out of the muddy water with a thumb and forefinger. She tried to shake the water off it, but it was too late – the ink was already smudged and blurred and the paper was pulpy.

She frowned for a moment at the now-unreadable message, then pushed the damp piece of paper into her pocket, and hurried on her way back towards Sinclair's.

By teatime, Billy was feeling tired and extremely hungry. Detective Inspector Worth was not the kind of man to bother with tea breaks, and he had kept Billy hard at work all day. The pages of Billy's notebook were crowded with notes, and his hand was aching from so much writing.

All the same, it had been fascinating seeing a real Scotland Yard detective at work. Worth might be brusque, but there was no doubt that he had approached the disappearance of the painting in a most systematic way. While a junior policeman took fingerprints in the Exhibition Hall, Worth conducted interview after interview, speaking to everyone at the store who might know anything about the robbery, extracting every single piece of information, however small. He had already talked to Mr Betteredge, Uncle Sid, and the nightwatchman who had been on duty. He even spoke to Joe about Daisy the guard dog. Most importantly, of course, he had spent a good hour talking to Mr Lyle himself.

Billy had been intrigued by the wealthy art collector, and eager to hear what he had to say – but it soon became clear that Mr Lyle was in no mood to chat. One moment he was spitting out angry remarks and the next falling into a tense, edgy silence. After he had snapped out sharp responses to several of Worth's respectful questions – Billy had noticed that the detective was a good deal more polite to Mr Lyle than he was to any of the Sinclair's staff – Lyle paused, mopped his forehead with a large silk handkerchief, and apologised.

'I'm sorry, Worth. This has been a shock. I'm afraid I'm not thinking clearly.'

'No need for apologies, Mr Lyle,' said Worth briskly. 'I understand this situation is putting you under a considerable amount of stress.'

'I had hoped we'd be able to keep it quiet but the whole place is crawling with newspapermen,' said Lyle. 'So typical of Sinclair! The man can't resist publicity. He probably telephoned them all himself. I daresay that this will be all over the papers tomorrow morning – why, I've already had a telephone call from His Majesty's private secretary!

The whole situation is a complete nightmare.'

'Please be assured, sir, that returning this painting is an urgent priority for Scotland Yard. We are exploring every possible avenue.'

'I know I can count on you, Worth. The Commissioner speaks very highly of you. There's already been far too much bungling here – I'm glad to have things in the hands of a man of your abilities. Please ask whatever you must.'

Worth nodded. 'Very well. Can you think of anyone who might have a grudge against you?' he asked. 'Someone who perhaps might have orchestrated something like this specifically to injure you?'

Mr Lyle looked sour. 'I hardly like to point fingers, but I suppose I can think of one or two.'

Detective Worth looked at him expectantly, and after a pause, Mr Lyle reluctantly went on: 'There is young Nicholls. He is – or he *was* – a third-year student at the Spencer Institute. I am afraid that he may hold me responsible for his recent expulsion.'

'Why is that, Mr Lyle?' asked Worth.

Mr Lyle pursed his lips. 'Well, it was I who spoke to the Principal about him and recommended that he be asked to leave. He is a gifted artist, but his conduct is quite outrageous! He gives the Spencer a bad name – it's quite unacceptable.'

'Do you think he could have taken the painting as an act of revenge?'

'I wouldn't put it past him. He's a wild young fellow, given to all kinds of idiotic behaviour.'

Worth nodded, and jotted down a note. 'Who else?' he asked.

You have heard, I suppose, that the painter Max Kamensky and I have not always seen eye to eye. I *had* hoped we had put all that business behind us, but recently he has been raking it up again. It's obvious he is still bitter – though goodness knows I've tried my best to set things right.'

'What exactly was the – er – business?' asked Worth, carefully.

'Oh, merely the small matter of a review,' explained Mr Lyle airily. 'Kamensky took a dislike to the way I had written about one of his exhibitions in an art magazine. It was trivial enough, but I'm afraid he has a tendency to hold a grudge.'

'And do you think either of these men might really have orchestrated this stunt with the paintings?'

'Goodness knows. I cannot imagine what kind of a person would trifle with a rare painting belonging to the King himself for a petty personal vendetta.' Mr Lyle flicked some imaginary specks of dust off his cuffs as he spoke, almost as if the very idea was dirt that he wished to brush away.

'What about the girl, Miss Fitzgerald? The student who painted the false picture?' asked Worth suddenly.

'Good heavens, I shouldn't think twice about *her*,' said Lyle dismissively.

'You don't think she might have had something to do with this? She was the last one to leave, wasn't she – she had plenty of opportunity to switch the paintings. And it was her painting, after all.'

'I highly doubt it. I did wonder, just at first. I thought it could perhaps have been a cry for attention. She is a little put out with me at present – I pointed out the weaknesses in her painting, and I'm afraid she's rather sensitive to criticism. But honestly, Inspector, I simply don't believe her capable of something like this. She has some talent: I've been trying to encourage her, to take an interest, but really I'm rather sorry for her. Afflicted, you know, and I think something of an outsider. She's the fanciful type – I shouldn't trouble too much about anything she has to tell you.'

'Well, is there anyone else you can think of, Mr Lyle? Anyone at all that you think could have done this to damage you?'

'I sincerely hope not,' said Mr Lyle, straightening a cufflink. 'In my field, it is rather difficult to avoid upsetting people sometimes – but I do hope that I have not made too many enemies.'

The art collector left not long after that, and Worth scribbled down a few brief notes of his own in the silent office. Billy watched him, longing to ask Worth what he was thinking, and whether he thought that one of the people that Mr Lyle had mentioned could really have stolen the painting. Of course, he did not dare: he didn't think Worth was the type to chat.

In any case, there wouldn't have been much time to ask. The next person had already arrived for their interview, and when the door opened, Billy saw that it was the art student he had noticed at the Exhibition Hall that morning – the one who had first discovered the missing painting. She was only young, he thought, probably about Lil's age. She wore a plain dark coat with the collar turned up, over a blouse with a floppy bow at the neck. She had a satchel over her shoulder, a leather portfolio tucked under one arm and her crutch under the other. There were shadows smudged under her eyes; Billy thought that she looked strained and nervous.

'Sit down, Miss Fitzgerald,' Worth said. The politeness with which he had addressed Lyle had vanished.

She went towards the chair he had indicated, but as she sat down, she fumbled with her portfolio, knocking her crutch clattering to the floor. Colour rushed into her pale cheeks, and Billy sprang up from his chair at Worth's side, picked up the crutch and leaned it against the desk for her. As he did so, he flashed her a grin, and rather to his surprise, she smiled back, though her face quickly returned to its tense frown.

'I am Detective Inspector Worth. This is Parker, who is assisting me today. He will be taking some notes during this interview – Parker, note down that I am speaking to Miss Leonora Fitzgerald, first-year student at the Spencer Institute of Fine Art.'

Billy nodded and began to scribble down notes, as Worth went on.

'You are one of the students who has been helping Mr Lyle with this exhibition?'

The girl nodded, but said nothing. She looked too anxious to speak.

'You volunteered, I understand?'

She nodded again. 'Yes.' Her voice was cut-glass: she sounded just like some of the wealthy customers at Sinclair's. 'Mr Lyle came to the Spencer and asked for volunteers to help with the exhibition. Professor Jarvis said it would be a good idea for me to take part.'

Worth nodded. 'I'll be speaking with all the students involved as a matter of course, but I've asked to speak to you first, Miss Fitzgerald, because I understand that you are the painter of the forgery substituted for the original of *The Green Dragon*.'

'It wasn't a *forgery!*' the girl burst out. 'I never intended to try and pass it off as the real painting!'

'Why paint it, then?' asked Worth, in surprise.

'I wanted to study it, and to see if I could create my own version.' Seeing that the detective looked sceptical, she went on: 'If I'm especially interested in a picture, I sometimes make a copy of it. It helps me learn, you see – and you notice all kinds of details about a painting that you might not otherwise have noticed.'

Worth pounced on this: 'So you had a special interest in *The Green Dragon*?'

'Yes – I did,' she said, lifting her chin. 'But so did lots of people. It's a very famous painting.'

'That's as may be, Miss Fitzgerald, but I don't imagine that many people have painted their own copy.'

'But it was never meant as an exact copy. It's more like a sort of . . . *tribute* to the original,' she explained. 'It was Mr Lyle who suggested I should try to paint my own version. He was interested in my work – and he knew I liked the painting – and he said that he might like my version to keep, as a kind of souvenir of the exhibition.'

Detective Worth looked up sharply at this. 'So at the time of the robbery, your copy of the painting was in Mr Lyle's possession?'

The girl shook her head. 'When he saw the finished version, I'm afraid that he didn't think much of it,' she said in a flat voice. 'He wasn't impressed with what I had done. So I – well, I threw the painting away,' she finished awkwardly.

'You threw it *away?*' repeated Detective Worth, incredulously.

'Yes – I put it in the wastepaper basket in the studio at the Spencer,' she said in the same flat voice. Her pale face had more colour in it now, and Billy realised that she was embarrassed.

'When was this?'

'Yesterday. We'd had a class in the morning, and then Mr Lyle came in. I showed him the painting and he told me what he thought. Then, after he had gone, I threw it away.'

Worth stared at her for a few moments, and the girl seemed to grow smaller under his gaze. He shuffled a few papers, and then abruptly changed tack: 'You were also the last person to see the painting – the real painting – *in situ* in the Exhibition Hall before it was stolen – is that right?'

She nodded.

'Can you tell me what happened yesterday afternoon?'

She shifted in her seat as though she was uncomfortable. 'We were all working in the Exhibition Hall, putting final touches to the exhibition. Mr Lyle left at about half past four. He said the rest of us could leave too, as soon as we had finished . . .'

Her words seemed to run out: she paused for a moment, and glanced up to see the detective's eyes fixed on her.

'Go on,' said Detective Worth, drumming his fingers on the table.

'We worked for another couple of hours, then the others wanted to go to supper before they went to the theatre, so I said I would stay and finish the last few things off.'

'You weren't going to the theatre with the others?' asked Worth, and she shook her head, glancing downwards.

'So the other students left – what happened after that?'

'Nothing!' she exclaimed. 'Nothing happened! I was there working by myself for about half an hour, and then I got my things and left.'

'What time was this?'

'Ten minutes past seven. I saw the clock in the Entrance Hall, on my way out.'

'What happened when you left?'

'I just . . . went out,' she said, sounding confused. 'Through the side door, the one that leads into the stable-yard. That's the way we leave if the store is already closed and the main doors are locked.'

'Did anyone see you on your way out?'

'Only Mr Parker – he came down and he locked the Exhibition Hall doors behind me.'

'You saw him lock the doors?'

'Yes.'

'He didn't go into the Exhibition Hall?'

'No – I'd already closed the doors behind me.'

'What things did you have with you that day?'

She shook her head, bewildered. 'My satchel . . . and

129

my umbrella, because it was raining. And my portfolio, of course.'

'That one there?' said Detective Worth, gesturing to the portfolio, which she had placed against the wall beside her chair. She nodded.

'What size is that portfolio?'

'Er . . . I don't know precisely,' she said, looking baffled.

'Could you fit a painting inside it? *The Green Dragon*, for example?'

'Yes, I suppose so . . . I mean, you could *in theory*,' she added hastily, seeing what Worth might be driving at. 'But I didn't, if that's what you mean. I didn't steal the painting!'

'I'm not suggesting you did, Miss Fitzgerald – I am merely establishing the facts.'

She looked twisted up with anxiety now, and Billy felt sorry for her. Suddenly, he was reminded of when Sophie had been interviewed by a Scotland Yard policeman, when she had been accused of being involved in the theft of the Clockwork Sparrow.

'What did you do after you left?' Detective Worth was asking.

'I went home.'

'You walked?'

She shook her head. 'I went down to the underground railway station and caught a train.' When she saw that he was frowning again, she explained: 'I find walking more than a short distance tiring.' She gestured awkwardly to her crutch. 'I usually take the underground – or sometimes the omnibus.'

Worth nodded. 'What time did you arrive home?'

'About eight o'clock, I think.'

'Did you go out again, or see anyone else, that night?'

'No. I just stayed in my room. I made some tea and then I went to bed.'

Worth paused for a moment and looked at her. Then he made another of his abrupt changes in tack: 'Are you enjoying your time at the Spencer Institute?'

'Yes,' she said, sounding surprised.

'Do you get on with your fellow students? Have you made friends there?'

'A few,' she said defensively.

'Do you ever feel lonely?'

'I don't really know what that has to do with this,' she said bluntly.

Worth gave a short nod, as if to say that was a fair comment, and went on: 'How do you get on with Mr Lyle?'

She shrugged and said nothing.

'He's been encouraging you, hasn't he?' went on Worth. 'Taking an interest in your work?'

'He *had.* Until I painted my version of *The Green Dragon*. Then he made it clear that he wasn't so impressed any longer.'

'And how did you feel about that, Miss Fitzgerald?' He stared at her searchingly.

'I was upset,' she said shortly.

'Did you feel angry with him?'

'Of course I did! I'd worked for weeks on that painting!' she flared suddenly. 'But I was no angrier than anyone would have been – and I certainly didn't try to get back at Mr Lyle by switching the paintings, if that's what you're trying to imply!'

Worth raised his eyebrows and scribbled down a few more notes. 'Was Mr Lyle anxious about the safety of the pictures in the exhibition?' he demanded suddenly.

The girl gulped, as though she was trying to swallow down her feelings. She nodded and said in a more composed voice: 'Yes – he wanted to make sure the Exhibition Hall was secure. He was always very cautious and particular about window latches being closed and so forth. Mr Parker was always very careful too. I think he wanted to be quite sure that Mr Lyle was satisfied with everything.'

'Miss Fitzgerald, can you think of anyone who might have wanted to steal this painting?'

She stared at him, frowning. 'No,' she said after a moment. 'No, I can't think of anyone. But – but there is something that I wanted to tell you about. Just as I was leaving the Spencer to come here, I got a note,' she explained, her voice unsteady. 'It was addressed to me at the Spencer, but it was anonymous. It said something like *If you want you and your friends to stay safe, tell no one about the dragon painting.'*

Worth raised his eyebrows. 'An anonymous note?' he repeated, his voice sharp with interest. 'Do you have it with you?'

'I'm afraid I dropped it in a puddle,' said the girl, blushing. 'It fell to pieces.'

Worth looked at her with a curious expression on his face – a sort of odd half-smile. She looked back at him uncertainly. Abruptly, Worth stood up. 'Thank you, Miss Fitzgerald. We'll take your fingerprints, and I daresay we'll need to talk to you again.'

'But, the note . . .' she faltered. 'Don't you think it's important?'

'It may be, Miss Fitzgerald,' was all that Worth said. 'That will be all for now.'

Billy tried to smile at her, but she scarcely looked at him as she got to her feet, leaning on her crutch for support.

For a moment she paused and hesitated, looking at Detective Worth, almost as though she was going to say something else – but then she turned abruptly, took up her portfolio, and made her way out of the room.

Leo blew out a long, wavering breath of air as she walked down the stairs. She scarcely knew what to make of

Detective Worth and his searching questions. Had he believed what she had said – or did he think that she could have something to do with the theft?

The nightmare feeling she had been experiencing ever since that morning seemed to have grown worse while she was in that room. Now she felt as though she were being pulled underwater by some invisible hands. The worst of it was that it was all her own fault. If only she wasn't always so stiff and spiky! If she had just agreed to go with Jack and the others to the theatre, instead of staying behind by herself – why, perhaps she could have spent last night making fun of Mr Lyle over tea and cakes, and then forgetting all about the painting at the theatre! Instead, she had been alone and miserable; and now she was being interrogated. All at once, she wished she had done everything differently – but more than anything else, she wished that she had never set eyes on Benedetto Casselli's *The Green Dragon*.

As she made her way through the store, she saw that the staff were already closing up for the evening. She felt for her gloves in her pocket, and her fingers closed upon the disintegrating scraps of damp paper that were all that remained of the anonymous note. She wasn't even sure that Detective Worth had believed it was real. But the note puzzled her. Why would anyone tell her to 'keep her mouth shut' about the painting – after all, she hadn't the slightest idea how it had been stolen. It might have been her picture on the wall in its place, but she was just as much in the dark about what had happened as everyone else.

The interview with Detective Worth had taken longer than she had expected, and when she stepped out on to the street, she realised it was already dark. The daytime crowds had vanished and Piccadilly seemed unnaturally quiet, with only a few figures hurrying by in the rain, their faces hidden beneath their umbrellas.

In a different mood, she might have thought that the way the yellow light from the street lamps shimmered on the wet road was beautiful. She might have wondered about how she could paint the hazy reflections in the shop windows, or the headlamps glowing in the dark. But for once, she wasn't thinking about painting. She was too distracted by her conversation with Detective Worth to pay attention to anything around her – and she certainly didn't notice the man in the bowler hat, who stepped out of the shadows in the stable-yard, and began to follow along behind her.

PART IV
Dragon Passant

The Dragon Passant, *sometimes known as* The Blue Dragon, *is named for the position in which the dragon is depicted, walking with its right forepaw raised. 'Passant' comes from the Old French 'striding' or 'walking' . . . Belonging for many years to the Royal Family of France, the painting was said to be a particular favourite of Queen Marie Antoinette and hung in the Royal Bedchamber until it was stolen during the attack upon the Palace of Versailles in 1792.*

Dr Septimus Beagle, *The Life & Work of Benedetto Casselli,* 1889 (from the Spencer Institute Library)

CHAPTER THIRTEEN

'Leo – *Leo!* Are you all right?'

'Someone fetch a doctor!'

Leo groaned. Her body ached all over. She tried to open her eyes.

'I say – I think she's coming round. Give her some room!'

Disorientated, Leo blinked up into their faces. She was astonished to find herself lying flat on her back on the underground platform. Someone had put her scarf under her head, as a sort of pillow. To her surprise, she realised Jack was crouched down beside her, and beyond, she could dimly make out the shape of other people – strangers, peering over at her and whispering to each other in low, fervent voices.

'Leo – are you all right?' asked Jack again. He was leaning over her, his dark hair flopping forwards into his eyes.

'I think so,' she managed to murmur. She felt a sudden rush of embarrassment and tried to sit up.

'Take care: you're hurt,' said an unfamiliar voice, and Leo saw to her surprise that there was a girl kneeling beside Jack – a girl who was so like him that, for a moment, she thought she must be seeing double. She blinked at this stranger, confused.

'This is Lil – my sister,' said Jack gently. 'We were on our way to the music hall and we found you here. Leo, what happened? They said you were lying on the tracks – and a train was coming. However did you get there? Did you slip and fall?'

Lil put an arm around Leo's shoulder and helped her to sit upright. The other girl felt warm and solid, and Leo leaned against her gratefully.

'There was a man,' she tried to explain, as the memory returned, with a sharp stab. 'He pushed me.'

'A man pushed you? On to the *tracks*?' repeated Lil in an astonished voice.

Leo clutched her head, trying to free her thoughts and get them to move properly again. 'Yes – he was following me.' She saw once more the dark shape of the man in the bowler hat; the red leather glove closing over her mouth; the train tracks coming towards her as she fell. For a second, she wavered.

'We ought to take you to a doctor,' said Jack, his face an anxious frown.

'No – no – I don't want that. I'm all right, really,' Leo

protested. She didn't want to see a doctor; she only wanted to get away from here, from the bright lights and all these inquisitive faces. 'I just want to go home.'

'All right. We'll take you. Be careful, you hit your head when you fell – you're a little dazed. Let us help you.'

Leo took his hand and between them, Jack and his sister eased her to her feet, to a murmur of interest from the crowd.

'Are you all right, my dear?' asked an elderly lady with violets in her hat.

But Leo didn't answer her. 'Where's my crutch?' she asked suddenly, looking around for it.

Jack's face was full of sympathy. 'I'm sorry, Leo – but it's gone.'

'*Gone?*'

'It was left behind on the tracks, and the train went over it.'

Leo gazed dizzily downwards at the railway tracks. There, among the rails, she could just make out the broken fragments of her trustworthy old crutch. She felt a lump rise up in her throat.

'Excuse me, clear the way please. There's another train coming through in a minute.' The station guard came pushing through the crowd that had gathered. 'Now then, miss. I'm glad you're feeling better, but you'd best take more care in future,' he said, wagging his finger at her. 'You could have been seriously hurt!'

'Look here – this wasn't her fault,' spoke up Jack, indignantly.

The guard ignored him. 'If it wasn't for the quickness of the driver – well! You shouldn't be gallivanting about on your own, if you can't manage to get about safely,' he said, gesturing vaguely to the way that she was leaning on Jack's arm for support. 'It's thoughtless, that's what it is. These kinds of incidents cause all kinds of problems – delays, trains backing up in the tunnel. Why, that contraption of yours down there could have done serious damage to the workings of the train!'

'I beg your pardon?' demanded Jack, incredulously. 'I think you'll find that your *train* could have done very serious damage to my friend!' Leo looked up at him in surprise. He sounded not at all like the free and easy art student she knew, but more like the young gentleman of Oxford University that she knew he had recently been.

'I won't have the likes of you taking that sort of tone with me!' blustered the train guard.

'Now then, what's all this?' came a loud voice, and Leo saw that a uniformed policeman had elbowed his way towards them along the platform. 'What's the to-do?'

'This young lady took an accident, constable,' said the train guard, before anyone else had the chance to speak. 'Slipped on to the train tracks, she did. Could have been nasty – very nasty indeed. And now this young *gentleman* seems to be saying it's *my* fault,' he added, with an unpleasant emphasis on the word 'gentleman' and a very dirty look in Jack's direction.

'Well, there's no need to go blaming anyone,' said the policeman, frowning around at them all. 'If the young lady has had an accident, the important thing is to make sure she's all right.'

Jack stepped forwards. 'Listen,' he said in a serious, grown-up voice. 'This is very important. My friend here was pushed on to the tracks deliberately. Someone tried to hurt her. It ought to be reported to the authorities at once.'

A murmur of interest ran through the crowd. 'Pushed on to the tracks?' repeated the policeman, scratching his head and looking rather baffled.

'Ha! That's what *she* says, I daresay,' the guard sniffed. 'I didn't see no one around here to do any sort of pushing – and none of these folks did either, I'll wager! I reckon she's confused in the head.'

The policeman seemed to take in the group properly for the first time, looking them up and down, glancing at Jack's hair – rather longer than a respectable young gentleman's ought to be; staring for several moments at Lil; and finally taking in Leo, the Suffragette ribbon pinned to her collar, her satchel, lying on the ground spilling out pencils: 'That's a nasty bump, that is,' he

143

said slowly. 'The likes of that could confuse anyone. You ought to get that seen to.'

'She's not confused!' protested Jack. 'She's telling the truth!'

'But if the guard here says there was no one about, and no one else saw anyone . . .'

'There was no one else on the platform,' Leo tried to say, but the policeman did not seem to want to listen.

'Perhaps you slipped, miss, and you just thought that someone pushed you?'

'She didn't slip!' exclaimed Lil. 'This is *serious* – why, she could have been killed!'

'Now, now, miss,' said the policeman. 'Don't take on so – I know your friend has had a nasty turn, but there's no need to get hysterical.'

'*Hysterical?*' demanded Lil, really angry now, but her voice was lost in the rattle of a train, rushing into the station. Most of the people standing around them on the platform scrambled to get on to it and Leo was buffeted as people pushed their way past, the little drama on the platform all but forgotten.

'Just take her home – and don't let her go wandering off by herself again, you hear?' instructed the train guard, as he turned away from them to slam shut the train doors.

The policeman was following the crowd on to the train. 'Hey!' Jack shouted after him, but Leo tugged at his arm.

She felt impossibly weary; she couldn't bear to stand here a moment longer: 'Please – can't we just *go*?'

Jack looked at her anxiously. 'Of course we can,' he said, squeezing her hand. 'We'll get a cab and take you home.'

They insisted on accompanying her up to her room, and Leo felt too exhausted to argue. Besides, she realised that without her crutch she probably would have found it difficult to make it up the stairs by herself. She breathed a sigh of relief as the door closed behind them. Jack helped her into the easy chair, and then Lil took off her hat and gloves and announced that she would make a fire and some tea.

'You don't have to do that,' said Leo helplessly. She felt thoroughly embarrassed at the thought of Jack's sister, who seemed such a glamorous creature, having to turn scullery maid to look after her. 'I don't want to ruin your evening,' she begged. 'Didn't you say you were going to the music hall?'

'We thought we might – after the exhibition opening was cancelled, we thought we'd do something else jolly instead to cheer ourselves up,' explained Jack. 'But we aren't leaving you, Leo. We can go to the music hall any old time. We have to make sure you're all right.'

'You aren't supposed to leave people alone if they've hit their head. It can be fearfully dangerous,' added Lil from over by the fireplace, where Leo saw that she was building a fire in a very efficient manner.

Meanwhile, Jack was wandering around the room picking things up – Leo's books, some of the drawings scattered across the table – and then putting them down again. 'Tell us about what happened,' he said. 'Who was the man who pushed you? Do you suppose it was some idiot's idea of a joke? I can't believe that that awful guard – and that fool of a policeman – wouldn't even *listen*.'

From over by the fireplace, Lil gave a little snort, as if to suggest that she was not quite as surprised by this as her brother. But before she could say anything more, Jack burst out suddenly in a pin-sharp voice. 'I say – Leo? What's this?'

'What's what?' asked Leo, confused. Her head was throbbing more than ever: she was beginning to wonder if perhaps she ought to have said 'yes' to visiting the doctor after all. She was glad that Jack was here – his presence was oddly comforting – but at the same time, she wished he wouldn't keep asking so many questions. She longed to close her eyes and rest.

'*Leo!*' exclaimed Jack more loudly and insistently.

She looked up. He was holding a single sheet of writing paper in his hand, and to her astonishment, he began to read aloud.

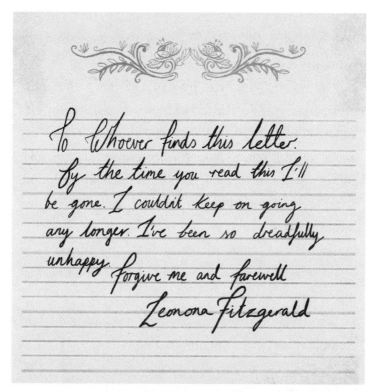

To Whoever finds this letter.

By the time you read this I'll be gone. I couldn't keep on going any longer. I've been so dreadfully unhappy. Forgive me and farewell

Leonora Fitzgerald

'Let me see that,' said Lil, dropping the poker and snatching it out of his hand. She looked at the paper for a long moment and then stared back at Leo.

Slowly, Leo realised what it all meant. 'I didn't write that!' she burst out. She staggered to her feet and grabbed the letter from Lil. 'I've never seen this before in my life. This isn't even my writing – though it looks a bit like it. And since when have I ever called myself *Leonora?*'

'But . . . it was just lying here – on your table. Are you saying that someone *else* wrote this – and signed your name?'

Leo's knees felt weak. She sank back into the chair again, still staring at the letter. 'Someone wanted to make it look as though I jumped in front of that train on purpose,' she whispered. 'They left this letter here to cover it up.' Her hands, holding the letter, were shaking now. The others were staring at her, and she tried to explain. 'I got a note earlier, when I was leaving the Spencer. It said something about keeping quiet about the dragon painting – otherwise I would be in danger.'

'The *dragon painting*?' repeated Lil, her brown eyes sparking with surprise and curiosity. 'The painting that was stolen from Sinclair's?'

Leo nodded. 'I told the detective from Scotland Yard about the note,' she went on. 'And then . . .'

'And then someone tried to push you under a train,' said Jack, staring at her in horror.

'But what on earth do *you* have to do with the theft of the painting?' asked Lil.

Leo felt her face flush. 'I was the last one to see the painting in the gallery,' she explained. 'The thief swapped the real *Green Dragon* for a copy I had made. But that's all. I don't know anything about the burglary – and I have no idea how they got their hands on my painting. I told the police that.'

'Well, whoever sent you the note must think you know something – and something jolly important too!' said Lil, her eyes widening. 'Let's have a look at the note.'

'You can't,' said Leo. 'I dropped it in a puddle and it fell to pieces. There's only a scrap left – and you can't read a word of it. I'm not sure Detective Worth even believed I was telling the truth.'

Jack was staring around the room. 'I don't understand how anyone could have got in here to leave that letter. The door was locked when we came in!'

'Well, if they're the same person that spirited a painting through the locked door of the Sinclair's Exhibition Hall, I hardly think breaking into Leo's room is going to cause them much of a problem,' murmured Lil.

'We have to do something,' Jack exclaimed, pacing up and down on the rug as though ready for action. 'We should go to the police at once!'

'Wait – I'm not so sure that's a good idea,' said Lil. 'The last time Leo spoke to the police, she ended up on a train tracks. It's obvious that whoever did this is serious about harming her. If she goes straight back to the police now – why, she could be in even more danger than before!'

Jack stared at her. 'But what do we do instead? We can't just ignore this!'

'I'm not saying we should ignore it,' argued Lil. 'I'm just saying that we should think before we go haring off.'

'It isn't just about me either,' said Leo, suddenly. 'The note said that my friends would be in danger too.

That's *you*, Jack – and Connie and Smitty.'

'But we have to go to the police – it's the right thing to do.'

'Gosh, I wish Sophie was here,' sighed Lil. 'She's far better at this sort of thing than I am. Look, the police aren't always helpful. What if we tell them and they don't believe us – like that policeman at the underground station? Or what if they believe Leo really did write this letter? If we wait, maybe we have a chance at working out who is behind all this. We could talk to Sophie – and we have a friend, Mr McDermott, who's a private detective. He's helped us before, and we know we can trust him. We could go to him, and he would help us keep Leo safe!'

Jack looked impatient. 'But – Lil – I'm really not sure about this. I know you and your friends like to think yourselves detectives – but this is *serious*.'

'*Serious*! Well, I like that! You don't know the first thing about it,' Lil stormed. 'This summer a girl was *murdered* – and Sophie and I could easily have been very badly hurt ourselves – while you were swanning about at Oxford! I jolly well know this is serious – that's why I'm taking it seriously, and using my *brain*.'

Jack opened his mouth to argue back, but Leo interrupted: 'Please stop,' she whispered. Her head was throbbing painfully again. 'I can't bear it – I can't face the police tonight. I just want to go to sleep – perhaps all this will make more sense in the morning.'

Jack looked at her sympathetically. 'Well, I suppose if that's what you want – it won't hurt to wait until the morning,' he said.

'You need a good rest, then you'll feel much better,' said Lil. 'You've had a simply awful time. But I'm afraid you'd better not stay here tonight.'

'Why not?' asked Jack, even as Leo stared at her in consternation.

Lil looked at him and sighed as though she thought him rather stupid. 'Think about it. Someone got in here and left this letter. They know where Leo lives – and for all we know, they may even have a key. This same person wants her *dead*. If they realise their plan failed, what's to stop them from coming back to finish the job? It's too dangerous for her here. You should come and stay with me tonight, Leo, where you'll be safe. We can get a cab there easily.'

Lil began putting on her hat and gloves, as though the decision had been made. Leo watched her, feeling a little dazed. Since the discovery of the false letter, her once-cosy room had begun to seem sinister. The pain in her head was worsening by the minute; there was a sort of roar in her ears. She was conscious that the other two were still talking – but she couldn't take in what they were saying. Then they were all on their feet: Jack was tucking the letter into his pocket. Unwillingly, she allowed Lil to help her out of the chair and lead her towards the door.

'Where are we going?' she heard her own voice say, sounding hollow and strange.

'You're coming to stay with me, remember?' said Lil. Her face seemed to sway; Leo stumbled on the stairs and almost fell, but there were hands there to catch her.

'I say,' came Lil's voice. 'Suppose whoever tried to kill Leo followed us back here – suppose they're outside waiting for us now.'

'Don't be silly. You're frightening Leo,' said Jack, in the dark.

The shadows seemed to loom larger than ever, as the two of them bundled Leo – sick, dizzy and confused – through the door, and out again into the night.

A few minutes later, Jack was walking briskly down the street. He felt much better now that he had seen Leo into the cab with his sister. He'd even tipped the driver sixpence to make sure they both got back to Lil's lodgings safely.

As he walked towards the police station, his hand rested over the letter in his coat pocket. It was obvious that Leo had been very badly shaken by her accident. He'd never had a friend quite like her before – she couldn't have been more different from the chaps at school, or the fellows he had known in Oxford – and he felt a strong urge to protect her. That was why he was taking the letter straight to the police. Whatever Lil might say, he knew that it was the right thing to do.

He turned down a narrow alleyway that he knew led towards the police station – he could see its blue lamp glowing in the distance. This fellow Worth, the detective investigating the theft, he would be the proper person to speak to. He would tell Worth the whole story and show him the false letter. Maybe the police would be able to analyse the handwriting, or check it for fingerprints.

He didn't hear the footsteps behind him in the alley until it was too late. Something bore down on him from behind – something very hard and heavy. He slipped, and all at once he was on his face on the cobbles. He heard himself groan. He was dimly conscious of hands rifling through his jacket pockets; he tried to push them away, to stand up and fight back; but then a gloved fist smashed into his face, and darkness fell.

CHAPTER FOURTEEN

Leo awoke with a sudden start. She'd been dreaming of the empty platform of the underground railway, of hands in red leather gloves, of rattling through the streets of London in a cab late at night.

She was astonished to find herself in a completely unfamiliar room. She was lying in bed in a small bare attic, with the autumn sun falling gently through a window set into the roof. The little bed she lay in was white; the walls were whitewashed too; and not far away from her, a white cat sat on a wooden stool, calmly washing one paw.

Even as she became aware of all this, she realised that there was a girl sitting at the end of her bed watching her. The girl wore a striped frock with a pinafore over it, and her black hair fell over one shoulder in a long thick plait.

Leo sat up in surprise, and then realised that she hurt all over. She winced, and sat back against the pillows.

'Sorry if I startled you,' said the girl. 'Mum said I oughtn't to let you sleep too long. Here – I got you some tea.'

She carefully handed Leo a mug full of steaming, fragrant liquid. Leo took it automatically, feeling it warm her hands.

'You're Mei,' she said suddenly, as the events of last night began to flood back to her. The girl's name was Mei; her parents were Mr and Mrs Lim; and her older brother was Song. She was at their home above a little grocer's shop, where Jack's sister Lil and her friend had brought her the previous night.

When she had got into the cab with Lil, Leo had thought they were going to Lil's home, but as soon as the cab door had closed on Jack, Lil had given the driver a different set of instructions. Instead, she had taken Leo to see another girl – a small, fair-haired person whose name, Leo remembered now, was Sophie. She had joined them in the cab, and the two of them had talked in low, earnest voices, while Leo sat opposite them, so tired now that she couldn't even speak. She only dimly remembered snatches of their conversation:

'There's every chance we could have been followed.'

'She could still be in danger. We have to take her somewhere *really* safe.'

'We can count on the Lims. No one would ever think of looking for her in China Town.'

So that was where she was now – in China Town, London's East End! She rubbed her eyes and stared around her, but the attic didn't look anything like she might have imagined China Town to be. In novels she had read, it sounded like a dark and rather creepy place, but this room was full of light, and the girl sitting at the foot of her bed was smiling at her.

'Don't worry,' she said in a voice pleasantly tinged with a Cockney accent. 'It's no wonder you're a bit confused. Mum says you must've taken a nasty bang to the head.'

'Is this your room?' asked Leo, glancing all around her once more.

'No – it's my uncle's. He's a sailor and he's away on a voyage at the moment,' explained Mei. 'So you can stay here as long as you like.'

Leo sipped her tea thankfully. Gradually she was becoming aware of sounds around them. Somewhere a bell was striking out the hours: she counted eight chimes. There was the distant honk of a horn, and someone shouting outside in the street. Closer by, downstairs, she could hear someone humming to themselves, a kettle singing, and what sounded rather like a bird squawking.

'Our parrot. She's a bit noisy,' laughed Mei, seeing Leo's bewildered face. 'I've brushed your frock for you. I'm afraid it got a bit dirty – that must've been from where you fell on the railway tracks. It's hanging up behind the door when you're ready to get dressed. But Mum says you're to take it gently and not hurry. She said you'd likely be all over bumps and bruises this morning.'

Leo tentatively put a hand up to her forehead and flinched as she felt a graze and a swollen place where she had hit her head.

'I'll leave you to get dressed,' said Mei, getting to her feet. 'Just come down when you're ready. There's breakfast waiting in the back room.'

'I'm not sure whether I'll be able to get down the stairs by myself,' Leo said awkwardly, thinking again of her smashed-up crutch.

'Just call and I'll come and help you,' smiled Mei. 'And I think Mum and Dad have something for you that might help too.'

Leo felt so stiff and sore that it took her a long time to get dressed. When at last she limped downstairs with Mei's help, she found that Mr Lim was still sitting at the big kitchen table reading the newspaper, while behind him, Mrs Lim bustled about at the stove.

'Good morning,' she said, feeling rather shy.

'Sit yourself down and Mei can fetch you some breakfast,' said Mrs Lim. 'You must be hungry.'

'Please don't go to any trouble,' said Leo, as she eased herself down into a chair. She glanced around, remembering that she had seen this room last night too. It was small and rather bare – the big scrubbed wooden table, and the selection of mismatched chairs and stools around it took up most of the space – and yet there was something she liked very much about it. There was a pleasing plainness, and a friendliness too, about the big brown teapot, the iron pans on the old stove, the green parrot clicking its beak on the perch in the corner.

Mei handed her a plate of bread and butter and Mrs Lim poured out another mug of tea. Leo found that she was very hungry. She murmured a 'thank you' and bit into the wedge of bread. For a moment, she found herself thinking back to the enormous breakfasts laid out at Winter Hall each morning by the army of housemaids – the great dishes of kedgeree, the bacon and eggs, the huge tureen of porridge served with sugar and cream. She wasn't sure that any of them had ever tasted as good as Mrs Lim's homemade brown bread.

'You might want to see this,' said Mr Lim, pushing the newspaper across the table towards her.

Leo put down her cup and read.

'Dad – have you got it?'

Leo looked up from the newspaper at the sound of Mei's eager voice.

Mr Lim grinned, and reached beneath the table. 'We heard about what happened to your crutch yesterday,' he said to Leo. 'We have something for you that we thought you might be able to use instead – at least until you get a replacement. Here.'

ANOTHER MYSTERIOUS THEFT AT SINCLAIR'S DEPARTMENT STORE!

Less than six months after the burglary at Sinclair's that saw the theft of the priceless Clockwork Sparrow, London has been stunned by news of another dramatic robbery at the capital's most famous store.

Our sources inform us that the target was the new exhibition of art, which was expected to open in the store yesterday evening.

The thief's prize was none other than the renowned painting *The Green Dragon*, a rare and priceless work of art, loaned to the exhibition from the Royal Collection of His Majesty the King.

We note that a companion piece, *The White Dragon*, painted by the same artist, was stolen from a Bond Street gallery earlier this year. Though the details of the robbery are currently unknown, our sources have revealed that the painting was stolen just hours before the exhibition was due to open. It is believed that no other paintings in the exhibition were taken by the villain behind this mysterious crime.

A spokesman for Sinclair's department store informed us that the exhibition has been cancelled ' for the foreseeable future'.

Mr Randolph Lyle, the exhibition's curator, declined to comment.

Detective Inspector Worth of Scotland Yard will lead the investigation.

Story continued on page 11

– What happened to The White Dragon?

Whereabouts of priceless painting still unknown –
Page 24

– Could Sinclair's be cursed?

Our clairvoyant Madame Anna Fortuna reflects on Edward Sinclair's run of ill luck – Page 37

He held out a walking stick. It was a good deal smaller than her crutch, but it looked very stout and strong. It was made out of some kind of dark wood, polished to a gleaming shine, and the decorative handle had been carved into the shape of a lion's head.

'It's beautiful,' gasped Leo, as he put the walking stick into her hands. She could feel that it was far lighter than the crutch, but all the same, substantial. It seemed heavier at one end than the other, as though it had been weighted, and the wood felt smooth in her hands. 'But I couldn't possibly take it. You've been too kind already . . . this belongs to you.'

'Actually it used to belong to my father,' said Mr Lim, with a sad smile. 'He passed away earlier this year. I think he would have liked you to have it. Leo – that is also a word for lion, isn't it? It seems as if it must've been meant for you.'

Leo hesitated, but before she could say anything Mrs Lim chimed in. 'Go on – you take it,' she said. 'Much better it gets used than cluttering the place up. After all, none of us have any use for a walking stick. Though I can think of a couple of lads who might benefit from a good slap of it across their backsides,' she added, in a teasing voice as two much younger boys ran into the room. 'What sort of a time do you call this?'

One of the boys grabbed a hunk of bread in each hand

as he hurried past the breakfast table. He shoved one of them in his mouth, and waved the other at Leo. 'Who's she?' he demanded, with his mouth full.

'I'll thank you to mind your manners,' snapped back Mrs Lim – though Leo had the distinct impression that her bark was worse than her bite. 'This young lady's name is Leo, and she's staying with us for the time being.'

'Leo?' asked the other boy, staring at her. 'That's a funny name.'

'When did she get here?' asked the first boy.

'Last night, after you had gone to bed. She's a friend of Sophie's. Now that's enough of your questions. Take some bread, Jian, and off you go.'

'Thank you so much for taking me in like this,' said Leo, as the two boys ran outside, banging the door behind them. 'It's awfully kind of you.'

'Nonsense!' said Mrs Lim.

'Your friends – Sophie and Lilian – they did us a very good turn in the past,' said Mr Lim, in his softer voice. 'We're always happy to help them – and their friends too.'

Leo shook her head. 'They're scarcely my friends. I hadn't even met them before last night,' she said. 'They've really got no reason to help me like this.'

'Well, that's what Sophie and Lil and the others do,' said Mei. 'They help people. They helped us too.'

'We know how it feels to be threatened,' said Mr Lim

161

soberly. 'You have a safe place with us here for us long as you need it.'

Leo was about to argue, but before she could say anything, Mrs Lim interjected. 'It will be nice to have you. Mei and her dad are so busy in the shop just now; and Song is always working, so I'll be glad of the company.'

She looked at Leo rather fiercely, as if daring her to try and protest, and Leo fell silent at once. There was something about Mrs Lim that reminded her rather of Nanny: she was the sort of person with whom one didn't dare to argue.

It was a strange sort of day. Eager to make herself useful to her new friends, who seemed to be so generous in spite of having so little themselves, Leo offered to help Mrs Lim in the kitchen. She soon found herself doing all kinds of things she had never dreamed of before – peeling potatoes, chopping onions, and even rolling out pastry. She was slow and awkward, and yet she took an odd pleasure in learning these new skills, even when the onion made her eyes sting, and when she burned her fingers on a hot dish. She felt rather proud when Mrs Lim praised the pattern she had made around the edge of the pie they were to have for lunch.

Mei had been helping Mr Lim in the shop, but after a time she came through to see Leo, and suggested a walk to the end of the street to test out the new cane. At first, Leo felt a little nervous – the lion's head felt strange in the palm of her hand, and walking without her crutch made her feel unsteady and self-conscious, but before long she found she was getting along far more easily than she had expected. The cane was light in her grasp, and she felt more agile than usual – in spite of her aching limbs.

But what Leo really enjoyed about their walk was the chance to see the East End neighbourhood where the Lim family lived. She was immediately fascinated by the crooked little buildings, all squashed up together. Mei's street was a wonderful jumble of shops, houses and even a tiny inn. In the distance she could see the tall shapes of the warehouses, the sharp lines of their cranes and pulleys – and beyond, the masts of the ships on the river.

The scene was begging to be drawn, and as soon as she had said as much to Mei, the other girl had run off and quickly returned with some paper and coloured chalks. A piece of a wooden packing crate made a drawing board; Mei brought her out a stool to sit on; and by the time the pie was baked, Leo had completed several drawings. She had also attracted quite a crowd of spectators – including a little girl with no shoes, two elderly sailors who were waiting for the Seven Stars Inn to open, and a mangy-looking stray dog.

Intrigued by the spectacle, Mei's brother Song soon poked his head out of the door of the Eating House across the street where he worked in the kitchen. He was so impressed with Leo's drawing that he brought his boss, Ah Wei, out to see it too. Shortly afterwards, Leo had earned her first real commission: to paint a picture of Ah Wei's Eating House for him to hang on the wall inside. It was a far cry from Mr Lyle's exhibition and the Spencer Institute, but she felt a real thrill of pride as she shook Ah Wei's hand.

It began to rain after that, but she settled herself comfortably at the table in the back room of the Lims' house and went on drawing. She made lots of quick sketches one after another – Mrs Lim kneading the bread, the green parrot, Mei with the cat sleeping in her lap. When Song returned from his day's work at the Eating House, the table was covered in drawings, and Leo was feeling light and unexpectedly easy. She hadn't enjoyed drawing nearly so much in weeks, and she hadn't thought about *The Green Dragon* or the man in the red gloves all day. But when Song spoke up, he jolted her sharply back to herself.

'I met the postman on the way in – there's a letter for you,' he said, handing her a little white envelope with her name on it. For a moment, her heart lurched. Was this another anonymous letter? Did the man in the red gloves know that she was here? Realising that Song and Mei were watching her in suspense, she quickly ripped open the envelope – and pulled out the letter inside.

CHAPTER FIFTEEN

'What a yarn!' exclaimed Joe. 'Even one of your Montgomery Baxter tales isn't a patch on that!'

Billy's eyes were wide as saucers. 'Gosh – just think what the clerks would say, if I told them!'

'You'd better not go jawing about this to anyone – especially those gossipy clerks,' Lil rebuked him from where she was sitting beside Joe on a hay bale. 'This has to be a *secret*! Leo is in danger – and she needs our help.'

'I don't *go jawing* about anything,' Billy protested. 'I can keep a secret just as well as anyone else!'

'Never mind that now,' said Sophie. 'We need to get to work!'

Even as she spoke the words, she felt herself pulsing with a new energy. When Lil had turned up the previous evening, with Jack's art school friend, and had poured out her extraordinary story, Sophie had been filled with resolve. Something very strange and frightening had happened to this girl, and she knew exactly how that felt.

Leo Fitzgerald needed their help. Now, the four of them were back together again at Detective HQ, and they had a real mystery to solve once more. She could hardly wait for Billy to get out his notebook and pencil.

'I wonder where Jack's got to?' Lil was saying. 'I told him to meet us here this morning.'

'Well, let's not wait – we need to get started,' said Sophie impatiently. 'Let's begin with what we already know.'

'Well, the most valuable painting in Mr Lyle's exhibition, *The Green Dragon*, was stolen from the Exhibition Hall a few days ago,' Lil reminded them. 'But no one knows how. At the time the painting was stolen, the door was locked, there was a nightwatchman on duty and a guard dog outside the door.'

'And this girl – Leo – she was the last person to see the painting?' asked Joe.

Sophie nodded. 'Then, on the same day that the theft was discovered, she received a threatening note, warning her not to talk to anyone about the painting. After she was interviewed by the police, someone followed her to the underground station and pushed her on to the railway tracks. They left a note in her room to make it look like she'd jumped in front of a train herself.'

'Someone obviously thinks she knows something important about the robbery,' said Joe. 'It looks like they'll stop at nothing to make sure she doesn't tell anyone what it is.'

'But what could it be?' wondered Billy, tapping his pencil thoughtfully against the notebook he used to keep track of their cases. 'In her interview with Detective Worth, she didn't seem to know anything much about what had happened.'

'She told us she didn't know a thing about the robbery too,' said Lil. 'But then, she was exhausted and confused.'

Joe nodded. 'Maybe when she's feeling better she might remember something – some sort of a clue?'

Sophie turned to Billy. 'Tell us more about the interviews. Does Detective Worth have any idea who might be behind the robbery, do you think?'

Billy shook his head. 'I don't think so – not yet at any rate. But there are some suspects.' He flicked through the pages of his notebook. 'He asked Mr Lyle about anyone who might have done this to spite him.' He quickly explained what he had learned about the expelled student, Nicholls, and the artist, Max Kamensky.

'So we've two suspects already – gosh!' exclaimed Lil.

'We should see what we can find out about them – and whether either of them have an alibi for the night of the robbery!' suggested Billy, with a vivid memory of his new Montgomery Baxter story.

It was Joe who sounded a note of caution. 'Don't you

think we should tell someone about this? I mean – what happened to this girl – it's pretty serious stuff. Maybe we ought to go to Mr McDermott – or the police?'

A new voice spoke up from behind them. 'Er . . . actually, I'm not so sure that would be a very good idea.'

They all turned around to stare.

'*Jack!*' wailed Lil. 'What *happened* to you?'

Jack felt his face reddening. He knew he must look a frightful mess. His eye was blackened; his lip was split; and his jacket was dreadfully stained from where he'd spent several hours lying semi-conscious in a muddy puddle. He'd felt like a prize fool when he'd come round. His pockets were empty – his wallet, the watch that Father had given him for his birthday, the letter they had found in Leo's room – they had all vanished. He'd hobbled down to the police station, but the constable on duty had barely listened to him. Without the false letter, he was aware that his story about Leo sounded not much more than a tall tale.

Eventually he had given up and come to meet Lil as he had promised: though this wasn't at all how he had imagined he would be introduced to her friends. Now, he looked around, finding himself in a loft, stacked with hay bales. Sophie was sitting on one of them near the window, beside a boy with a notebook balanced on his knee.

Opposite them were Lil and a tall young fellow wearing working clothes. 'Blimey!' he exclaimed now, in a Cockney accent. 'Someone's given you a proper walloping.'

Jack felt his face grow redder than ever. 'I'm Jonathan Rose – Lil's brother,' he tried to say in his usual confident voice.

'Are you all right?' demanded Lil, getting to her feet and rushing over to him.

'I've been better,' Jack admitted, and then sank down on one of the hay bales. 'I rather think I did something stupid. After I put you and Leo in the cab last night, I thought I really should take that letter to the police station. But as I was walking there, some cad jumped on me out of nowhere. He didn't give me a chance – just knocked me down from behind and then went for me. He took everything – including that letter.'

'Oh, you *idiot*! Whatever did you do that for?' exclaimed Lil, all her sympathy evaporating in a moment. 'I *told* you not to go the police – I said it wouldn't be safe!'

'I know,' said Jack helplessly. 'I thought I was doing the right thing!'

'You must have been attacked by the same person who tried to push Leo in front of the train,' said Sophie. 'They saw you heading to the police station and decided they had to stop you.'

'Did you get a look at the person who clobbered you?'

asked the taller fellow, who Lil now introduced to him as Joe. Jack shook hands with him, rather surprised. Somehow he'd expected Lil's friends to be actresses, or shop girls like Sophie – not a fellow like this.

'I wish I'd had a chance. He was a big chap – that's all I know. And as strong as a horse.'

The other boy, introduced as Billy, spoke up next: 'It was probably the same person who attacked Leo,' he said excitedly. 'And maybe the *same person who stole the dragon painting!*'

There was a buzz of eager chatter: it was Sophie who cut through it. 'We have to act quickly. Whoever is behind this is obviously very dangerous. We need to find out who it is – before anyone else gets hurt.'

'Do you think we should take a look at the Exhibition Hall?' suggested Lil. 'It's the scene of the crime, after all – perhaps there's a clue there?'

'But Scotland Yard have already done all that,' said Billy, looking up from his notebook. 'Detective Worth had a policeman in there all day yesterday with a fingerprinting kit.'

'Well, then, couldn't you find out what he discovered?' asked Lil promptly. 'You are working with Scotland Yard, after all.'

'Not any more, I'm not,' said Billy, looking glum. 'PC Potts is better now. He's back at work today – so it's back to Miss Atwood's filing for me.'

'All the more reason for us to take a look, then,' said Lil. 'Sophie – why don't you and I do that? We could meet this afternoon.'

Sophie nodded. 'I'll find some excuse to slip away from the Millinery Department.'

'Jack, you should come too,' suggested Lil. 'You know the exhibition after all – you'll know if there's something out of place that could be important.'

'But – you can't really mean that we're going to go and hunt about for clues?' said Jack in surprise. He laughed. 'We're not in a detective novel!'

The others all stared at him. The two boys looked wary; Sophie a little disappointed. As for his sister, she had her hands on her hips and her lips pursed.

'I mean – you know best, of course,' he said hurriedly. 'We'll go to the Exhibition Hall – we'll look for clues – and I'll help.'

Sophie looked pleased, and he felt better. 'We'll see you outside the Exhibition Hall, then – let's meet by the fountain at four o'clock.'

Jack tried to flash her his most charming smile, but he had forgotten about his split lip, and the effect was rather spoiled when he winced in pain.

'Don't worry,' she said, as they all got up to go. 'We'll get to the bottom of this.'

'Oh, I wasn't *worrying*,' he said quickly. But no one

was listening. They were all busily talking about the theft of the painting as they went back down the ladder and out of the door.

CHAPTER SIXTEEN

At four o'clock that afternoon, Sophie was hurrying down the stairs to the Exhibition Hall. She felt sharper and more alert than she had for weeks, and her pulse was racing at the prospect of doing some real sleuthing with Lil. It had proved a little difficult to get away from Mrs Milton, who had been in rather a temper with her after she had arrived late that morning, and had been watching her with an eagle eye all day. She'd managed it at last by slipping out while the Head Buyer was distracted by an especially demanding customer.

Now, she soon caught sight of Jack, who was leaning against the edge of the fountain, staring rather too conspicuously at the door to the Exhibition Hall, marked with a sign reading *Closed to the Public*. A very young uniformed policeman was standing outside the door, looking miserable and blowing his nose at intervals upon a large white handkerchief.

'Hullo,' said Jack as she approached. 'I went over there

to see if we'd be able to have a squint around inside, but I'm afraid I haven't had much luck.'

Even as he spoke, Lil came hurrying over to them too. She was wearing her outdoor coat and hat, and her cheeks were red as if she had been hurrying. 'I say, am I late? Awfully sorry,' she began. 'Is that PC Potts over there? That's a spot of bad luck. It'll be harder to sneak in with him on the lookout.'

'I know,' said Jack. 'I did ask him if I could just pop in and have a look – but no dice! He says that no one's allowed in under any circumstances.'

Sophie and Lil looked at each other and then Lil giggled. 'Did you really think they were just going to let you stroll in and have a look around?'

'Well, I don't see why not,' said Jack. 'I mean, I had been working on the exhibition after all. And I don't see how else we're going to get in.'

'Oh, I think we'll probably manage,' said Lil airily.

All the same, they would have to be careful, Sophie thought. Mr Sinclair was back at the store now, and had spent most of the day shut up in his office with Detective Worth and Mr Lyle. She was quite sure that none of the three would be at all impressed if they were caught sneaking into the Exhibition Hall and interfering with the scene of the crime. She looked at Lil, nodded in the direction of the policeman, and Lil grinned back at once.

174

'Just be quick about it,' she murmured. 'I have to be back at the theatre soon.'

Jack looked rather confused, but all the same, he went with Sophie as she beckoned him to follow her behind one of the large marble mermaids that surrounded the elaborate fountain. From here, they were out of sight of PC Potts.

'What are we doing?' asked Jack.

But Sophie didn't answer. She was watching the Exhibition Hall door. A few moments later, Lil reappeared and strolled quite casually over to the young policeman. As they watched, she paused and spoke to him.

'He won't let her in,' said Jack. 'No one's allowed in there, except for Scotland Yard.'

'She's not asking him to let her in,' Sophie whispered back. As they watched, Lil laughed and the policeman laughed too. 'She's creating a diversion. It's one of the things she's rather good at.'

The policeman had stepped a little way from the door now. Lil was pointing up at the big golden clock on the wall, and his attention was fixed on what she was saying to him. Seizing her opportunity, Sophie darted out from behind the mermaid, and across towards the unguarded door, Jack following hastily behind her.

'We could scarcely believe it, but you know it turned out that a bomb had been rigged up to the clock, and set to go off when it struck midnight,' Sophie heard Lil saying, as she slipped past them. 'It was simply terrifying! But I suppose *you* must be used to that kind of thing in your line of work . . .'

The young policeman didn't even blink as Sophie and Jack silently opened the door and stole through into the Exhibition Hall.

'I say!' exclaimed Jack. 'That was jolly clever.'

Sophie grinned. 'Look – here we are. We ought to be quick – Lil won't be able to keep him busy forever. Let's have a scout around.'

Jack was already staring around the big room. 'Looks like most of the paintings are gone. I suppose their owners have taken them back – they probably weren't too keen on leaving them here, once they heard about the robbery.'

'Where was *The Green Dragon*?' asked Sophie.

Jack pointed to a blank space on the panelled wall that had been carefully roped off by the police. 'Leo's painting has gone too. They must've taken it away to test for fingerprints or something.'

Sophie glanced for a moment at the one or two remaining pictures on the walls in their heavy gold frames, and then began to walk quickly from one side of the room to the other, closely examining the panelled walls, the large windows. She had half-wondered whether there might be any truth in the rumours about the thief getting in through a ventilation shaft, but it was clear that they were far too small to admit a person – even a child couldn't have fitted through. The windows too appeared completely intact.

'It's all very interesting,' she said after a while.

'What is?' asked Jack, puzzled. 'There's nothing here – nothing out of the ordinary at all.'

'But that's just it, isn't it?' said Sophie. 'Nothing. No broken window panes. No forced locks. No secret way in. And that all suggests one thing.'

'What's that?'

'Whoever stole this painting probably got in here exactly the same way we did – by walking through the doors.'

'But how?' asked Jack.

'I don't know. I suppose they must have had a key. But what it also suggests is that this crime was *planned*. It wasn't a quick smash-and-grab, where the thief saw an opportunity, grabbed the nearest painting and ran for it. What's more, the thief only wanted the dragon painting. There were lots of other paintings here but they didn't touch any of those.'

'That's true,' said Jack, realising what she meant. 'And they must have been prepared. They had Leo's painting with them, ready to switch for the real one.'

'Right,' said Sophie. 'The question is, why did they want this specific painting so much?'

'Well, it's probably the most valuable picture in the exhibition. It's priceless.'

'But whoever stole it couldn't be planning to sell it – at least, not in any ordinary way. This is a famous painting, and the robbery has been all over the papers. If the thief tried to sell the painting, they'd be discovered.'

'Perhaps they already had a buyer in mind?' suggested Jack. 'Someone unscrupulous who didn't care what methods were used to get the painting. I've heard of some collectors like that. They develop a kind of obsession with a particular artwork – they would happily keep it locked in a safe and never show it to anyone – for them, it's the sheer thrill of *owning* the thing that matters. Maybe that's what happened here? After all – couldn't it be that the person who stole this painting was also the person behind the theft of *The White Dragon* a few months ago? Perhaps they wanted the pair?'

Sophie frowned and stopped short for a moment. The word *collector* had immediately conjured up a vision of someone very familiar: the Baron. He was a collector: she knew that for sure. She had never known someone as fixated on strange and beautiful objects as he was. She thought of the strange room where he had once locked her up, full of queer old clocks and clockwork devices; of the hidden underground bunker where he stored stolen treasures in wooden crates; of the library they had found in his mansion, full of old books and antiquities. Could it be possible that he had become interested in paintings too –

and that these dragon paintings had been his latest target?

Aware that Jack was watching her, she pushed her suspicions away. She knew only too well what Lil and the others would say if she started bringing up the Baron again. Anyway, in the unlikely event that he was here in London, surely even the Baron was not arrogant enough to revisit the scene of a previous crime? All the same, she had a sudden picture of him back at Sinclair's – stealing into the Exhibition Hall and removing the dragon painting from the wall. Even though she knew that the Baron was the last person to get his own hands dirty, the image made her shiver.

'But if whoever did this wanted to cause trouble for Mr Lyle, then perhaps they didn't even want to sell the painting,' she said quickly, trying to focus her attention back on the here and now. 'They simply wanted to embarrass him.'

Jack looked thoughtful. 'Lyle does seem to have rather a habit of making enemies. We were all surprised how beastly he was to Leo about her painting. It was one thing to criticise it – we're all used to that. Why Professor Jarvis is always tearing our work to shreds! But there was something about the *way* he spoke to her in front of everyone like that. It seemed rather cruel.'

'So you think it's reasonable that someone could have held a grudge against him?'

Jack shrugged. 'Perhaps. Nicholls – the student

that got expelled – he certainly didn't seem very happy with Mr Lyle when we saw him at the Café Royal. He said that Mr Lyle would get his comeuppance – and that he hoped the exhibition would be a failure. And he's got a track record of getting in trouble with the police.'

'Let's suppose he did this – to ruin the exhibition and embarrass Mr Lyle,' said Sophie thoughtfully. 'He took the dragon painting because it's the most famous, and belongs to the King. But why would he go to the trouble of taking Leo's picture from the art studio, and leaving it in the place of the real painting?'

'Nicholls is a painter himself,' said Jack. 'He would never think that Leo's painting would pass muster as the original.'

'Besides,' Sophie went on, 'if he really wanted to *embarrass* Lyle, why would he care if people did notice the painting had gone? Surely that would be the whole point.'

Jack was staring at her again. 'I say – Lil was right. You *are* awfully good at this.'

Sophie felt embarrassed for a moment, and then suddenly realised the time. 'Gosh – we ought to go!' she said hurriedly. She had been so busy thinking that she had almost forgotten about Lil trying to keep PC Potts distracted outside.

As they tentatively pushed open the door of the Exhibition Hall, she could see that Lil was still gamely chattering to the policeman. But then the door made an unexpected loud creak – and they both froze for a second, holding their breath. For a moment it seemed that PC Potts would turn around and see them, but to their relief, his attention stayed fixed on Lil.

'Let's get out of here!' whispered Jack, and to Sophie's surprise, he grabbed her hand. A moment later, the two of them were running across the Entrance Hall and into the crowd of shoppers, without the policeman realising they had ever been there at all.

As Sophie made her way back to the Millinery Department, her heart still bumping and her hair now rather untidy, she hoped her absence had gone unnoticed – but to her dismay, she found that Mrs Milton was waiting for her.

'I don't know *what* is the matter with you, Sophie Taylor,' the Head Buyer scolded, as the other shop girls went about their work, pretending they weren't listening to every word.

'First you're late to work – and then you disappear for hours, and now I hear you've been seen gadding about the store with a young man! This isn't like you! You had better pull your socks up, miss. You know this isn't at all how Mr Sinclair expects his salesgirls to behave.'

'Ooh – Sophie's got herself a young man,' Edith taunted

her, as soon as Mrs Milton was out of earshot. 'Is yours a stable boy too?'

But Sophie had no time to listen to her. It had been a long time since she gave a button for what Edith thought. She ignored her and held her head high as she went through into the storeroom. Mrs Milton had told her she was to clean it from top to bottom as her punishment – a dull task, but she didn't mind that. She had plenty to occupy her mind, now that she was solving a mystery again. As she swept and dusted, she buried herself deep in thought about what could have happened to the dragon painting and every now and again, she found herself smiling at the memory of Jack's warm hand, clasping her own.

CHAPTER SEVENTEEN

At precisely noon the next day, as per the instructions in the letter, Leo, Mei and Song were stepping down from the omnibus outside the British Museum. Leo had said she would go alone, but the others had insisted on coming too.

'It could be dangerous,' said Mei, her eyes very wide.

'Sophie would never forgive us if we let you go by yourself,' said Song in a very decided voice. 'I'm afraid you've no choice in the matter. We're coming with you.'

And in the end, she had been glad of their company. Even with Mei and Song beside her, Leo found she was rather nervous as they made their way through the great gates of the British Museum, and across the courtyard. It was strange being back here in Bloomsbury. The tall, narrow houses; the leafy squares; the rain-washed pavements that had all begun to seem so home-like felt cold and strange all over again. She felt her chest beginning to tighten as she made her way through the crowd, but she pushed herself onwards. Mei and Song followed close behind her, staring around them. Neither of them had ever seen the British Museum before, and they looked awed as they went up the stone steps between the immense columns at the museum entrance, and into the bustling foyer.

The British Museum was always busy and today was no exception. Scholars were hurrying to the library; a group of tourists with copies of *Baedeker's Guide to London* tucked under their arms were listening to a lecture from a learned-looking reverend; and a governess was shepherding three young girls in matching sailor hats. Footsteps echoed on the marble floors, and the ceiling arched high above them.

'It's like . . . an enormous church,' said Mei, gazing around her. 'Or a palace!'

Song looked as startled as she did. 'I've never been anywhere like this before . . .' he said. He looked around almost nervously for a moment and then collected himself. 'Come on – we need to find the Coins and Medals room. That's where we're meeting everyone. Look, there's a map over there.'

The map pointed them up the big stone staircase. As they went upwards, Leo noticed again how much lighter and swifter she felt with Grandfather Lim's cane at her side, instead of her crutch. The shape of the lion's head was beginning to feel pleasingly familiar against her fingertips.

The upper floors of the museum were quieter. They took

a wrong turn at first, and found themselves walking through the Prehistoric Saloon. The air seemed heavier here, and their footsteps echoed as they walked on, into a long empty gallery exhibiting terracotta antiques. Leo began to wonder uncomfortably if they had been wise to come here. After all, how could they be sure that the letter she had received had really come from Lil and Sophie? What if it had been another trick?

Her heart began to beat faster, and then to her horror, she saw before her the shape of a man, wearing a bowler hat. At once, she stopped dead.

'Leo – what's the matter?' whispered Song.

To her enormous relief, she saw that it was a tall thin young gentleman, eagerly examining some Assyrian vases – nothing at all like the man with the red gloves.

'Nothing,' she whispered back. She was idiotic to panic, she told herself. This was a public place – there were people everywhere – and Mei and Song were with her. The red-gloved man could not reach her here.

She walked on. Behind her, Mei called Song's attention to a Chinese vase displayed in a glass cabinet. Going on a little way ahead of them, Leo turned a corner and suddenly found herself confronted with a dead end. She was about to turn and retrace her steps, when with a horrible heaviness, a man's hand gripped her shoulder. Leo cried out in alarm.

The hand shot back at once. 'I beg your pardon, miss.

185

I didn't mean to startle you,' said an anxious voice from behind her, and Leo turned around to see the young gentleman in the bowler hat standing behind her, politely holding out something to her in his gloved hand. 'It's just – you dropped your handkerchief.'

'I'm sorry – thank you very much,' Leo managed to stammer out, before she hurried back to Mei and Song.

Her hands were still trembling when Mei finally spotted the plaque reading COINS AND MEDALS. Her heart gave another nervous flutter as Song turned the door handle. Inside, the room was dark: she could see the golden shapes of the coins glimmering in glass cases. A dark figure standing before a display turned to face them, and she saw to her relief that it was Jack. But then she realised that his face was cut and bruised, and she started back in surprise.

'What happened?'

Jack looked a little ashamed. 'I'm afraid that the fellow who pushed you on to the train tracks paid me a visit too,' he said.

Leo stared at him, horrified. She knew that the anonymous note had threatened her friends, but she had never imagined anything like this. 'Are you all right?' she blurted out.

'Of course – I'm fine. Just awfully worried about *you*, Leo. Come in and meet everyone.'

For a little while, it seemed as though everyone was

talking at the same time, and the Coins and Medals room was quite a hubbub of noise. It was Lil who eventually silenced everyone: 'Sit down,' she said to Leo, thumping the bench beside her. 'We've got an awful lot to talk about.'

But Leo was staring at Billy with an anxious expression on her face. 'Do you work for Scotland Yard?' she asked him.

'Oh no,' Billy explained hurriedly. 'I work at Sinclair's – I'm an office boy. I was just helping Detective Worth take some notes the other day. I'm Billy – Billy Parker.'

The others were introducing themselves too: Song shaking Jack's hand, Lil introducing Joe to Leo, as she took a careful seat beside them on the bench.

'We wanted to talk to you because we thought we might be able to help,' Sophie began, from where she was sitting opposite them, with Song on one side of her and Jack on the other. 'I know it might sound unlikely but we've solved a few strange mysteries before – and we thought we might be able to solve this one.'

Leo stared at her for a moment. Then she said, in a rather gruff voice, 'Mei was right about you.' She was fingering the head of her cane, as if the shape of it was comforting. 'I'd be grateful for any help from anyone. I just don't know what I ought to do – or why any of this has happened to me.'

'It's obvious that it's all linked back to the theft of *The Green Dragon*,' said Lil.

'But that's just what makes no sense to me at all. I don't know anything about what happened to the painting.' Leo looked over at Billy. 'You were there when I talked to Inspector Worth – I told him that. I don't know the first thing about how the painting was stolen – or why mine was put there in its place.'

'Well, whoever tried to push you on to the train tracks obviously feels sure that you do know something. Maybe you know something you don't *know* that you know.'

Leo stared at Sophie, obviously confused by this cryptic statement, but then Song said: 'Look, why don't we go back to the beginning. Tell us what you *do* know. Perhaps there will be a clue.'

It didn't take them too long to revisit exactly what had happened on the afternoon of the robbery. Although Billy had typed up proper notes to give to Detective Worth, he still had his notebook, and Leo and Jack chimed in where any details were missing.

'So when you left – at about ten minutes past seven – Uncle Sid locked the Exhibition Hall door,' Billy reminded Leo. 'Are you absolutely certain that you didn't see – or hear – anything unusual on your way out of the store?'

Leo shook her head, trying to remember. 'It was very quiet and empty,' she said slowly. 'I know it sounds rather silly, but it was *creepy* somehow, with everyone gone. I believe I did hear some footsteps up in the gallery, and for a moment I felt a little bit scared – but I think it was just Mr Parker, on his way downstairs to lock up.'

Billy looked thoughtful. '*Footsteps in the gallery*,' he murmured as he scribbled it down. Then he went on. 'So then Uncle Sid locked the doors behind you. Daisy and the nightwatchman were on duty overnight – and the doors were not unlocked again until the next morning. But when the doors were opened, the painting had vanished.'

'I don't suppose there's any way that the painting could have been stolen that morning, *after* the door was unlocked,' suggested Sophie. 'Could someone have swapped the paintings then, without being seen?'

'Not a chance,' said Jack, shaking his head. 'There were far too many of us there. It would have been impossible for anyone to do that without being noticed.'

'So that means the robbery must have taken place between ten past seven the night before – and the next morning when the door was unlocked,' said Song, working it out.

'Yet there are no signs of a break-in in the Exhibition Hall – nor of any secret way into the room,' said Sophie. 'So whoever stole the painting must have got in through the doors.'

'It's a locked-room mystery,' said Billy, suddenly. The others stared at him and he explained. 'Just like the new

Montgomery Baxter serial. It's about how a diamond is stolen from inside a locked bank vault.'

'So, go on – how did they do it in the story?' asked Joe at once, as if this was going to provide all the answers they needed.

'I don't know yet, do I?' said Billy, feeling rather silly for having even mentioned it, especially as both Leo and Jack were staring at him as if they hadn't the slightest idea what he was talking about. 'They've only published the first chapter.'

'Oh, never mind Montgomery Baxter now!' said Lil. 'It's *this* locked room that matters. We have to know how the thief got through that door.'

'Well, there's one way into a locked room,' said Sophie pragmatically. 'You need a key. So, the question is – who could have got hold of keys to that door? We know there's a master set in the safe but apart from Mr Sinclair, only Mr Betteredge knows the combination.'

'There's no way that Betteredge could have had anything to do with this,' said Billy promptly. 'He was completely flummoxed when Mr Lyle told him the painting was gone. He didn't even understand what he meant!'

'Unless he's an awfully good actor,' argued Lil. 'Perhaps he was bluffing? Remember Mr Cooper? No one had the first clue about what he was up to, after all,' she said, alluding to the former store manager – who had turned out to be mixed up in the theft of the Clockwork Sparrow.

'Well, I'll note it down, but it doesn't seem very likely,' said Billy, scribbling away. 'Then – well, Mr Sinclair has his own set of keys with him at all times, of course. But he was still away in the country.'

Jack frowned suddenly. 'No he wasn't,' he said. 'We saw him in London the evening before, at the Café Royal.'

'That's right,' remembered Leo.

Billy screwed up his face. 'You can't have done,' he said. 'It must have been someone else that you saw.'

'It was definitely him!' exclaimed Jack. 'We all saw him.'

'He's been away for weeks and he only got back yesterday – everyone knows that,' Billy scoffed.

Jack looked annoyed, but Lil interrupted him before he could say anything else. 'It hardly matters whether Mr Sinclair was in London or not. *He* wasn't going to give anyone his keys, was he?'

'Maybe they could have been stolen from him?' suggested Leo tentatively.

'Or he might give his keys to someone if he *wanted* to have the painting stolen,' suggested Mei suddenly.

The others stared at her in surprise. 'But – why on earth would he do that?' asked Billy.

Her face reddened at this sudden attention. 'Maybe so that the store would be in all the newspapers?'

'I say – that's rather smart,' said Lil. 'It reminds me of

something that happened at the theatre, once. What if the Captain did arrange this? As a sort of . . . publicity stunt?'

'That's ridiculous,' scoffed Billy. 'He wanted to befriend Mr Lyle, not upset him. Besides, I know the Captain likes to get lots of attention for the store, but surely if he was going to plan a publicity stunt, it would be something that shows Sinclair's in a good light – not a burglary that would upset the King and spoil the whole exhibition!'

'Still, it's worth a thought,' said Lil. 'You'd better write it down anyway.'

Rather reluctantly, Billy scribbled down the words – *Mr Sinclair – publicity stunt??*

'Who else?' asked Sophie.

'The only other person who had keys was the nightwatchman,' said Billy. 'Uncle Sid always hands his keys over to him when he leaves for the night.'

'Now that is something,' said Joe. 'I reckon a nightwatchman doesn't earn much. Could he have been paid to give up his keys – or even to let someone into the Exhibition Hall?'

Billy scribbled the word *NIGHTWATCHMAN?* down in his notebook and underlined it with a flourish.

'But even if he did give someone else his keys – or let someone else in – there's another problem isn't there?' said Lil. 'How would the thief have got past Daisy?'

Joe nodded. 'We didn't hear a peep out of her all

night long. And it's not as though we could have missed it. When she barks – my word! You could probably hear her out in Limehouse. I don't see how anyone could have got past her without her making a right old racket.'

'Wait a minute,' said Sophie suddenly. 'Daisy wouldn't have barked at someone she knew though, would she? Wasn't that what Mr McDermott said to you?'

Joe caught what she was getting at. 'You mean that if it was someone from Sinclair's who went into the Exhibition Hall – someone Daisy had met before – she wouldn't have made a fuss? I reckon you're right. So what you're saying is that it could have been an inside job?'

Sophie shrugged. 'Maybe. It's certainly one possible explanation.'

'Well, that leads us right back to the nightwatchman again,' said Billy. 'Maybe he stole the painting?'

Song spoke up now. 'What I don't understand is what all this has to do with Leo. She doesn't know any more about the theft than anyone else – so why is she being threatened like this?'

Sophie turned to Leo. 'Tell us about the note you got, and what happened at the station,' she said.

They all listened as Leo related her story. She looked as though she hated remembering it. 'It came just as I was going back to Sinclair's for my interview with Detective Worth. Just as I was leaving, the secretary handed it to me.'

'What did it say?' asked Joe at once.

'I can't remember exactly – I dropped it in a puddle and it was ruined – but it was something like *Keep your mouth shut about the painted dragon if you want you and your friends to be safe.*'

'Do you remember anything unusual about the note?' asked Sophie keenly. 'Anything about the handwriting – or the paper?'

'It was just a little slip of white paper. Nothing unusual about it. The message was written in ink, all in capitals. The only thing I remember is that there was a mistake in it – whoever had written it had spelled *friends* wrongly. I told Detective Worth about the note, but he didn't seem to take it very seriously.'

'What happened after that?'

'I walked down to the underground railway station. There was someone following me – a man wearing a bowler hat. I thought I'd lost him by the time I got to the station. I was waiting on the platform for my train – and then all of a sudden, he came up behind me, and pushed me on to the tracks. After that, I don't remember anything until I woke up on the platform and Jack and Lil were there,' she finished up in a rush.

'The man who pushed you – did you see his face? Do you remember anything about him?' asked Billy.

Leo shook her head. 'Not really. I didn't get a good look

at him – it was dark outside, and then he was behind me in the station. All I know is that he was very strong. Oh, and he was wearing leather gloves – red ones,' she added, feeling a prickly shiver run over her at the memory.

'Wait – did you say *red gloves?*' Joe spoke up suddenly. He looked very interested – and also rather uncomfortable.

'What is it?' asked Lil eagerly.

Joe bit his lip. 'I think I might know who came after you. If you're sure about those gloves – well, I think it might have been a man called "Red Hands" Randall.'

Song looked up at him in surprise.

'"*Red Hands*" Randall?' repeated Lil, incredulously. 'Who on earth is that?'

'He's a proper nasty piece of work. The sort of fellow other people pay to do their dirty work. He always wears red gloves – leather ones.'

'And that's why he's called "Red Hands"?' asked Lil.

Joe shifted uncomfortably. 'Well . . . that and other reasons. I reckon the nickname came first and then the gloves probably followed.'

Jack was frowning. 'How exactly do you know all this?' he demanded, shooting a very suspicious glance at Joe.

'I used to know him,' explained Joe, frankly. 'Everyone did – I mean, you've heard of him, right?' he said, looking at Song who nodded.

'I've heard the name, that's for sure. Didn't he sometimes work for . . .?'

'For *the Baron*?' finished Sophie excitedly.

'Yes – but not only him,' Joe went on hurriedly. 'He worked for all sorts. He's the sort of fellow who'd do anything for anyone, as long as the price was right.'

'Who's the Baron?' asked Leo.

'He's someone we've come across before – twice, actually. A criminal,' explained Lil. 'But he's gone now. He left the country, so he can't *possibly* have anything to do with this.'

Billy wriggled awkwardly. Lil might have been answering Leo, but she was looking at Sophie while she spoke – and Sophie just frowned and said nothing. Meanwhile, Jack was scowling at Joe, as if he did not at all care for the revelation that the boy his sister was so friendly with knew so much about thugs and criminals. The atmosphere in the gallery had suddenly become a little strained.

'So d'you think this Red Hands could have been the one who stole the painting?' Billy spoke up quickly, wanting to break the silence. 'As well as attacking Leo and Jack?'

'Maybe,' said Joe, nodding slowly. 'He's a bad lot, all right. But he isn't the sharpest tool in the box. He's mean and tough – but he's not so clever. I reckon if he did take the painting, it must have been on someone else's orders.'

'Anyone could have paid him to do it – as long as they had the money,' said Song.

'But it still doesn't make sense though, does it – I mean, if he took the painting, why didn't Daisy bark?'

Everyone was silent for a moment. Sophie was staring at one of the cabinets, lost in thought. It was Lil who said: 'What shall we do now?'

'Maybe we could see if anyone saw Randall around the store that night?' suggested Joe. 'I could talk to the lads at the stable-yard. If anyone saw him coming in, it would likely have been one of them.'

'And we still have to find out more about our other prime suspects,' Billy reminded the others. 'Nicholls and Kamensky. Perhaps one of them was paying Randall?'

'I've thought of something else too,' Lil chimed in suddenly. 'On the day before the painting was stolen, I saw a group of women hanging about outside the store. There were four or five of them, and they were behaving in the queerest way, staring up at the building. Then, as soon as Mr Lyle appeared, they all shot off. I thought they were maybe trying to peep through at the window displays but now . . . you don't suppose they could have been planning the robbery?'

'A group of women?' repeated Billy, frowning.

'Yes, and I'm sure I recognised one of them. She had an awfully familiar face. I thought that she must be an actress and that I recognised her from the theatre papers, but afterwards I realised it wasn't that at all. It was that famous Suffragette – Mrs St James.'

'Mrs St James?' exclaimed Leo in surprise.

'But how on earth would the Suffragettes be mixed up in the theft of a painting?' asked Jack. 'Are you sure you weren't mistaken?'

Lil shook her head. 'I'm sure of it – it was *her*,' she said. 'I don't know what they were up to – but it was definitely Mrs St James.'

'Well, I suppose I could ask Connie about it,' said Jack, rather reluctantly. 'Perhaps she'd know what it was all about.'

'You could ask around at the Spencer too,' suggested Lil. 'Find out a bit more about that student, Richard Nicholls. After all, if he actually *said* to you that he wanted Mr Lyle to get what was coming to him, and for his exhibition to be ruined – well, he's probably got the clearest motive of anyone, hasn't he?'

'We'll get to work this afternoon,' said Leo decidedly.

The others looked at her uncertainly. 'Do you think it's a good idea for you to go back to the Spencer?' asked Lil, voicing what they were all thinking. 'I mean – you might still be in danger from this Red Hands Randall character?'

But Leo's voice was steady as she said, 'I'm not going to let Randall, or whoever is behind this, frighten me away from the Spencer. I don't want to miss any classes. I won't let this get in the way of my work. Besides, I have to help find out what happened to the painting. If you're all planning to investigate, I want to be part of it too.'

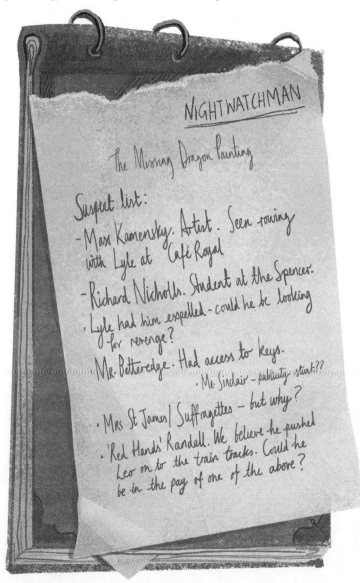

NIGHTWATCHMAN

The Missing Dragon Painting

Suspect list:
- Max Kamensky. Artist. Seen rowing with Lyle at Café Royal
- Richard Nicholls. Student at the Spencer. Lyle had him expelled - could he be looking for revenge?
- Mr Betteredge. Had access to keys.
    - Mr Sinclair - publicity stunt??
- Mrs St James/ Suffragettes - but why?
- 'Red Hands' Randall. We believe he pushed Leo on to the train tracks. Could he be in the pay of one of the above?

*The painting depicted a dragon in the 'courant' position –
running at full stride. Occasionally called* The Golden Dragon
or The Hunting Dragon *because of its background of trees,
its whereabouts have been unknown since the late 1600s.*

Dr Septimus Beagle, *The Life & Work of Benedetto Casselli*,
1889 (from the Spencer Institute Library)

CHAPTER EIGHTEEN

On Piccadilly Circus, Sinclair's was back to business as usual. Mr Lyle's exhibition might be cancelled; *The Green Dragon* might still be missing; but Sinclair's was a great machine, chugging and steaming onwards. Even now, behind the silk curtains, Claudine was busy transforming the Living Paintings display into a clever arrangement of new season shoes and hats; while in the Book Department, Mr White had dismantled his presentation of art books and replaced them with tantalising stacks of mysteries and romance novels. The string quartet in the gallery played merrily on and the coloured flags on the roof rippled in the breeze as regally as ever. In both the Ladies' Lounge and the clerks' offices above the shop, even the gossip had moved on to the latest news - whether it was the Suffragettes smashing windows at the Home Office or the news that the Honourable Miss Phyllis Woodhouse had just become engaged to dashing young Hugo Devereaux.

Of course, the store was still busy with journalists,

sniffing around for any news about the robbery. Mr Sinclair had given a carefully worded statement to the papers, calling for the painting's immediate return. Yet there was still no real information about who was behind the crime, and the press were becoming impatient. Detective Worth looked increasingly annoyed by their presence as he made his way about his investigations.

What Detective Worth didn't know, however, was that he was not the only one investigating the crime. While Joe quizzed the stable boys about anything they might have seen on the night of the robbery, in the tea shop next door to the Spencer, Leo and Jack were gathering information over hot coffee and Fuller's walnut cake. They were sitting at a small table in the window with Connie and Smitty, who had given Leo a rapturous welcome.

'You're back!' Connie exclaimed, with unusual warmth.

'Jack told us all about what happened,' added Smitty. 'We were worried about you. How are you feeling?'

'Much better now, thank you,' said Leo, surprised and touched by their concern. It was true that she did feel better now that she was back at the Spencer. She realised how attached she had already become to the art school, with its distinctive smell of oil paint, ink and turpentine, its chatter of voices in the Antiques Room.

The only place she still felt a little uncomfortable was the studio. Somehow, she could not quite forget the last time she had been here, when Mr Lyle had poured scorn on her painting, and she had thrown it into the wastepaper basket. Someone at the Spencer must have seen her do it, and then taken the painting. The thought made her uneasy: as Professor Jarvis paused behind her easel, his looming presence had made her even more anxious than usual. It was all she could do to keep drawing until he at last strode away.

Now, Jack was telling the other two what they had found out so far. 'We want to talk to you about the robbery. We believe it's possible that a fellow called Randall might have been involved – but we suspect he was paid to do it by someone else. We need to work out who that is – and we want your help.'

'We wondered if it might be Richard Nicholls,' said Leo. 'Remember what he said about Mr Lyle when we saw him at the Café Royal?'

'He was angry – and he even talked about wanting Mr Lyle to get his comeuppance,' added Jack.

Smitty frowned. 'But that can't be right. There's no way that *Nicholls* could be the one to pay this Randall fellow.'

'Why ever not?'

'He's completely broke! He can scarcely scrape a shilling together – the third years had to all club together to cover his rent and stop him getting chucked out of his lodgings.'

Jack and Leo looked at each other. 'I say – I wonder if

that would rule out Nicholls?' said Jack. 'If someone was paying Randall – or bribing the nightwatchman – they would have needed plenty of money.'

'But we wanted to ask you about something else too,' said Leo, turning to Connie. 'Lil saw a group of women behaving strangely outside Sinclair's on the day of the robbery. She rather thought one of them was Mrs St James.'

To her surprise, Connie's face suddenly turned white. 'I – I didn't think anyone would ever find out about that,' she whispered faintly.

'Find out about *what*?' demanded Jack, staring at her in surprise.

Connie looked around at them, and then took a deep breath. 'I suppose I have to tell you now – though I'd be in fearful trouble if they ever found out,' she began. 'Look – the thing is that when I went to the Suffragette meeting a few weeks ago, everyone was talking about something Mrs Pankhurst had said – *deeds not words*. Mrs St James said we needed to do more to draw attention to our cause. Everyone agreed we ought to do something really big – not just giving lectures and circulating newspapers, but something that would make people sit up and take notice. Mrs St James had heard about the exhibition at Sinclair's and – well – she thought it would make a good target.'

'A *target*?' repeated Leo in surprise.

Connie looked unhappy. She lowered her voice to

a whisper. 'You mustn't tell anyone,' she said. 'They wanted to take action – and they had the idea of disrupting the exhibition. They wanted to throw stones through the windows and upset the Living Paintings display. They even talked about storming the exhibition launch and damaging the paintings. They wanted to make the point that women could be artists, not just pose for paintings. When they found out that I was involved with the exhibition, they asked me to help sabotage it.'

'But – how *could* you?' demanded Jack.

'I didn't, of course!' Connie shot back at once. 'I said I wouldn't have anything to do with it – and that they should find another target. Smashing windows is one thing, but Lil and the other mannequins could have been badly hurt! Besides, I don't believe that works of art should be destroyed – however important the cause.'

Jack looked a little ashamed of himself, as Connie went on. 'Of course, they were all fearfully annoyed with me. They said I didn't care about votes for women if I wasn't prepared to do whatever it takes. I didn't go to any meetings for a while after that – but when the painting was stolen, well, at first I wondered if it might have been them.'

'And was it?' asked Leo excitedly.

'No – of course not. I went to talk to Mrs St James straight away – that's why I couldn't come with you and Lil to the music hall the night that Leo got hurt,' said Connie, turning to Jack. 'Of course, she didn't know a thing about it. When they heard the exhibition was cancelled, they changed their plans and decided to target the Home Office instead. I ought to have known – it would be no good to the Suffragettes to steal a painting in *secret*. We want to get as much attention for our cause as possible.' She turned to Leo and spoke earnestly. 'I know I ought to have told someone about it – but I just *couldn't*. I made a promise that I wouldn't give them away. But when you said that about Mrs St James being outside Sinclair's – well, I think that must have been why. That's all. I'm awfully sorry I didn't say anything before.'

'You haven't got anything to be sorry for,' said Leo, thinking of Mrs St James's rousing speech. 'You were trying to do the right thing.'

'And looking out for your friends – nothing wrong with that,' said Smitty, giving Connie a reassuring thump on the shoulder. Then he frowned. 'Well, I don't know a thing about who did this. But I do keep thinking that whoever was behind it *must* have had some connection with the Spencer. They must have known about your painting, Leo.' He shifted uncomfortably in his seat and his voice dropped to an anxious whisper. 'And that means it's likely they are *someone we know*.'

Jack nodded vigorously. 'But if it isn't Nicholls, then who?'

To her surprise, Leo saw that Connie was staring at

them, a rather grim look on her face. As the two boys got up from the table, ready to head into the studio, she pulled Leo back. 'Wait,' she whispered. 'I want to talk to you.'

Leo stared at her in surprise. 'I've got something I have to tell you,' Connie said hurriedly. 'There *is* something else – something that I didn't tell the police – but I couldn't say anything in front of the others. I know who took your painting out of the wastepaper basket at the Spencer. I saw them – and Leo, *it was Smitty!*'

Back at Sinclair's, Billy was spending the afternoon catching up with Miss Atwood's filing. It was a dull task in comparison with investigating a mystery, but at least he had plenty to think about as he worked in the small archive room that adjoined Miss Atwood's office.

The main thing occupying his thoughts was his conversation with PC Potts in the Sinclair's refectory earlier. He had found himself sitting beside the young policeman as they ate their lunch, and they had soon fallen into an interesting conversation about the latest *Boys of Empire*. Billy had discovered that PC Potts was quite a fan of detective tales, and after they had spent some time discussing their favourite Montgomery Baxter adventures, he had turned the conversation to the real investigation taking place – and had been surprised how readily Potts had begun to chat about it.

'We've had the picture – the false one – tested for fingerprints, of course. A fellow from the Fingerprinting Bureau did it for us specially. Detective Worth had two suspects in mind – but the queer thing is there aren't *any* fingerprints on the confounded thing. Not except for the prints of the girl who painted it, the students who worked on the exhibition, and Mr Lyle of course,' he confided.

'Does that mean that the thief could have been wearing gloves?' Billy had asked, thinking straight away of Red Hands Randall.

'You'd think that, wouldn't you?' said PC Potts. 'But that's the funny thing. If they'd been wearing gloves, likely they'd have smudged the other fingerprints. But they didn't – those prints are perfect. It's almost as if whoever did it never touched the picture at all. Well . . . unless . . .'

'Unless what?' said Billy eagerly.

Potts lowered his voice to a confidential tone. 'Unless it really *was* the girl who painted the picture that did it. She had the best opportunity of anyone, after all. Or maybe it could've been one of those other students. I reckon Worth is thinking now that one of them must've been involved.'

Billy nodded, but inside he felt nervous. If Worth really did suspect Leo or Jack, or one of their friends, there was even more reason for them to try to find out who was in fact behind the crime – and quickly.

'But how could someone switch the paintings without even touching them?' he said aloud to himself now.

He looked down at Lucky, who was keeping him company while he worked. The little dog had been banished from her master's office after chewing up several important documents and making a nuisance of herself during the Captain's meeting to discuss the robbery, barking at Detective Worth and trying to eat Mr Lyle's trouser leg. Now, she was sitting on the floor, scratching and looking hopefully at a sales ledger as though she thought it might taste interesting.

'Well, you wouldn't make a very good police dog, would you?' Billy admonished her. 'Cheer up – once I've finished this lot, I'll take you out for a walk. We're meeting the others at the park – maybe your friend Daisy will be there too, what do you think to that?'

Lucky gave a little yap, almost as though she was saying 'yes', and Billy grinned as he turned back to the pile of paperwork.

Smitty's face had turned as red as his hair. 'You've got this all wrong!' he kept saying.

'You can't pretend any longer,' said Connie sternly. Telling Leo her suspicions had fired her up to such an extent that she had insisted they follow the two boys to the Spencer and confront Smitty. 'I saw you with my own eyes.

You were the one who took Leo's painting out of the wastepaper basket.'

'Well – yes, I suppose I was,' said Smitty, redder than ever. 'But it's not what you think. It wasn't anything to do with the robbery – I promise you that.'

'So why did you do it, then?' asked Leo, baffled.

'Because it was a good painting!' he burst out. 'Mr Lyle was talking rot. It was beautiful, Leo – and – and – well, I suppose I thought you might regret throwing it away.'

Leo stared at him in astonishment.

'But, if that's true, then why did you hide it?' demanded Connie. 'I saw you – you put it secretly away!'

'Don't be so daft, Con. I wasn't *hiding* it. I just put it with the rest of my things. I meant to give it back to Leo later, when she'd had a chance to calm down. But then I got called to see Professor Jarvis – and when I got back, the painting was gone.'

'Why didn't you tell us any of this before?' asked Leo.

Smitty looked embarrassed. 'At first I thought you must have come back and taken it yourself. I knew you were upset – I didn't want to make a fuss about it. And then – well, I know it was stupid – but when we saw the painting hanging in the gallery, I didn't like to say anything about it to Detective Worth. I thought he might decide that I'd had something to do with the robbery.'

'So that still means that whoever took the painting must

212

have had access to the Spencer,' said Jack, musing over this new information thoughtfully.

Connie looked close to tears. 'You idiot!' she burst out. Then, rather to Smitty's astonishment, she flung her arms around him in an enormous hug. 'Why didn't you say anything to me? All this time I was fearfully worried that you had somehow got yourself all mixed up in the robbery!'

'You ought to have known better,' said Smitty, his voice sounding rather muffled.

Jack and Leo just grinned at each other, and left them to make it up. They were due to meet the others at the park and tell them what they had found out.

Back in Miss Atwood's office, Billy heard the telephone beginning to trill. For a moment, he wondered if he ought to go through and answer it, but then he heard Miss Atwood herself come in from the clerks' office to pick up the receiver. 'Sinclair's department store, good afternoon. This is Miss Atwood speaking. Mr Lyle? Yes, of course. Please wait one moment.'

Billy could hear her skirt swish as she swept out of the room. A moment later, the door opened again and he heard footsteps, then Mr Lyle's voice.

'Hullo – Lyle here.'

His voice was brisk and normal, but when he next

spoke, he sounded quite different. '*Why would you call me here?*' he hissed.

Curious now, Billy put down the stack of papers he was holding, and cautiously peeped around the bookshelf. He could see that Mr Lyle had pushed the office door closed, and was whispering into the telephone receiver in a low, urgent voice. It was quite obvious that he had not the slightest idea that Billy was there and could hear every word he was saying.

'Yes – *yes*. No one suspects. I've just seen Worth's latest report and . . .'

Behind Billy, Lucky gave a low growl. '*Hush!*' Billy admonished the dog in a whisper, darting back to pick him up in the hope of keeping him quiet. Lucky squirmed and licked Billy's ear happily, as Billy crept back towards the door.

'I've done everything you told me, exactly as you wanted,' he heard Lyle saying. 'Look, you *know* I can't talk properly here. Anyone could be listening!'

There was a long pause. 'Fine. I'll report at the meeting tonight,' Lyle said finally. As Billy watched from behind the bookshelves, he scribbled something on Miss Atwood's blotting pad. 'Very well. I'll be there.'

Mr Lyle replaced the receiver with a click. His shoulders seemed to slump down, and Billy whisked quickly back behind the shelves before Lyle could look up and notice him.

His heart was beginning to race. When he heard the office door close again, he hurried back out and darted across to the telephone. He wanted to see what Mr Lyle had written – would there be anything on Miss Atwood's blotting pad? But, to his disappointment, the top sheet was gone – of course, Mr Lyle must have taken it with him.

Lucky had followed him out of the room, and had begun yapping again, and growling at a pencil that had fallen on to the floor. The sight of the pencil gave Billy a sudden idea.

'Hang on a minute, Lucky,' he whispered in excitement. 'Give me that.'

He bent down and grabbed the pencil, then carefully tore the top sheet of paper from Miss Atwood's blotting pad. 'This always works for Montgomery Baxter,' he murmured, as he used the pencil to very lightly shade over the sheet of paper. 'Let's hope it works for me.'

In the park, the others were taking it in turns to throw sticks for Daisy. The weather had grown colder in the past few days, and Sophie's breath puffed out in little clouds as the others shared what they had found out so far, while Daisy bounded through the autumn leaves around them, woofing in delight. She didn't have the slightest idea that she was rather in disgrace at Sinclair's, having failed in her duty to guard Mr Lyle's exhibition.

'Nothing to report from the stables,' said Joe, as he flung the stick across the grass, and Daisy raced after it joyfully. 'No one remembers seeing anything out of the normal way.'

'What about you two?' asked Lil eagerly, turning to Jack and Leo. 'What did you find out at the Spencer?'

'Well, we're pretty sure it wasn't Nicholls,' said Jack. 'It sounds like he would never have had enough money to pay Randall. And even if Randall wasn't the one who stole the painting, we know he must be mixed up in this somehow.'

'We know that the Suffragettes weren't involved either,' added Leo, quickly explaining what they had learned from Connie.

'So it really was Mrs St James that I saw outside the store!' said Lil. 'I say – I'm jolly well in favour of votes for women, but just the same I'm fearfully relieved that the Suffragettes didn't end up chucking bricks at us. So who's left on our list?'

It was at that moment that Billy came running towards them across the wet grass. He had evidently decided that Lucky was too slow to keep up with him, and had tucked the little dog under his arm while he ran. His face was pink and he was very out of breath, and when he reached them, he had to stand still for a moment, puffing in a way that suddenly reminded Sophie of his uncle Sid.

'Got – something – to – tell – you!' he panted, setting Lucky down on the ground. 'Look!'

He pushed a piece of blotting paper into Sophie's hands.

'Whatever is this?' she asked in astonishment.

'It's a *clue*! I think I might know who could have stolen the painting!' Billy managed to say. 'What if it was *Mr Lyle*?'

CHAPTER NINETEEN

They all stared at Billy as he gasped out his story.

'I was in Miss Atwood's office, and Mr Lyle came in to take a telephone call,' he began. 'He sounded strange – *shifty*. He kept saying things about how no one suspected anything. *I think he was talking about the robbery. I think he was the one behind it!*'

'*Mr Lyle?*' repeated Jack. 'But – it can't be! That doesn't make any sense!'

Several different thoughts seemed to click together in Sophie's mind, and she felt a sudden fever of excitement. 'He left at half past four – but what if he came back later that evening, after the store was closed and took the painting?' she said, working it out. 'He had access to the Spencer studios, so he could easily have taken Leo's painting. He could have bribed or tricked the nightwatchman into giving up his keys. And Daisy knows him – she's seen him at Sinclair's – so she wouldn't have barked.'

'Why on earth would he have wanted to steal a painting from his own exhibition?'

'It wasn't his own painting, was it?' said Lil. '*The Green Dragon* belongs to the King!'

'But he made such a fuss about the robbery, and the damage it would do to his reputation. He was so angry about it – he was the one who insisted on getting Scotland Yard's top man! If he was the one who stole the painting, why would he do that?'

'He was bluffing,' said Sophie. 'That's the cleverest part of it.'

Joe nodded vigorously. 'It's like if you pick someone's pocket. It's much easier if you put their attention somewhere else. Tell 'em you're lost, and ask for directions – they'll be so busy trying to help that they don't notice you've nabbed their pocket watch. Not that *I* go nabbing any pocket watches, mind,' he added hurriedly, seeing Jack's expression. 'I'm just saying, that's how it works.'

'Don't you see?' Billy went on. 'By making all this fuss, he's throwing attention away from himself – making sure he's the last person anyone would ever suspect!'

'But *why*?' Jack protested. 'He's a wealthy man – with a huge art collection. Why didn't he try to *buy* the painting, if he wanted it so much? I know it's rare – and special – but surely no painting would be worth becoming a criminal for.'

'That's if he is *becoming* a criminal,' said Billy eagerly.

'We don't know that this is the first time that he's done something like this. What about the other painting that got stolen? Couldn't he be behind that too? Maybe he even arranged the exhibition to give himself an opportunity to get his hands on the painting!'

'*The Green Dragon* is hardly ever exhibited in public,' said Leo slowly. 'This is the first time it's been on show for years.'

Jack stared at her incredulously. 'But if it was Lyle, why on earth would he put your painting in place of the stolen picture? He of all people would have known that it wouldn't fool anyone for a second!'

'But it makes sense of something,' said Sophie suddenly. She turned to Leo: 'Mr Lyle was angry with you when he saw your version of the painting – he said he was disappointed. Do you think that maybe the reason he was so angry was that he'd hoped you'd paint an exact copy of the painting that he could use to cover up the theft of the real painting?'

Leo stared at her in astonishment. Suddenly she saw Mr Lyle's angry face in quite a different light. *This is no good to me* she heard him say again. She remembered him standing next to her, and she remembered the gleam of his lapel pin, the rich spicy scent of his cologne – and then she recalled that peculiar smell as she had left the Exhibition Hall.

'Those footsteps I heard when I was leaving that night –

what if it was Mr Lyle?' she burst out. 'I smelled something too – I didn't think about it at the time – but I think it might have been his cologne!'

The others looked at each other in excitement. 'I say – he really could be the one responsible!' exclaimed Lil.

'But I tell you what,' said Billy more soberly. 'If he is behind this, he didn't do it alone. The person he spoke to on the telephone was definitely involved too.'

'Was it Red Hands Randall, d'you reckon?' asked Joe.

'No, I don't think so. He sounded as if he was *receiving* orders – not giving them. I heard him say that he was going to some kind of a meeting tonight to talk about it. He even wrote down the time and place on Miss Atwood's blotting pad. He took the note away with him of course, but when I shaded over the next sheet of paper, the indentations of his writing became visible!'

Sophie read the message aloud:

'What a funny name! What does Wyvern mean?' asked Lil.

Rather surprisingly, it was Leo who answered her. 'It's a sort of dragon,' she said breathlessly.

'A *dragon*?' repeated Lil.

'Yes. *Wyvern* is an Old English word for a dragon. It's a kind that only has two legs, rather than four. I read about it in a book from the Spencer Library when I was researching the dragon paintings.'

Sophie stared at her in amazement. '*Wyvern* – *dragon*. It all fits together!' she exclaimed. She turned to Jack impatiently. 'Surely you see – it's too much of a coincidence. There *has* to be some kind of a connection to the robbery.'

'Wyvern House is a gentlemen's club,' added Billy. 'It's near the Bank of England. Mr Lyle is a member there.'

'So the people he's meeting at this club tonight – they might be involved too!' exclaimed Lil. 'Come on, Jack – maybe we are wrong and Lyle has nothing whatsoever to do with this, but you have to admit it's a perfectly splendid clue. We should take this to Mr McDermott and tell him about it straight away.' She turned to Leo and explained. 'He's a friend of ours – a private detective, the one we told you about. He'll be able to help us.'

Billy nodded in agreement. 'Mr McDermott may not be involved in the investigation this time – but I'll bet he could pass on word to Scotland Yard about this,' he said eagerly.

At last, Jack nodded too. 'I still don't believe it could be Lyle,' he said. 'But telling this detective fellow certainly couldn't hurt.'

It seemed right to Sophie that it was she and Lil together who went to take the news to Mr McDermott. She felt a glow of excitement and pride, as the two of them hurried side by side up the steps to the detective's house, with its familiar shiny black front door. She was quite certain that they had worked it out, although she could still scarcely believe that Mr Lyle had the sheer front to do it. He had tried to fool everyone into believing that he was the victim – but recasting him as the thief explained so much. It even made sense that there were no other fingerprints on the false painting beyond the students' and Mr Lyle's – after all, Mr Lyle had been the one who had hung it in the Exhibition Hall.

She saw it all quite clearly now. After Leo had left the store, Mr Lyle had gone back into the Exhibition Hall, had stolen the painting himself and crept away again. The next day, he had made sure he was on the scene with plenty of witnesses to discover the theft, who would see him display all the appropriate horror and outrage. Then he had directed the police towards other possible suspects –

Richard Nicholls, Max Kamensky, perhaps even Leo and the other art students.

Now all she and Lil had to do was tell Mr McDermott what they had discovered. She knew he would spring into action, just as he always did. He would be able to tell Scotland Yard what they had discovered – and Detective Worth would listen to him. The police could investigate Mr Lyle – maybe they would even be able to go to the meeting at Wyvern House and arrest him. Leo would be safe; the painting would be found; and best of all, she would know that they had solved another important mystery. Thanks to Billy's sharp ears, they had been able to work out the answer more swiftly and easily than ever before.

'We're here to see Mr McDermott,' Lil announced to the housemaid who answered the door. 'Is he at home? It's very urgent.'

The housemaid showed them through to Mr McDermott's study, where they found the private detective writing at his desk. He looked up in surprise as they came in.

'We came at once – we had to tell you,' Lil began excitedly. 'We believe we know who stole the dragon painting!'

McDermott listened as they related the story. Finally, he sat back in his chair, and examined the scrap of blotting paper for a long moment. Then, to her surprise, he reached for Sophie's hand, dropped the paper back into her palm, and closed her fist around it.

'I'm sorry,' he said soberly. 'I can't help you with this. There's nothing I can do.'

CHAPTER TWENTY

'**B**ut what do you mean, *he can't help?*'

'Doesn't he care that Mr Lyle might be the one who stole the painting?'

Sophie found herself pacing up and down in the hayloft. She felt intensely frustrated. The visit to Mr McDermott had been unnerving: she had been unable to do anything more than stare at him, as he had explained:

'My hands are tied. It's out of the question for me to suggest any kind of investigation into Lyle's business – especially without a shred of evidence to back it up.' He sighed, and looked at them both seriously. 'You must understand. Randolph Lyle is a man of very good standing, with friends in high places. He's made his feelings about me abundantly clear – he's insisted I have no part in this investigation – and I have to respect that.'

Sophie had had to turn away to hide her surprise, and disappointment. It had been Lil who had tried to argue:

'But if Lyle really is behind this – and Scotland Yard haven't the slightest idea –'

McDermott had held up his hands. 'I'm not worried about Scotland Yard. Worth is a smart man. He takes his time, but he's an exceptional detective. If what you say is true, I have every confidence that he'll get to the bottom of it.'

'But how can you be sure of that? If we could just tell him what Billy heard –'

'What did he hear – *really*? Lyle sounding a little odd on the telephone? A person with every reason to be upset and agitated? It's not enough. Go to Worth and tell him about it, if you want – but what you're suggesting is extraordinary. You'll need some concrete evidence to convince him.' Mr McDermott paused for a moment, and looked at them both seriously. 'But if you want my advice, you should stay well away from Lyle, and away from Wyvern House. These are powerful men – you shouldn't make enemies of them. Just leave it to Worth this time.'

But staying out of this and leaving it to Detective Worth was hardly an option, Sophie thought now. Here they were, with a mystery unfolding right under their very noses – they couldn't just walk away.

'But that doesn't sound like Mr McDermott at all,' Billy was saying fretfully.

'All that talk of powerful men – and – and "friends

in high places",' said Lil, shaking her head in disbelief. 'I didn't think McDermott was like that.'

'Look,' Sophie said briskly. 'If McDermott says he can't help – he can't help. But that doesn't mean *we* have to give up, does it?'

She spoke decidedly, but the truth was she didn't feel so certain. Mr McDermott's behaviour had rattled her, but she knew that he had been right about one thing: a man like Detective Worth would never listen if all they had to offer him was an outlandish tale about a man in red gloves pushing a girl off a train platform; a bit of blotting paper; the scent of an unusual cologne; and a telephone conversation overheard by Miss Atwood's office boy. If they were going to prove that Mr Lyle really was behind the theft of the painted dragon, they would need some real evidence.

'There's only one thing to do,' she announced. 'We have to go to this meeting at Wyvern House, and discover what's going on for ourselves.'

Rather to her surprise, no one said anything. There was an awkward pause, and then Lil spoke up: 'I'm not sure that would be an awfully good idea. Mr McDermott seemed really worried about us getting mixed up in this. I know he behaved strangely today, but I trust him and I think we ought to listen. I don't think we should go to Wyvern House tonight.'

Sophie frowned in disbelief. The last person she had

ever expected to disagree with her about this was Lil. She was usually the first to want to plunge into an adventure.

'The meeting is in less than two hours – and we don't have any kind of a plan,' Lil was saying. 'I don't mean we shouldn't investigate Lyle – I just don't think we should risk tearing after him tonight. Besides,' she added. 'I couldn't go anyway. I've got to be on stage at half past seven – I need to go and get ready at the theatre.'

Sophie stared at her, disappointed, but then Jack weighed in too. 'I think Lil's right,' he said, causing his younger sister to turn and stare at him in disbelief.

'I don't think you've ever said that in your life before,' she muttered.

Jack ignored her and went on: 'Wyvern House is one of the most important gentlemen's clubs in London. It's strictly private – and its members are some of the richest and most powerful men in the city. It's not somewhere we can just . . . stroll in off the street. Why, women aren't even admitted at all! We'd get in very serious trouble if we were caught trying to get inside – and I for one don't want to spend the night in a police cell.'

'But we might have the chance to find out what's really going on!' Sophie protested. She hated how small and high-pitched her voice sounded in comparison to Jack's confident tone.

Leo chimed in too. 'What happened to Jack – and to me

– was simply awful,' she said quietly. 'I don't want anyone else to get in any more trouble because of this.'

'Look, let's all sleep on it tonight,' suggested Jack more gently. 'We can think about what to do tomorrow – and how we can put all this to Detective Worth.'

He tried to put a hand on Sophie's arm and smile, but Sophie shrugged him off. She wasn't going to be patted and dismissed, like she was some sort of silly little girl.

Lil was putting on her coat and hat. 'I'm awfully sorry, but I have to go or I'm going to be late. But I do think this is the right thing to do,' she said, without meeting Sophie's eye. 'Look, let's all meet back here tomorrow morning. We can talk about this properly then.'

'We should go too,' said Jack to Leo. 'We're supposed to be meeting Connie and Smitty.'

Sophie stared after them miserably. What had happened to being the captain, bravely leading the regiment into battle? When they had taken on the Baron, they had done some terribly dangerous things – but they had never faltered. They had always felt like a team, but now all that seemed to have changed. Now, even Billy and Joe were eyeing her with a hint of nervousness – not in the least like she was someone whom they trusted to take charge, but instead rather as though she was a fluffy kitten that might be about to scratch them.

'Well, I'm going to Wyvern House – even if I have to go

by myself,' she found herself saying in a determined voice, as she got to her feet.

'But wait – Sophie – you can't do that,' spluttered Billy.

'We agreed – we aren't going,' said Joe anxiously. 'Sophie – come back!'

For a moment, the two boys looked uncertainly at each other. Then they scrambled to their feet and hurried after her.

A short time later, the three of them were walking together through the City. The streets around the Bank of England were a maze: a labyrinth of narrow lanes and crooked little passageways. Everything seemed to be all jumbled up together: shops, old-fashioned coffee houses, little eating places, even church spires. But there was no mistaking the grand edifice of the Bank of England itself, with its enormous statues and immense columns.

'No wonder they say it's the safest place in England,' said Joe, in awe. 'It scares you just looking at it.'

'We must be nearly there now,' said Billy. 'I think it's down this way.'

He led the way along a narrow street that twisted away from the main road. It was lined with tall, elegant, red brick buildings – and Sophie noticed that the finest of them all had a sign hanging outside, in the shape of a twisting golden dragon.

'Look!' she exclaimed. 'The sign of the dragon – that must be the place!'

'Are you sure?' asked Billy. 'But there's no name up anywhere.'

'I'm not sure there would be. If this club is as exclusive as we've been told, I can see that they might not want anything obvious to mark it out. You'd have to know the dragon symbol to find it.'

'So what do we do now?' asked Billy, stuffing the map into his pocket and eyeing the forbidding black front door – very firmly closed. 'Do we wait and watch for Mr Lyle?'

'Whatever we're going to do we can't just stand on the street like this,' said Joe, who was becoming restless. 'We're making ourselves obvious – and it's not far off eight o'clock. Mr Lyle might turn up at any moment. Let's wait back here.'

He turned swiftly into a narrow passage running along the side of the building, which Sophie hadn't even noticed. Following him, she saw to her surprise that it led through into what at first she thought was a small garden, and then she realised was in fact a little churchyard, with several trees and a scattering of old gravestones.

'There's a church!' exclaimed Billy.

But Sophie's attention was still fixed on Wyvern House. Thinking about how they could find their way inside distracted her from remembering how Lil had just gone off to the theatre like that. 'Maybe there's a back door – we might be able to sneak in that way,' she suggested.

Joe crept forwards, to scan the big building – but if there was a back door, it was clear that it wouldn't be easy to reach it. The building was separated from the churchyard by a tall fence of spiked iron railings. Higher above, on the upper floors, Sophie could glimpse balconies and brightly lit windows – but down at ground level, all was dark and still.

'Well, I reckon there's only one sure way to get in there,' said Joe, after a very long pause. 'And that's by climbing up.'

Sophie stared up apprehensively. She could see what Joe meant – the back of the building was all corners and window ledges, pillars and porticoes, little balconies and ornamental drainpipes. There were certainly plenty of footholds and handholds, but you would have to be a skilful climber, with a good head for heights. And that was something that Sophie did not have. She might be able to manage to get a cat down from a tree – but the thought of climbing several storeys up the outside of a building made her cold with fear.

'One of those sash windows should be easy enough to lever up from the outside,' Joe was saying. 'But we'd have to creep through without anyone seeing or hearing us.'

Billy gave a sudden shiver. Sophie knew that he was

remembering what Jack had said earlier. She didn't like to think what might happen to them if they were caught. Jack's vision of a police cell would probably be the least of their worries: if these really were the people who had set Red Hands Randall on Leo's tail, there was no doubt that they were very ruthless indeed. For a moment she wondered whether they had done right to come here, but she shoved the thought aside.

'Climbing it is, then,' she said firmly.

'It's a shame Mei isn't here,' said Billy, staring upwards nervously. 'She's the best of all of us when it comes to climbing.'

Sophie was wishing very much that both Mei and Song were there. Song was always so calm and sensible. And Mei was certainly a good climber, she thought, remembering how the other girl had clambered so boldly over the rooftops during their last adventure. She was conscious that Joe was watching her and knew that he was remembering the same thing. He was the only one who knew how much she hated heights.

'One of us had better stay down here,' said Joe quickly now, looking at her and raising his eyebrows. 'Someone who can give the rest of us a warning, if they spot anyone coming. Soph, what about you?'

Resolutely, she shook her head. She could see what Joe was trying to do, but she had to go through with this now.

She had made them come here, and she wasn't going to be left down here waiting and watching, while Billy and Joe finished what she had started. 'No,' she said stoutly. 'I'm going up.'

'Well, I suppose *I'll* have to stay down here, then,' said Billy, with a rather huffy sigh. All the same, Sophie suspected that he was a little relieved; he had not looked any more enamoured by the idea of climbing the building than she was herself. 'I'll do the owl hoot if I hear someone coming,' he suggested.

Joe nodded. 'And look sharp,' he said. 'We don't want anyone to spot us. It's a good job it's dark.' He turned to Sophie. 'All right – I'll go first. Then you come after – Billy can give you a leg up. Follow my lead – I'll show you how to go. I reckon if we can get up to that first-floor balcony, we might be able to get through one of those windows.'

Even the first-floor balcony looked frighteningly high. Sophie folded her hands to try and stop them trembling, nodded nervously to Billy and then followed Joe as he went towards the fence. He deftly levered himself up, finding a foothold between two of the spiked iron railings. With his foot braced, and a drainpipe to help him, he managed to swing himself upwards and grab the edge of the window ledge. Once there, he pulled himself up and then crouched down to lend a hand to Sophie, who was doing her best to follow him, cursing her long skirt and petticoats as they tangled with the sharp points of the railings. Not for the first time, she wished she could wear trousers like the boys did: girls' clothes really were not made for detective work.

Her legs were not nearly as long as Joe's, and there was an unpleasant moment as she stretched up towards the window ledge, and for a split second lost her balance.

'Careful,' whispered Joe, grabbing her hand and steadying her. 'Now, up you come.'

No longer caring if he could see her hands shaking, Sophie scrambled with relief on to the ledge. The ground already seemed horribly far away: she could just see Billy, watching them anxiously from the shadows beneath one of the trees in the churchyard.

The window beside them was in darkness: they tried to peer through, but it looked as though it had been covered by heavy curtains. There wasn't even a faint glimmer of light to be seen inside.

'Could we get in this way?' she murmured to Joe in a low voice.

Joe was examining the window with care. 'Not without making a racket,' he whispered into her ear. 'Let's go over to that one – it looks more likely.'

He went onwards, sliding across from the window ledge to the next window, which had a narrow iron balcony all twisted with ivy. Before he edged on to it, he laid a warning hand on Sophie's arm, and she nodded, understanding what he meant. This window was brightly lit – they would have to be on their guard, in case someone was inside.

Cautiously, they clambered over the edge of the iron balcony, and then crouched down low in the shadows. Sophie breathed a sigh of relief.

'What now?' she whispered.

'Let's try to take a look inside.'

Moving slowly on their hands and knees, they worked their way forwards until they were just beneath the window. It had begun to rain again, and Sophie wiped a few drops off her face, before gathering the courage to peep upwards.

Cautiously, she lifted her eyes to just above the window ledge – and immediately wished she hadn't. Facing the window was a table, and sitting at the table was none other than Mr Lyle himself. He appeared to have been writing letters, but now was staring ahead of him out of the window – apparently right into Sophie's face.

After one horrified glance, she dropped down into the shadows, her heart thumping. At any moment, she expected to hear Lyle shouting, to see him fling open the window and drag them inside. But nothing happened, and she realised that he had seen nothing. From inside the brightly lit room, everything outside the window must simply have looked black.

A moment later she heard a voice from inside the room.

'Mr Lyle, sir – it's time for the meeting. The gentlemen are assembling next door.'

She heard the scrape of his chair as he stood up, and then his footsteps as he walked away. Joe was already jerking his head at the next window along, and she realised he had heard it too. 'Next door!' he whispered.

Sophie followed his gaze across to the next window. There was no balcony there, nor even a proper window ledge, only an iron drainpipe running down one side of the window. It looked solid enough, bolted to the wall of the building at regular intervals with big ornamental brackets. All the same, she felt a rush of fear when she saw Joe looking at it speculatively.

'It'll have to be you,' he whispered. 'I don't reckon that'll hold my weight.'

Sophie nodded grimly. With Joe holding one hand, she stepped up on to the edge of the balcony – then, trembling fiercely, she made the step across to the drainpipe. The thing to remember was that she *must not look down*. Her hands scrabbled against brick and peeling paint, as her feet found a place to rest upon one of the brackets. She managed to work one arm around the drainpipe, squeezing her hand through the gap at the back, until she was almost hugging it, the cold metal pressed against her cheek. She felt better that way, clinging on like a spider to the pipe.

She realised with a sudden flutter of excitement that she could see very clearly into the room next to her. The window curtains were closed, but not properly – there was a gap through which she had a clear view into the room. She could even make out Mr Lyle, sitting at a long polished mahogany table. Better still, she realised that the sash window had been left open an inch or two, meaning she could hear the hum of voices inside.

She forgot to worry about how high up she was as she stared in. She could only see Mr Lyle and three others, but it was obvious that the room held around half a dozen men. Those she could see were smartly dressed, with all the trappings of wealthy gentlemen: silk top hats, pocket watches, gold monocles. One looked rather a dandy, with a carefully arranged silk necktie and jewelled cufflinks; another, with a long grey beard, looked as serious as a schoolmaster. As Sophie looked, she realised that there was something that united them all – each wore the same gold lapel pin. Squinting, she could just make out the shape of a twisting gold dragon.

'Are we all assembled? Good – thank you, Evans. Close the door behind you.'

Sophie could not see the speaker, but she could hear him clearly: a powerful voice from the head of the table. As she listened, the voice intoned. '*Salve*, my brothers. You are welcome to this meeting of the *Fraternitas Draconum*,

British Division. The Black Dragon is still away, dealing with urgent business in the Paris office: in his absence, I shall lead this evening's meeting. The first item for the agenda, is of course, an update from White.'

To Sophie's surprise, it was Mr Lyle who spoke. 'You will be pleased to hear that the painting has been retrieved exactly as planned,' he announced in a satisfied voice. 'It is now safely in my possession. You will have seen for yourselves the reactions from the press. It has been just as Black anticipated.'

Sophie's heart began to beat faster. They had been right. Lyle *was* the one who had stolen the painting!

'Very good,' said the first man coolly.

'Where is the painting now?' demanded the man with the long grey beard.

'Locked in my personal safe at home, under all the proper conditions and guarded by my manservant.'

'It ought to be placed in the bank vault at once!' exclaimed another man, with a white moustache and an angry red face.

'Black wishes to examine it himself first,' came the low, authoritative voice of the man in charge. 'Besides, surely it is obvious some delay is necessary. White can scarcely stroll into the bank with a valuable painting to deposit, the very day after the robbery.'

'Scotland Yard are bound to be watching the banks –

you should know that as well as anyone, Green,' said Lyle indignantly. 'I shall wait a week – I'll make the deposit on Friday morning, ten o'clock. Tell your people to expect me. I want to do this as quickly and discreetly as possible. Once it is safe in our vault, there can be no further concern.'

'Black will be satisfied,' said the man in charge.

The red-faced man said nothing more, but the grey-bearded man spoke up. 'You may *say* that this has gone to plan, White – but that's not how I've heard it. What's all this about a girl getting mixed up in it – and Randall being brought in to deal with her?'

A murmur of agitation ran around the table and Sophie leaned forwards eagerly. Surely he must be talking about Leo!

'There's no need for anyone to be concerned about that,' said Lyle in an annoyed voice. 'The problem is in hand.'

'What exactly *is* the problem?' demanded the red-faced man.

'One of the art students was lurking around late in the Exhibition Hall on the night I retrieved the painting. I'm afraid she may have seen something,' said Lyle shortly. 'She had already been asking awkward questions about the painting. Black and I agreed that Randall would be brought in – to make sure she stayed quiet.'

'Quiet?' said the man with the grey beard sharply. 'Exactly how *quiet* do you mean?'

'He was instructed to do whatever was necessary,' said Lyle tightly. 'After all this trouble, you know we can't take even the smallest risk of the truth coming out. Anyway, it worked – the girl was frightened off.'

'Who is she, this student?' asked the red-faced man.

'No one to concern us,' said Lyle. 'Not someone who would ever be taken seriously. I've made quite sure the police understand that.'

'That's not what I heard,' spoke up the young fellow with the necktie suddenly. 'I heard she was Fitzgerald's youngest.'

'*Fitzgerald!*' burst out the grey-beard. 'You can't seriously mean you set Randall after Horace Fitzgerald's daughter!'

'It's not as though he'll ever know a thing about it,' protested Lyle crossly. 'He takes no interest whatsoever in the girl.'

'I don't like this,' said grey-beard, primly. 'Fitzgerald – Randall – it's too messy!'

'These are the instructions from the Black Dragon,' came the firm voice of the man in charge from the far end of the table.

'Well, perhaps Black has gone too far this time,' said grey-beard in a tetchy voice. 'The methods used last time were bad enough – but this whole business has been too showy, from beginning to end. We're taking needless risks, drawing too much attention to ourselves.'

Lyle spoke in a low, angry voice. 'You know how important it is that we complete the set of paintings,' he hissed. 'We have been working towards this for years – and we're only a few days away from attaining our goal.'

'I don't set store by all that mystical nonsense. It's nothing but superstition.'

'I doubt very much you would dare say that if Black was here,' said the man with the red face. 'Besides, superstition is hardly the point. The secret information the paintings conceal is what matters. Once Black returns from Paris, he'll be able to examine them, and we'll be able to complete the instructions at last. You know what that means for us.'

He sat back in his chair, pleased with himself, as if he had spoken the last word, but the man with the grey beard was still grumbling. 'We've managed well enough for all these years – why unsettle everything now? Why disturb the status quo? Wherever the paintings may lead us, is it really worth risking everything that we have spent so long building? This last year has hardly been smooth sailing for us – why, it's been little short of a disaster! The last thing we need is any more attention coming our way – and frankly, Black's mania for these paintings is becoming a liability.'

'You must not question the word of the Black Dragon,' said the cold voice of the man at the head of the table. 'You swore an oath, Blue.'

There was a strained silence and in that quiet moment, Sophie could hear her heart pumping. The rain was falling more heavily now: she could feel a cold trickle of it sliding down her neck. Her hands were slippery against the wet drainpipe.

'I wasn't *questioning* him,' said the grey-beard hurriedly. He paused, suddenly panicked. 'You aren't going to tell him about this . . . are you? All I meant was that perhaps the methods used were a little –'

But the rest of his sentence was lost. To Sophie's horror, the ornate iron bracket that she was standing on suddenly slipped sideways. Her weight was too much for it – one of the screws must have come loose. She clutched on tightly with her arms, scrabbled for purchase with her feet. The other screw was about to give way – she could feel it.

'What on earth was that?' came a voice from inside, and there were the sound of footsteps coming towards the window.

Sophie pressed herself against the drainpipe, clinging on for dear life – even as below her, she heard the distant, but very definite, hooting of an owl.

CHAPTER TWENTY-ONE

Leo lay awake that night. Even though she was still staying in the Lims' cosy attic room in China Town, she found it difficult to sleep. Ever since her experience at the underground railway station, shadows seemed darker than usual, the hollow sound of the wind blowing outside more sinister. What was more, she had a great deal to think about. Now, she lay back into her pillows, listening to horses' hooves rattling on the cobbles outside, and the distant hooting of a fog-horn on the river, as she tried to make sense of all that had happened to her in the past few weeks.

In the very first moments, she had felt as disbelieving as Jack at the idea that Mr Lyle could be the one behind the theft of *The Green Dragon*. But the more the others had talked, and Jack had argued, the more she had begun to feel certain they were right. She thought again of the ghostly pad of footsteps, the spicy scent in the Entrance Hall. She felt sure now that it was Mr Lyle's cologne that she had smelled. Then she thought again of how swiftly

Lyle had shifted from the kind friend who had encouraged her, to the cold-eyed man in the studio. She had always thought that Vincent was cruel, but she now realised she would take a thousand of his jibes over the way that Lyle had manipulated her.

It seemed so obvious now, the way he had built her up with his admiring remarks until she was ready to do whatever he suggested. He had manoeuvred her into making that copy of *The Green Dragon*, she was sure of it. She wondered if perhaps Sophie was right, and he really had believed she was capable of painting a version convincing enough that he would be able to switch it for the original painting. She wasn't sure whether to be flattered or horrified. No wonder he had been so angry when she had decided to take her painting in a new direction.

She turned over restlessly on her pillows. Had Mr Lyle seen something in her that had made him sure he could shape her to exactly what he wanted? She had always thought of herself as resilient. She thought again of Mrs St James's lecture. *I have learned for myself the strength, the integrity, the independence and the wisdom of today's young women.* But she wasn't strong, she thought now – and she certainly wasn't wise. She had thought she had built an armour to protect herself, like the hard shiny carapace of an insect – or even the scales of a dragon. Now, she saw in a clear flash how cleverly Mr Lyle had managed to pierce that protective shell. Beneath it she was weak and stupid. She had been desperate for approval, and to feel like she belonged. Mr Lyle had known that, and he had taken advantage of it – then discarded her when she was no longer of value. The letter that had been left in her room the night she had been pushed on to the train tracks now seemed crueller than ever before.

Mr Lyle would never have tried to do something like this to Jack or Smitty, she thought now, thinking of Mrs St James again. *We are merely to be represented by our fathers, brothers and husbands, as if our thoughts and beliefs have no value of their own.* Lyle thought he could manipulate her because she was a girl – but as she lay there and thought about it, she realised that he was wrong in that. She certainly couldn't imagine that it would be easy to manipulate someone like Jack's sister, Lil – nor even Sophie, who might seem quieter than her boisterous friend, but who had a sort of steeliness about her. Leo had seen that tonight, when Sophie had been so determined to go to Wyvern House. Now, Leo found herself wondering uncertainly if she and the others had been right not to go. If Lyle was behind all this, she felt a sudden and very powerful wish to see him exposed and punished. It was her last thought before she turned over again, and finally fell into a troubled sleep.

*

'What on earth did you think you were doing up there?' demanded a voice in the dark above her.

A hand reached towards her, and Sophie gripped it gratefully as Lil pulled her up from where she had slipped over on the wet stones of the graveyard. 'Honestly, Sophie! I don't think I've ever been half so frightened in my whole life!'

She must have come straight from the theatre, Sophie realised. She had thrown her coat over her costume, and her face was shining with greasepaint. She was at once a very peculiar, and very, very reassuring sight.

'If it wasn't for Joe, you'd be splattered on these paving stones by now. Or captured by Lyle and his cronies – and I don't know which is worse,' Lil was now saying in a cross voice. Joe, who had clambered down after Sophie, began to look rather pleased with himself, but Lil put a stop to that at once. 'Oh don't think I'm all too pleased with you either,' she said, turning on him. 'How could you let her do this? We all agreed it was too dangerous!'

Joe took a step back, looking alarmed. 'I didn't *let* her do anything!' he protested. 'We just . . . er . . . came too . . .'

But Sophie felt that Lil could scold as much as she liked, just as long as her own two feet were planted firmly on the ground. After that awful moment when she had been quite sure the drainpipe was going to give way altogether, it seemed extraordinary that she had made it back down here at all. It was certainly true that if it hadn't been for Joe, her adventure would have ended in disaster. He had managed to reach out and grab hold of her just as the bracket had slipped from under her feet. With his help, she had scrambled back over on to the balcony – and by the time the gentleman with the silk necktie had made it over to the window to look out, they were both safe in the shadows.

Climbing back down the building again had been nerve-wracking. She had slipped several times, grazing an elbow, bumping her knee and scraping her hand – but none of that mattered now. When she had finally reached the ground, her knees had given way and she'd slipped forwards on to the wet ground, even as she stared across the graveyard at Billy, who seemed to be having a whispered argument with someone very familiar.

'How was I supposed to know that it was you? I thought we'd been discovered! That's why I did the owl call!'

To her astonishment, she had realised that it was Lil.

'How did you find us?' Joe asked her now.

'What about the show?' Sophie gasped, in a voice that sounded rather more wobbly than usual.

'Oh, I'm not on again until the third act,' said Lil. 'I can get back in plenty of time, if I jump in a cab.'

'But why are you *here*?'

'I just had a feeling you were going to do something

249

mad – and I had to come, in case you needed my help. There's no need to look quite so astonished. I do know you quite well, you know, Sophie,' she said, still sounding cross. 'Then, when I got here, I saw you dangling off a drainpipe! You could have been awfully badly hurt!' Lil's voice made a sort of cracking sound, and all at once, Sophie realised that she wasn't only annoyed with them – she was frightened and worried too. 'If you had been – well, it would have been my fault. I'm awfully sorry, Sophie. I ought to have backed you up – and I shouldn't have just left like that.'

Sophie stared at her in astonishment. 'No, *I'm* sorry,' she burst out. 'I was the one who was in the wrong. It was silly and dangerous to come here – but I couldn't bear not doing anything. It's different for you – you've got so much else,' she added in a smaller voice. 'The theatre, and your brother, and everything. This – being a detective, I mean – it's all I've got.'

'Of course it's not all you've got, you mutton-head!' said Lil, sounding much more like her normal self again. 'You've got *me*, haven't you? We're in this together!'

Sophie smiled. She was wet and cold, her elbow and knee ached, but just the same, she suddenly felt flooded with happiness.

Joe put a gentle arm around Lil's shoulder. 'Er – girls, I'm glad you're patching things up – but do you think you could do this somewhere else?' he said tentatively. 'I think it's time for us to get out of here.'

The meeting in Detective HQ the next morning felt quite different. Sitting side by side on a hay bale, and occasionally finishing each other's sentences, Sophie and Lil told Jack and Leo the whole story – with a little help from Joe and Billy.

'So it's really true,' breathed Leo, when they at last finished talking. 'Mr Lyle is the one behind this.'

'Him and the rest of – what did you say they were called, Sophie? The *Fraternitas . . .* something or other,' explained Lil.

'I think they said *Fraternitas Draconum*,' Sophie remembered. 'At least that's what it sounded like. They seemed to be some kind of secret society.'

'*Fraternitas Draconum*,' said Jack slowly. 'It's Latin. It means something like the dragon brothers – or perhaps the Dragon Brotherhood.'

'Dragon!' exclaimed Lil. 'Like the dragon painting – and Wyvern House.'

Sophie turned to Leo. 'Those footsteps you heard on the night the painting was stolen – I think they must have been Mr Lyle's. He thinks you saw him, at Sinclair's! So he hired Randall to frighten you off.'

'It was *Randall* who sent you that note, telling you not

251

to talk to anyone,' said Lil. 'Then when he saw it hadn't stopped you talking to the police, they must have got frightened you would point the finger at Mr Lyle. That's why he pushed you on to the train tracks.'

'Mr Lyle and the other men at the meeting talked about the painting holding some kind of a secret,' Sophie went on. 'I think that's why they want it so much – and why they've gone to such elaborate lengths to get it.'

'I still can't believe you really did all that – climbing up there and eavesdropping on their meeting,' said Jack, who was gazing at Sophie in amazement.

'For goodness' sake, Jack, whatever you do, don't encourage her to do any more mad things,' said Lil with a giggle. 'I've had quite enough of that for a while!'

The others laughed, but Billy was eager to make more plans. 'What ought we to do next?' he wondered, putting down his notebook and pencil.

'Well, we still don't have a scrap of real evidence,' said Sophie. 'And I'm afraid I don't even know the names of any of those men. I think they were using code names. One was Green and one Blue. Lyle was called White, which confused me awfully at first. And their leader was called the Black Dragon.'

'*More* dragons!' said Lil. 'I say – the Black Dragon sounds rather fearsome, doesn't he?'

'One of the paintings in Casselli's original sequence

was of a black dragon,' Leo remembered. 'All the paintings have a different colour – black, green, white, blue and so on.'

'Gosh!' said Billy, even as he scribbled this down. 'So their code names could have come from the dragons in the original series of paintings!'

'But even the code names aren't going to help us convince Worth,' said Sophie. 'We need more. The only good thing is that I do know exactly where the stolen painting is now – it's in Mr Lyle's apartment, locked up in his safe, and guarded by his manservant.'

'Should we tell Detective Worth about that?' suggested Jack. 'He could send the police to go and look for it?'

'We know he isn't going to listen to us if we don't have any real evidence,' said Lil. 'Mr McDermott told us that.'

'But we have to do *something*,' protested Leo. 'Now that we know Mr Lyle really did this – he can't be allowed to get away with it!'

'What worries me is that if Mr Lyle deposits the painting into this bank vault on Friday, we may be too late,' said Sophie. 'Once the painting is locked away, there will be no way for us to find it – and I suppose even the police would need a jolly good reason before they could search a private vault. Besides, from they way they talked, it seemed like one of the men themselves might work at the bank – which I suppose would make it even harder.'

'But what can we do?' asked Leo anxiously. 'Friday is only a few days away!'

'Could we try and intercept him as he's taking it to the bank, somehow?' suggested Billy.

But Joe looked doubtful. 'There's no way that he's going to just stroll off down the bank with it by himself. He's bound to have some protection. That manservant of his will be with him – and maybe Randall too.'

Leo and Jack exchanged glances. Neither of them felt in the least that they wanted to cross paths with Red Hands Randall again.

Sophie spoke up. 'Well . . . I do have a sort of plan,' she said, a little more shyly than usual. 'It's not going to be easy – and you might all think it's another wild idea – but I do think there's a way we could get inside Mr Lyle's apartment and get hold of the painting. But it would only work if you all agree to it.'

The others looked at her with interest. ''Well, go on – tell us what it is,' said Lil at once.

Ten minutes later, the others were all staring at her with a mixture of astonishment, admiration and sheer perplexity.

'It sounds . . . *mad*,' said Joe.

'Mad? It sounds *brilliant*,' exclaimed Lil.

'Even Montgomery Baxter couldn't have come up with that,' said Billy, grinning.

'I think we should do it,' said Jack. 'It's our only chance.'

Leo didn't say anything, but she just smiled at Sophie and nodded vigorously.

'All right, then,' said Sophie. 'We'd better get to work – we've got rather a lot to do.'

The next two days certainly were very busy ones – and they all had a part to play. While Miss Atwood was occupied with a telephone call to one of their most important suppliers, Billy quickly searched the Sinclair's records, and after work that evening, he and Joe caught the omnibus out to an address in Chelsea, where they spent several hours watching a certain mansion block overlooking the river. Meanwhile, Jack and Leo spent the evening telling Sophie absolutely everything they could remember about Benedetto Casselli's dragon paintings. The next morning, Lil set out to several elegant West End residences to pay afternoon calls upon some old friends; while Sophie and Joe headed East, to pay a visit of quite a different kind to a former acquaintance of Joe's. While Jack and Leo whispered plans to Connie and Smitty under cover of the chatter in the Antiques Room, Billy slipped down to a very familiar room in the Sinclair's basement to collect some supplies. That night, Sophie sat up late reading an old book entitled *Tales from Greek Legend*.

'Everything's in place,' reported Jack in a low voice to Sophie in the Millinery Department the next morning, while nearby, Connie and Leo pretended to be interested in a display of hats. 'We've begun to spread word about the auction. We think we've got a good idea about the right thing to tempt Mr Lyle.'

'Do you have anything like this in blue?' asked Connie in a loud voice. More quietly, she whispered. 'The Suffragettes are planning to march down Piccadilly on Thursday afternoon. Mrs St James has organised a big demonstration at Trafalgar Square. It couldn't be better timing.'

'How about this style, madam?' suggested Sophie politely, holding out a hat. 'Can Song and Mei help us?' she asked Leo in a low voice.

Leo nodded at once. 'Of course. I've told them all about the plan.'

Jack pretended to admire the hat as Connie tried it on. 'What about your other friends?' he whispered to Sophie. 'Will they help us too?'

Sophie grinned. 'Oh yes. Actually, Lil said they are rather excited about it.'

'We're really going to do this, then?' said Leo nervously. 'We're going to get the painting from Mr Lyle's apartment?'

Sophie felt the familiar, shivery prickle of excitement run through her. 'I think we really are.'

Beyond them, Connie was admiring her reflection in the mirror, fluffing out her curls. 'Do you know, I think I really do like this hat,' she said to them suddenly. 'I rather think I might buy it.'

PART VI
Dragon Combatant

Also called The Silver Dragons, *the painting is thought to have been destroyed during the Sack of Rome in 1527. The only painting to depict a pair of dragons, it showed them standing beneath an arch through which a background of blue sky and an Italianate landscape of castles and hills could be seen. The dragons were facing each other, as though ready for combat.*

Dr Septimus Beagle, *The Life & Work of Benedetto Casselli*, 1889 (from the Spencer Institute Library)

CHAPTER TWENTY-TWO

On Thursday afternoon, Mr Randolph Lyle was walking up the steps of the auction house in St James's, feeling a pleasant tingle of anticipation. He never tired of the fever of excitement he always experienced just before an auction, where there was a real prize to be won. The very thought of getting his hands on the rare and unusual Watteau drawing that he had heard was going to be auctioned today was thrilling.

He took his customary seat in the best possible spot, where he could keep a close eye on the auctioneer, but also had a good view of the rest of the bidders. He could only hope that none of them knew what a treasure was on offer, though looking around the room, he could see no one who was likely to pose him a real threat. They seemed to be mostly wealthy socialites, not serious collectors. Indeed, even as he looked around, two fashionably dressed young ladies squeezed themselves and their excessively large hats into the seats beside him, whispering and giggling as though they were at some sort of theatre entertainment. No doubt they considered that attending an art auction was no more than the latest fashionable society pursuit.

Ignoring the chatter of the young ladies, he ostentatiously flicked opened the auction list, and began scanning the list of the works on offer. He felt pleased to be here, thinking about something normal, rather than worrying about what was back at home in Chelsea, locked in his safe. The horrible prickling anxiety that had been keeping him awake night after night seemed to have faded to something gentler and more bearable – a low hum he could almost ignore. He would feel much better once he had paid a visit to the bank tomorrow, he told himself. Once he had made the deposit exactly as the Black Dragon had instructed, it would no longer be his problem.

Blue was right, he thought: the whole affair had been messy and dangerous. Under normal circumstances, he would never have agreed to such a pantomime, but Black had a way of making you do things. Worst of all was the unfortunate business with Leonora Fitzgerald. He ought never to have got that thug Randall involved. His palms became a little sweaty as he thought about it, and he had to take out his silk handkerchief to wipe them.

He shook the thought of Miss Fitzgerald away. He would not think of her now, nor of Randall – and especially not of the Black Dragon. He turned his attention back to the programme, and began combing it for information about the Watteau drawing. But however carefully he looked, he could not see it listed anywhere. Could it be a last-minute addition that had arrived too late to be listed in the programme?

The auctioneer had appeared at the lectern now, and was calling the room to order. The first few lots did not interest Mr Lyle very much: there was some poor quality Chinese porcelain, a few anaemic watercolours, a seemingly endless series of oil paintings of dogs and horses. There was no sign of the Watteau at all, and he soon began to feel impatient.

After at least a dozen different lots had been sold, he leaned forwards and tapped on the shoulder of a young man sitting in front of him, whom he recognised as a clerk from the auction house.

'Excuse me,' he murmured. 'I understand that a Watteau drawing is to be auctioned today – do you know when that lot will come up?'

The young man turned around. 'Oh, good afternoon, Mr Lyle,' he said, immediately recognising one of their best customers. 'I'm terribly sorry but we don't have anything by Watteau in today's auction – and no drawings at all. I'm afraid that you must have been misinformed.'

Lyle sat back in his chair, frowning. He had been so sure the drawing was going to be here today. Why, he'd heard it from at least three different people at the Café Royal. Could he have got the wrong day – or even the wrong auction house? But if the Watteau wasn't here, there was no sense in sitting watching all these awful oil paintings being auctioned off. He got to his feet at once.

'Excuse me!' he said brusquely to the two young ladies seated beside him. They gaped up at him in surprise, and then confusion, as he gestured that he wished to get by. 'Could I possibly come past, if you please?' he said through gritted teeth.

Understanding at last, the young ladies moved out of his way, a fluster of skirts and ribbons and parasols, and more impatient than ever, Mr Lyle squeezed past them and out of the room. He did not even take a second glance at the young lady with the red-gold hair, who was even now glancing quickly across to another young lady, standing by the wall on the other side of the auction room. He certainly did not notice her swift signal – three quick taps of her closed fan against her gloved palm.

Across the room, the other young lady nodded smartly, then slipped her hand through the arm of the well-dressed young gentleman beside her, and steered him quickly out of the auction room, towards the foyer.

Mr Lyle was feeling quite out of temper, as he marched back towards the door. His plans had been upset, and now he had nothing to distract him from his anxious thoughts of dragon paintings. He decided he would go back home: perhaps he would feel better there, knowing that his safe was just a few feet away. But, rather to his surprise, before he could leave the auction house, a young couple stepped into his path.

'Oh hullo – Mr Lyle, isn't it? I don't know if you'll remember me, but I'm Hugo Devereaux,' said the smiling young man. 'We met at one of my mama's little soirées, as I recall?'

Mr Lyle nodded briefly, mumbling the usual pleasantries.

'I want to introduce my delightful fiancée, the Honourable Miss Phyllis Woodhouse,' said Mr Devereaux, presenting the young lady on his arm, his face pink and shiny with pride. 'We're only just engaged you know – the announcement was in *The Times* yesterday.'

'How do you do, Miss Woodhouse? My congratulations,' said Lyle, politely, with a small bow. He made as if to go on his way, but the young gentleman stopped him.

'I say, Mr Lyle, it's frightfully lucky we bumped into you like this,' he began. 'We were wondering if we could ask you about something. I know you're quite the expert on art, you see. Miss Woodhouse and I, well, we're both awfully keen to buy some really good paintings for our new home – aren't we?'

'*Awfully*,' agreed the young lady, nodding her head so fervently that her yellow curls bounced.

'Father says it's a jolly good investment, and all that – but the thing is, well I have to confess that we're both rather duffers when it comes to what to choose. So I wondered whether perhaps you might be able to give us some good advice – on what to buy, or whatnot?'

Mr Lyle paused thoughtfully. Up until that moment, this conversation had been nothing more than an annoying interruption in what was fast becoming an extremely irritating day – but he suddenly felt a prickle of interest. He liked to encourage young men like Mr Devereaux, who in his experience tended to have deep pockets and to be rather easily led. A society couple like these two could easily be persuaded to buy work by some of the young artists for whom he wished to act as benefactor.

'Of course, Mr Devereaux,' he said, smiling in his most avuncular manner. 'I'd be only too delighted to offer you any assistance that I can. Perhaps we might arrange an appointment when we can talk a little more about it?'

But Mr Devereaux and Miss Woodhouse seemed a great deal more interested in talking to him then and there, and it was some time before he could extract himself from their flood of questions. But at last, he managed to bid them farewell, and made his way swiftly out of the door, Mr Devereaux's card tucked safely inside his waistcoat pocket.

As he came down the steps of the auction house, and

on to the street, he noticed to his surprise that St James's was unusually busy. Pall Mall seemed quite crowded with carriages and motor cars, and in the distance he could hear music – it sounded like a marching band. On the pavement, he encountered his neighbour, Colonel Wentworth, evidently on his way to his club.

'Hullo, Lyle old chap. Good hunting today, was it?' he asked, gesturing to the auction house behind them.

'Not very, I'm afraid,' said Lyle, managing rather a weak smile. 'Busy, this afternoon, isn't it?'

'Huh!' exclaimed Wentworth. 'All the fault of those harpies, you know!'

'Harpies?' repeated Lyle confused.

'Those blasted *women*,' said Wentworth, swinging his swordstick in an aggressive manner. 'Mrs St James and her *Suffragettes*! Pack of nonsense! They're marching down Piccadilly to Trafalgar Square today, banners flying, singing their songs, making speeches, causing no end of fuss. No one can get through! This is why women ought to stay in the drawing room, where they belong – never mind trying to meddle with matters they don't understand.'

Seeing that Wentworth was working himself up into one of his diatribes, Mr Lyle swiftly made his excuses and went on his way. He hurried across to where his carriage was waiting, feeling that if the roads really were blocked because of this march, he wanted to get back home as soon as possible.

But as he approached his carriage, he saw that his driver, Groves, was waiting for him on the pavement, holding his cap in his hands and looking rather anxious. A large, very flashy-looking motor car had been parked directly in front of the carriage, blocking it in completely.

'What's all this?' Lyle demanded. 'Whose car is that?'

'I'm sorry, Mr Lyle, sir,' said the driver nervously. 'That's young Mr Pendleton's new car. His driver said he'd only be stopping for a moment, sir – but now they've both vanished, and well I don't rightly see how we're to get out.'

Lyle felt a stronger surge of irritation than ever. 'Where did Pendleton go?' he demanded crossly.

'Over there, sir,' said the driver, pointing to one of the best-known St James's clubs, famed for its popularity with young men about town with a taste for cards and champagne.

'Well, go inside and have him fetched,' stormed Lyle. 'I'm not going to stand here cooling my heels on the pavement while he finishes his beastly card game.'

Groves did as he was told, and after some time Mr Pendleton emerged, wreathed in smiles and reeking of cigar smoke. 'Hullo, Mr Lyle!' he exclaimed cheerfully. 'I say – how awful of me to have blocked you in like that.

Whatever was I thinking? I only meant to be a moment, but I bumped into a pal and rather lost track of time – you know how it is. Now, where has my man gone off to? Not to worry, Mr Lyle – I can move the vehicle myself. Rather a splendid creature, isn't she? Brand new, you know – only got her last week. Couldn't let old Devereaux beat me in the motor-car stakes any longer. I say, have you heard the news about his engagement? Splendid, isn't it! A jolly fine girl, Miss Woodhouse . . . Now, all I need to do is remember how to turn the dashed thing *on* . . .'

Although really it couldn't have been much more than ten minutes, it seemed like an age until Mr Pendleton (with the help of his man, who had finally turned up) managed to move the motor car out of Mr Lyle's way. By the time Lyle was able to climb up into his own carriage, he was feeling no longer irritated, but strangely *twitchy*. He didn't know exactly why, but for some reason he felt he needed to get home, as quickly as he could. Something didn't seem quite right.

'Home at once, Groves,' he said, as he clambered inside the carriage. 'Keep us from getting stuck in all this traffic, if you can.'

He sat back on the comfortable padded seat, and heaved a sigh of relief as Groves urged the horses forwards. But then all at once, he froze. There was someone in the carriage with him – someone who was sitting opposite, regarding him with an ironic smile.

'Good afternoon, White Dragon,' said a familiar voice.

CHAPTER TWENTY-THREE

Mr Lyle might have felt better if he could have seen just how peaceful it was at his home at that very moment. It was a picture-perfect October day on the river in Chelsea: the leaves of the trees were richly coloured enough to please any artist's eye, and the sunlight was soft and golden. Far from the busy streets of St James's, only the occasional carriage or motor car passed by the elegant mansion block where Mr Lyle resided. Birds were singing in the garden, and in the hall, the concierge took advantage of the peace to put his feet up behind his desk and settle down with a novel. Every now and again a boat drifted by on the river, and on the bank a young lady in a picturesque new hat was sitting under the dappled shade of a tree, painting the scene before her in soft watercolours.

It was not until just before four o'clock that a smart delivery van, drawn by two glossy brown horses, drew up outside Mr Lyle's residence. Four delivery boys got out, all smartly dressed in the distinctive blue-and-gold livery of Sinclair's department store. They went around to the back of the van, from which they removed a large – and evidently very heavy – wooden crate.

If anyone had been listening especially carefully, they might have heard a voice from somewhere inside the cart whisper something that sounded rather like 'Good luck!' followed by a sound that might have been a very quiet woof.

The four carried the crate on to the pavement, and one of them rang the bell beside the gate. Presently, the concierge appeared to answer it.

'Yes?' he asked, a little crossly. He had just settled down with his book and was not best pleased by this unexpected interruption.

The smallest of the delivery boys touched his cap. 'Delivery for Mr Randolph Lyle, from Sinclair's department store, sir,' he announced.

'I'm afraid that Mr Lyle is not at home – and I don't believe he was expecting any delivery,' said the concierge in a chilly tone. 'His manservant is out too.'

The delivery boys glanced at each other, and then the smallest one said: 'We were told his manservant would be at home to receive the delivery.'

'Yes, well, I'm afraid he was called away unexpectedly. A note arrived for him earlier sending him out on an urgent errand.'

Another of the delivery boys spoke up now: 'But we're

under orders to get this to Mr Lyle right away. It's a delivery of paintings – very important.'

The concierge looked at him in surprise, thinking that surely this young fellow was rather well-spoken for a delivery boy. But then a third went on: 'We can take it away again if you'd rather, but I reckon Mr Lyle won't be too pleased when he gets back. We were told it was urgent.'

'Well . . .' hesitated the concierge.

'Look, whatever you want to do, can you make your mind up quick?' groaned the fourth boy. 'This weighs a tonne!'

'Oh, very well,' said the concierge at last, unlocking the big gate so they could come through. The last thing he wanted was to get in some sort of row with Mr Lyle, who now he thought about it, had been rather out of temper this last week, what with all that fuss over his exhibition. Probably these were some of the paintings from his own collection, being returned home, he thought. 'As no one is at home, I'll show you to Mr Lyle's apartment,' he said briskly. 'Follow me please – and take care. The hallway has only recently been redecorated.'

The boys carefully carried the big crate along the neat gravel path, and up the steps into a large hallway, elegantly painted in duck-egg blue with gilt decorations. One of the delivery boys bumped his side of the box against the banister on the way up the stairs, and another elbowed him quickly. 'Careful!' he exclaimed. 'You, er – you want to watch out for the paintwork!'

On the landing, the concierge was unlocking the door to Mr Lyle's large first-floor apartment. 'In here please,' he instructed, holding the door open. 'You may leave it there, by the door.'

The boys obediently shuffled inside, and gently set the large crate down on the rug. They were certainly taking good care of the delivery, the concierge thought approvingly – you couldn't fault them for that. He supposed Sinclair's really did provide the best service.

All the same, he was glad to see the back of them, and felt pleased when Mr Lyle's door was locked again, and they were all trooping down the garden path and back into their delivery van, leaving him to return to his patch of sun, his novel and his quiet afternoon.

Upstairs, in Mr Lyle's empty apartment, all was very quiet too. Then, unexpectedly, from the large wooden crate there came a loud sneeze.

'*Lil!*' hissed a horrified voice.

'I couldn't help it!' protested another. 'I've been holding that in for simply ages. The straw keeps on tickling my nose!'

'But what if someone heard you?'

'Oh that fellow is long gone. I heard him lock the door ages ago. We're all alone here – surely we can get out now?'

Even as she spoke, the lid of the crate slowly lifted,

creaking a little as it did so. A moment later, two figures –
one tall, the other rather smaller – could be seen emerging
from inside.

'Gosh, that wasn't much fun, was it?' said Lil, as she
clambered out and stretched, then brushed a few bits of
straw off her frock. 'I'm glad we didn't have to spend even
a moment longer squashed up in there. It was horrid being
carried up those stairs like that – when the boys bumped
the box, I really thought I was going to squeal and give
the whole game away.' She paused and looked around her.
'I say . . . so this is where Mr Lyle lives . . .'

Sophie was already staring around too, taking in the
big bright room, with its polished parquet floors and
large windows, overlooking the attractive gardens below.
She was not at all surprised to find that the apartment
was luxurious and elegant – she had heard enough about
Mr Lyle to have expected that. What she had not perhaps
imagined was the air of disorder about the place. She knew
Mr Lyle kept a manservant: they'd had to be clever about
getting him out of the way for the afternoon. In the end,
they'd decided that Leo would carefully copy Mr Lyle's
handwriting, and Song had delivered a note sending the
servant out on a complicated errand to purchase several
art volumes from bookshops around London, which they
knew would keep him busy for some time. But now, she
reflected that he couldn't be much good at his job if he

had left Mr Lyle's room in such a state of lavish disarray.

Looking around, she saw an expensive-looking dressing gown with an oriental print, tossed over a green velvet chaise and the morning's newspaper strewn across a table still set with the remains of breakfast. The mantelpiece was cluttered with expensive cigar boxes, an abandoned pair of cufflinks, a carved jade ornament, a silver ashtray, a vase of camellias, spilling petals. A door led through into what was evidently the bedroom, offering a glimpse of an unmade bed with linen sheets and a satin counterpane.

But what was most noticeable about Mr Lyle's apartment were the walls. Every inch of the rich silk wallpaper seemed to be covered by pictures, reaching almost from the floor right up to the ceiling. Sophie paused to look at them, but she knew she didn't have time to linger. Lil was already over by the door to the small balcony that Billy and Joe had told them about. 'This is our escape route,' she murmured. The key was in the lock: she softly turned it, and the door opened silently. 'Oh jolly good!' she exclaimed, relieved. 'Now all we have to do is find the painting – and then we can get out of here.'

'We'd better find it fast,' said Sophie, glancing at the clock on the mantelpiece. 'The auction will be almost over already – and we don't know how long Phyllis and the others will manage to stall Mr Lyle.'

'There's the big Suffragette march that Connie told us

about too, remember,' Lil reminded her. 'That should slow him down on his way home.'

'Even so – we have to be quick. Let's find that safe.'

They started in the big room, hunting everywhere they could think of for Mr Lyle's safe. But finding it proved trickier than either of them had expected. 'It doesn't seem to be anywhere,' whispered Lil, frustrated, after she had even searched through Mr Lyle's wardrobe without success.

'It must be hidden – somewhere secret,' Sophie whispered back. She glanced up at the clock again, and tried not to panic as she saw how many of their precious minutes had already ticked away. She had been sure that Mr Lyle had said the painting was in his safe at home – was there any chance she had been mistaken, and the safe was somewhere else entirely? She paused for a moment, and closed her eyes.

'What are you doing?' demanded Lil in astonishment.

'I'm trying to think like Mr Lyle,' hissed Sophie. 'Wait. Couldn't the safe door be hidden behind one of the paintings?'

They began lifting picture after picture, Lil clambering on a chair and reaching up a long arm to the very highest paintings. They had checked almost one whole wall when Sophie suddenly heard Lil's excited squeak. 'I say! I think I've found it!'

She spun around to see that Lil had unhooked a large

painting of a vase of flowers. Underneath was an iron door, set into the wall itself.

Sophie ran over to her, her heart pounding. They had found the safe – now the next part of the plan was all down to her. She blew out a long breath as she stared at the safe door in front of her.

It had been Joe who had insisted she had to be the one to learn to crack the safe. 'No good trying to teach Lil something like that. You've got to have patience to be a cracksman,' he said. He'd taken her to visit an old East End acquaintance – a spry, elderly man in a dirty attic, whom they found sitting at a workbench squinting at something through an eyeglass. His face had wrinkled up into a toothless smile at the sight of Joe.

'Well, well – I never thought I'd see you round these parts again, young feller,' he'd said, looking Joe up and down, blinking at him with watery blue eyes.

'Never thought I'd be back here neither,' Joe had admitted. 'Still – the Boys have gone now, and the top man too.'

The old man had nodded. 'For now,' he said.

'What do you mean, *for now?*' asked Sophie.

'Well, they never caught him, did they? If I know the top man, he'll be back afore long. Like a spider in a web, he'll be biding his time.'

His words had sent a chill down Sophie's spine. She knew he meant the Baron – and it seemed she wasn't the only one who believed he wasn't gone for good.

'Well now, it looks like you've landed on your feet, Joey,' said the old man, looking him up and down.

Joe rubbed a hand through his curly hair. 'I've had a bit of luck, all right.'

'I can see that, lad. This your young lady then, is it?' he said, winking at Sophie.

Joe flushed, embarrassed. 'This is Sophie – she's my friend – but listen, we didn't come here to chat. We came to ask for your help,' he said gruffly.

'My help, eh?' repeated the old man, frowning. 'And how am I supposed to be helping you?'

'I need you to teach her what you do,' said Joe, nodding to Sophie.

Samuel suddenly began to laugh. 'Teach her – what to be a cracksman?' he guffawed. 'That's a lark, that is! Mind, you,' he added to Sophie. 'I dunno why I'm laughing really. Best little lock-pick I ever saw was a young lady, round about your size. And I don't deny you've got the hands for it,' he said, seizing one of Sophie's hands suddenly. She tried not to shrink back as his long yellow fingers felt the shape of her own. 'Good fingers. Long and thin – see – like mine? You play the piano, miss? Piano players, they got good hands for this line of work.'

'She's smart too,' said Joe quickly. 'She'll pick it up fast. And we'll pay you.' He clinked something in his pocket, and the old man's face lit up.

'So, what is it you want to do?' he asked Sophie, looking at her with his small blue eyes. 'Crack open a lady's jewellery box? Pick the lock to her boudoir, eh? Something like that?'

Sophie shook her head. 'I need to crack a safe,' she said, trying to sound confident.

Samuel looked startled. 'Crack a safe!' he exclaimed. He looked at Joe. 'That ain't easy to teach. You better have something better than a sixpence in that pocket of yours, boy.'

'Half a crown,' said Joe, holding out the coins in the palm of his hands. 'It's yours if you just show her what to do.'

The old man scratched his head. 'All I have to do is just talk her through it – show her the ropes?' he said slowly. 'Then you're gone – and that's the end of it?'

'That's the end of it,' promised Joe.

'All right,' said Samuel, nodding finally. 'Well, I'll be blowed – this is the queerest way I reckon I've earned half a crown this week. Now mind you, young miss, I can't teach you to be a proper cracksman in a couple of hours. But I can show you a way to get into a safe.'

*

Sophie took a deep breath and tried to remember everything that old Samuel had taught her. He'd shown her an old safe and talked her through how the mechanism worked – the spindle, the dial, the drive pin, the wheels, which he called the 'tumblers', one for each number in a combination – and finally the lock-drop that kept the door shut. The safe in front of her now was brand new, but otherwise not so very different to the one Samuel had shown her. She could see the same sort of numbered dial, the same metal handle.

She tried to organise her thoughts. The first thing was to work out how many numbers were in the combination. She flexed her hands, and then moved forwards swiftly, turning the dial clockwise several times. Then she pulled the doctor's stethoscope out from where she had stowed it in the pocket of her frock.

'What on earth's that for?' demanded Lil, who was hovering at her shoulder, watching.

'Listening,' said Sophie. Samuel had given her the stethoscope – he had half a dozen, which he'd told her with a wicked grin he had half-inched from the doctors up at the Christian Mission. Now, she slotted the earpieces into her ears, then placed the end of the stethoscope as close as she could to the dial. Carefully, she rotated the dial counterclockwise, listening out for any clicking sounds. It was difficult, but after she had repeated this process several times, she thought she had at last identified the place on the dial where the clicks were coming from.

'Can't you go any faster?' came Lil's voice from behind her. 'We're running out of time!'

Sophie looked up to where her friend was jigging about impatiently. 'I'm cracking a safe, Lil, not boiling an egg. I can't just do it in three minutes flat!' She paused to wipe her sweating hands. 'Look – you go over to the balcony and keep an eye out for the others. Listen for the owl hoots – they'll signal if there's any sign of Lyle coming back.'

She turned her attention back to the safe. Carefully, she turned the dial around until it was positioned opposite the place that the clicking sounds seemed to be coming from. That was called *parking the wheels*, she remembered Samuel saying. Then she turned the dial back all the way around once more, and when she passed the park position, she heard a distinct, loud click. That was the first wheel engaged.

'*One* . . .' she breathed aloud, as she turned the wheel again. '*Two* . . . *three* . . . *four* . . .' But the fifth time she turned the dial, there was no click to be heard.

'Four numbers!' she exclaimed, looking up excitedly at Lil. 'There are four numbers in the combination.'

Lil stared at her. 'You mean it took you all this time just to work out *that*? But – Sophie – it's almost five o'clock. Lyle could be back at any moment!'

Sophie blew out a long breath of air. The next stage of

the process was far more complicated, and Lil was right – they were running out of time. Then she remembered what the old cracksman had told her. 'You know, the best way to crack any safe is to know the combination. Most people ain't that clever when it comes to setting it – so think of a number what matters to your mark. If you know his kiddie's birthday – or his wife's – then try that first. Nine times out of ten it's something you can guess, if you only use your loaf.'

Could Sophie guess the combination? Lyle didn't have a child, or a wife, or any family as far as she knew. She couldn't really think of anything that mattered to him very much – except for paintings. She tried a few of the combinations that Samuel had told her people sometimes used out of laziness – like 1234, or 1111 – but none of them worked. She stared around the room desperately, hoping for inspiration, looking at the paintings hanging on the walls. Could he have used the year that a favourite painter had been born? Or the date that a famous picture had been painted? She wished that Leo or Jack were here – she didn't know nearly enough about the history of art to take a guess.

Just then, her eye was caught by the painting that Lil had removed from the wall – the vase of flowers. For the first time she noticed that the vase in the picture was a blue and white jar, painted with a design of Chinese dragons. Whether he had done it deliberately or not, Mr Lyle had hidden the painting in the safe behind another dragon image. *The Green Dragon* was at least one painting she knew about, she thought suddenly – and it was certainly one that was important to Mr Lyle. For a moment, she thought back to what Leo had told her about *The Green Dragon*. Carefully, she began to turn the dial – and then she pulled the handle.

There was a loud clunking sound, and a moment later, the safe door swung open.

CHAPTER TWENTY-FOUR

At his desk in the office above Sinclair's, Detective Inspector Worth was working busily, reviewing his notes. There was no doubt about it, this case was a puzzler. Something about all the different information he had gathered just didn't add up – but he was jiggered if he could see quite what it was. He frowned, and turned back yet again to the notes from Mr Lyle's interview.

Just as he began to read, there came a nervous tap on the office door.

'What is it?' barked Worth, annoyed at yet another interruption.

'Er – there's someone here to see you, sir,' came Potts's tentative voice.

'Well, if it isn't Mr Sinclair or Mr Lyle then tell them to go away again. I'm busy!'

'But they're insisting they see you, sir. They've got some important information about the case.'

Worth heaved a sigh. 'Very well,' he said. 'Send them in.'

He was sick of well-meaning members of the public coming to him with tall tales about shady characters who might or might not have stolen the painting – but he didn't want to risk missing even a shred of real evidence. Not that anyone had brought him the least bit of that so far.

To his astonishment, a child came into the room and stood before his desk, where she bobbed a small curtsey. A Chinese child, plainly but neatly dressed in a striped frock and a pinafore.

'Er . . . hullo,' said Worth, quite startled by this vision.

'I've got a note for you, sir,' announced the girl in a distinct Cockney accent. 'It's important.'

She handed Worth a small envelope. It was neatly addressed *For Detective Inspector Worth Only – Urgent*.

'Did *you* write this?' he asked the girl in surprise.

She shook her head. 'I'm just here to make sure you read it,' she said.

More baffled than ever, Worth ripped the envelope open. Inside was a brief note – unsigned:

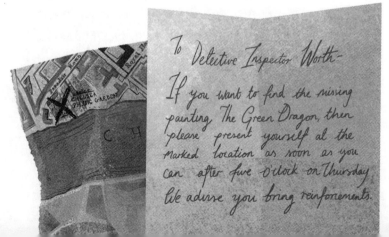

To Detective Inspector Worth –

If you want to find the missing painting *The Green Dragon*, then please present yourself at the marked location as soon as you can after five o'clock on Thursday. We advise you bring reinforcements.

'Whatever's this?' demanded Worth. The note was attached to a small square torn from a map of London. A red cross marked the Chelsea Physic Garden. He frowned and looked up at the child to see if she could offer him any kind of an explanation, but she had vanished.

He glanced at his pocket watch: it was a quarter to five. 'Probably just another wild goose chase, but you never know,' he muttered to himself, as he shrugged on his jacket. Then: 'Potts!' he yelled authoritatively. 'Stir your stumps! We're going to Chelsea.'

In Mr Lyle's apartment, Sophie was gazing at the safe in delight as the door swung open.

'You did it!' gasped Lil. 'You cracked the safe! But – what on earth was that number?'

'1-4-5-5. In other words, 1455 – the date that *The Green Dragon* was supposed to have been painted,' said Sophie triumphantly. 'It had to be something to do with the painting. That's what matters to Lyle, you see.'

Together, they pushed the big door all the way open and peered into the dark crevice. Lil reached inside, pulling out a sheaf of official-looking documents – envelopes sealed with red wax. Beneath was a bag that proved to contain a surprisingly large number of gold sovereigns. Behind them were a couple of large, flat parcels, each carefully wrapped in paper. She pulled out the top one, and with shaking hands, together they pulled the wrappings off.

'It's the painting!' squealed Lil in excitement.

Sophie stared down at *The Green Dragon*. It was extraordinary to think that such a small painting could have caused so much trouble. But as she looked at it, she began to see why Leo had been so intrigued by it. The bold green and gold paint; the inscrutable expression on the dragon's face; the painting was at once strange and beautiful. She gazed at it, almost spellbound as it lay on the floor of Mr Lyle's apartment, surrounded by a jumble of papers, and a velvet bag spilling out coins.

'*Sophie!*' exclaimed Lil, and then she heard it too. Somewhere outside, someone was hooting like an owl.

The Sinclair's delivery van might have left Mr Lyle's mansion block – but it had not gone very far away. Just around the corner, out of sight of the apartment, it came to an abrupt halt.

'D'you think they've got out all right?' asked the boy in the driver's seat, taking off his Sinclair's cap and anxiously running a hand through his thick curly hair.

'Of course they have,' said Billy stoutly. 'And Connie is on the lookout for Mr Lyle at the front of the house. If she catches sight of him, she'll signal.'

'I still think we ought to have come up with a better signal this time,' said Joe, shaking his head. 'Funny sort of owl, hooting before it's even got properly dark.'

'Never mind about that now – we've to get *going*,' said Billy, climbing down from the seat. 'We need to be ready for Sophie and Lil as soo as they've got the painting.'

A sudden volley of yelps was heard from inside the van, and Joe heaved a sigh as he jumped down too. 'Why did you bring Lucky?' he demanded. 'You know she's only going to make a nuisance of herself.'

'I couldn't help it!' exclaimed Billy indignantly. 'Miss Atwood said I had to take her out – and I couldn't very well say "oh no, sorry, I've got to go and rescue the stolen painting", could I? Besides, Daisy's here.'

'Yes, but Daisy is a trained police dog, isn't she?'

'I think you'll find that actually *Lucky* is the one who helped me find Mr Lyle's message. And actually now I think about it, she also tried to attack Mr Lyle's trouser legs. So really . . .'

Jack emerged from the back of the van. 'Er – if you two have quite finished bickering about your pets, I think we'd better hurry,' he said. 'Leo thinks she heard an owl call.'

'We have to get out of here!' exclaimed Sophie. 'Quick – you go first and take the picture. If I close the safe again, and hang this painting back over the top, maybe Mr Lyle won't immediately notice that *The Green Dragon* is missing.'

Lil nodded, and clutching the painting, still in its paper

289

wrappings, she dashed over to the balcony door. Behind her, Sophie hastily stuffed papers and sovereigns back into the safe, pushed the door swiftly closed and turned the handle to lock it. She could hear the sound of footsteps coming up the stairs and men's voices approaching.

On the balcony, Lil was looking anxiously for Joe and Billy. To her relief, she saw the two of them slipping stealthily through the garden, keeping to the shrubbery. '*Hurry*!' she called out in a low voice. 'Lyle's here!'

When they were directly beneath her, she leaned over the balcony, and carefully dropped the painting into their waiting arms. Billy took it and darted off back through the garden, while Joe took a length of rope from around his waist, and tossed one end of it up to the balcony. Lil caught it deftly and fastened it to the balcony railing, with one of the knots that Joe had taught her. Carefully, she climbed over the edge of the balcony and gripped hold of the rope.

'Even if I wasn't top of the class for anything else – it's a jolly good thing I came first in gymnastics,' she muttered to herself. She looked back into Mr Lyle's room before she climbed down, and saw to her astonishment that Sophie was still kneeling on the floor in front of the safe. 'Sophie – *come on*!' she hissed, alarmed. 'What are you doing?'

But Sophie didn't move. As the voices came closer up the stairs, she became more and more certain that she knew one of them. She had heard that voice before; it was a voice that she had heard many times in her nightmares; and it was a voice that she had known that she would hear again. *I daresay we'll meet again*, the voice said in her head.

The door began to open. Lil gave a little squeak of horror, but had no choice but to begin clambering down the rope. On the other side of the room from the balcony, Sophie got to her feet and darted quickly into Mr Lyle's bedroom, closing the door behind her.

'Where's Sophie?' hissed Joe urgently, as Lil jumped down from the rope.

'She's still in there!' said Lil anxiously. 'Everything went just as we planned it until Lyle turned up – and then she just froze. I don't know what happened!'

Inside the apartment, Sophie was standing behind the bedroom door listening with all her might, her heart thumping so fast and loud that it almost deafened her. *The Baron is here, the Baron is here, the Baron is here*, her heartbeats seemed to be saying.

'What's this doing here?' came a startled voice – Mr Lyle's of course. He had seen the crate. 'I wasn't expecting a delivery.'

'Everything seems to be in rather a mess, doesn't it?' came the familiar voice.

'I hired my manservant for his abilities as a security guard, not a domestic,' said Mr Lyle tightly. 'But wherever has he got to now? I gave him strict instructions to stay

291

here. 'I say – whatever can this be all about? This crate is open. And – it's *empty*.'

'Where's the painting?' came that voice again – suddenly incisive and sharp. The very sound of it made Sophie turn cold all over.

There was the patter of footsteps as Lyle hurried across the room. 'It's here – in the safe of course – just as always,' he said, sounding rather frightened. She heard him entering the combination, and the clunk as the heavy door opened. 'Look – here it is – it . . .' his voice faded suddenly away.

'Where's the painting?' came the Baron's voice again, louder this time.

'I – I – it's *gone*,' whispered Lyle. He sounded as though he was going to be sick. 'But – it *can't be!*'

'You *fool*,' snapped the Baron's voice, hard and cruel. 'You've been hoodwinked. That empty crate is a *Trojan horse*, you imbecile. I would have thought that you of all people would remember your Greek myths. Someone's used it to get in here. No doubt they were hiding inside.' Sophie heard him step over to the window. 'Luckily for you, it's not too late. I see them – a couple of young ruffians, down in the garden. I daresay they tricked your fellow into leaving the painting unguarded. Randall, I'm sure you can take care of this.'

'Of course, sir,' came a third voice – a deep grunt. 'Leave

it to me.'

Red Hands Randall! Sophie felt a stab of horror. He was here with Lyle and the Baron too – and now he was going after Lil and the others, while she was trapped here in Lyle's bedroom.

Lyle was still talking, his voice shaking. 'It isn't possible!' His voice sounded so frightened that it made Sophie cringe. 'The painting was hidden away in my safe – I promise you, Black, I . . .'

It was all Sophie could do not to gasp aloud. The Baron was the Black Dragon – the leader of the *Fraternitas Draconum*! He had been the one who had instructed Lyle to take the painting.

'I'm not interested in your excuses,' came the Baron's voice. 'Deal with this. We must check the premises. We need to make sure that the place is secure.'

Sophie froze as his footsteps turned in the direction of the bedroom door.

CHAPTER TWENTY-FIVE

Sophie heard the door handle turn. There was only one place to hide: she threw herself to the ground and rolled under Mr Lyle's bed.

The carpet was thick with dust and she had to swallow down a cough. She pressed a hand over her mouth to stop herself breathing in any more of the stuff. There were voices above her, and she tried to lie perfectly still, so she could hear what they were saying.

'Who could it be?' Lyle was saying, in a panicky voice. 'Has someone betrayed us? It couldn't be one of the *Fraternitas* – could it?'

'I sincerely doubt it. They have sworn an oath – as have you,' came the Baron's cool voice. 'We shall come to that later. For now all that matters is that we get the painting back. I have been waiting for this moment for months and I'm not going to let some young hooligans stand in my way. Is Randall out there?'

She heard their footsteps going over to the bedroom

window. They had turned away from her, and were talking in voices so low she could no longer hear what they were saying. She looked sideways: she was close to the door, which now stood open. Did she dare to slip out and try and make her escape while Lyle and the Baron were looking the other way?

She would have to try. She could not risk staying here. Without giving herself time to think better of it, she shuffled a little closer to the door – and then squeezed from under the bed, leaped to her feet and made a dash for the balcony door.

The two men spun around at once.

'*Randall!*' cried Lyle.

But Sophie was already sliding down the rope, taking most of the skin off the palms of her hands in the process. A second later, she was running across the garden – but Red Hands Randall was running after her.

'What the devil are *you* doing here?'

As Detective Worth came striding towards the pond in the Chelsea Physic Garden, Mr McDermott looked up from the note he was examining in some surprise.

'Listen, McDermott – if this is *your* scheme –'

McDermott gave a short laugh, as if he was surprised – but rather pleased – to see Worth there at all. 'Come on, Worth. You know me of old. Lyle can drip poison in your ear as much as he likes, but you know I'm no more interested in *schemes* than you are.'

'Well, look here, if it's not anything to do with you, then what's this all about? I got some anonymous missive, sending me down here if I wanted to get back *The Green Dragon*. A child brought it – and then vanished. It said to bring reinforcements. I've got a couple of men searching the gardens as we speak.'

McDermott shrugged. 'I don't know any more about this than you do. I got a note too. The only difference is that my note was signed.'

'Signed by who?'

'Miss Sophie Taylor.'

'And who the blazes is that?'

'A young friend of mine – who I rather think I have disappointed already this week. I thought the least I could do was do as she asked me.'

'Well, it appears that your girl has sent us both on a fool's errand,' said Worth in a tetchy voice. 'It's a quarter past five – and there's not a soul here. I've got better things to do than waste my time standing about chatting in a park, you know.'

'How's the case going?' asked McDermott.

'The case is a *headache*,' snapped Worth. 'I've got newspapermen on my tail wherever I go. I'm surprised they haven't followed me here – I daresay they'll pop up

296

any moment, flashbulbs going off in all directions.'

'Ah well, you get used to that when you work for Mr Sinclair,' said McDermott with a grin.

For the first time Worth looked a little awkward. 'Look here, McDermott – I'm sorry Lyle has been so bullheaded over this case. I'd have liked your help, you know. We always did work well together.'

McDermott gave a small smile, as if he was remembering something. 'We did,' he said. Then, suddenly: 'You don't think that Lyle's behaviour has been a little . . .'

Worth looked up at him keenly, but the rest of his sentence was cut off. Just at that moment, a young man came racing down the garden path towards them, with something flat tucked under one arm. To both of their astonishment, he stopped, bowed and then presented the package to them, with something of a flourish.

'Compliments of Miss Sophie Taylor and Miss Lilian Rose, gentlemen,' said the young man with a grin. 'I believe you've been looking for this.'

Worth pulled away the paper wrapping around the painting. 'Bless my soul,' he murmured, looking from the painting to McDermott, and back again. 'It's the painting – the real one this time. There's no doubt about it. This is *The Green Dragon!*'

'You might like to know that they found it hidden in

Mr Lyle's apartment, just over there,' said the young man, pointing back in the direction he had just come from. 'Now, if you wouldn't mind coming along quickly – and bringing your men with you – I rather think the girls could do with some help.'

Sophie pelted across the garden, her feet slipping and sliding on mud, grass and wet leaves. Spots danced in front of her eyes, and her chest felt as though it was going to burst, but she kept running, as fast as she could. She could hear Randall behind her: he was gaining on her. The garden wall was so close now – she could see Joe and Billy leaning over, their hands reaching out towards her; she could hear Lil shrieking her name. She made one desperate last leap forwards, and their hands grabbed her wrists. She had made it!

But even as they began to pull her up, Randall's leather-gloved hands grabbed her ankles. She could feel the grip of his fingers, as he pulled her back again. She screamed out in pain.

Then, all at once, a blur of something dark rushed over the wall, and she could hear a resounding bark – it was Daisy! Randall let go of her ankles, and the two boys dragged her over the top of the wall. Even as they did so, she heard the bright, sharp sound of a police whistle – and another answering it – and then another.

'Stop right there, Randall!' came Detective Worth's booming voice. 'You're surrounded!'

Waiting in the shadows of the Sinclair's van, with Lucky close at her side, Leo could hear the commotion. Whistles – and voices shouting – and Daisy barking. Lucky gave a little bark, and then a whine, as though she wanted to go and help her friend, but Leo shushed her. 'We can't. We have to stay here and keep lookout – remember?' she said.

She had to admit, it wasn't the most exciting task. At first, Sophie and Lil had suggested that she should join Connie on the riverbank, but Jack had pointed out that Lyle was far more likely to recognise Leo than anyone else – and if he saw her as he approached the mansion block, he might guess that something was up. Clearly she would be no use at all when it came to disguising herself as a Sinclair's porter, nor hiding inside packing crates and climbing down ropes and over garden walls – so there was nothing left for her to do but to lurk here, keeping Lucky out of trouble and watching out for any danger. She wasn't sure what danger there could be now that both Lyle and Randall were definitely inside the apartment, but she meant to do her part anyway. The most important thing was that Lyle was captured and punished for what he had done, she reminded herself – and that the painting was returned to its rightful owner. Still, she rather wished that she could have been in the thick of the excitement too.

She might never even have noticed the figure slinking down the street, if it hadn't been for Lucky beginning to bark. She looked up, and caught sight of a person stealing stealthily out of the front gate, under cover of the growing dusk. There was a flat parcel tucked under one arm.

Leo let out a little gasp. It was Mr Lyle - she would know that sweep of grey hair anywhere! He was escaping - and he had the painting! Her heart began to pound: there was no sense in doing the owl call now, she realised. No one would hear it among the commotion - and even if they did, Lyle would be long gone before they reached her. There was only one thing to do - she would have to try and stop Lyle herself.

Without really having an idea of how she was going to do it, she edged forwards. As Mr Lyle approached, looking anxiously around him, she stepped out of the shadows and struck out with her cane. The weighted tip hit him hard across the shin; Lyle gave a yelp of pain, staggered and fell forwards, the parcel slipping out of his grasp.

'The painting!' he murmured, trying to reach for it - but Leo stepped in front of it. She jabbed his arm back with the point of the cane, as Lucky ran in circles around them both, barking loudly.

'No you don't,' she said through gritted teeth. 'That's not yours.'

Lyle gaped up at her. 'Miss Fitzgerald – *Leonora?*' he panted in astonishment. 'But – what are you doing here? Please – I beg of you – this is not what it looks like . . . it's tremendously important that I get this painting away from here – where it will be safe. You must help me, Leonora.'

'You aren't going anywhere,' said Leo firmly. 'I know everything. I know about Randall – and what you tried to do.'

'I'm sorry about Randall,' gasped out Lyle. 'The man's a brute – I had no idea he was going to do that to you, Leonora – really, I didn't. I would never have let him hurt you – I –'

But Leo stopped him. There was something about the way he kept saying *Leonora* that made it all perfectly clear. 'Of course you knew!' she spat out. '*You're* the one who wrote that note he left in my room – you must have been. I suppose Randall stole a key and got inside to leave it, but you had to be the one who wrote it. Randall sent me the note at the Spencer. I've seen his writing – and he can't spell. *You* wrote the second note. *You* copied my writing, because *you* knew what my writing looked like. And you're the one who signed it *Leonora.*'

'I swear it wasn't me – there's been a terrible misunderstanding! Listen – if you help me, I can help you too. I can make you the best-known young artist in London. You're talented – you could be my star.'

Leo stared down at him. He looked very feeble, and very ridiculous sprawled on the pavement. All his elegance was gone now, and his stylish suit was smeared with dirt. 'I don't need your kind of help,' she told him shortly. 'And I certainly don't want to be your *star*.'

Lyle looked up desperately. There was anger in his eyes now, and for a moment Leo thought he was going to make a break for it, even if it meant leaving the painting behind – and she had no idea how she would stop him. But at that very moment, she heard the sound of footsteps, and to her enormous relief she saw Connie and Smitty running towards her, alerted by the increasingly frantic sound of Lucky's barks.

'It's Mr Lyle!' exclaimed Smitty.

'Quick – grab the painting. And someone fetch Detective Worth! We mustn't let him get away!'

It was Smitty who ran for the detective, and when he and some of his men came running up a moment later, they found that Connie was preventing Lyle from escaping by the simple method of sitting on his legs, while Leo pointed her cane threateningly at his chest. Meanwhile, Lucky was at long last having a very satisfying chew of Mr Lyle's expensive trouser leg.

Soon, Lyle was being led away by two burly policeman, protesting all the while that everyone had misunderstood, that this was nothing whatsoever to do with him, that he had been attacked, and that he wasn't at all used to being treated in this rough manner. Leo felt that she was not in the least bit sorry to see him go.

Just then, Jack came rushing over. He was followed by Billy and Joe, Daisy bounding after them looking as pleased as Lucky at her part in the adventure. 'Jolly well done for stopping Lyle!' Jack burst out. 'Randall has been arrested too – and we've got *The Green Dragon!*'

Leo stared at the painting Lyle had dropped, which she was now cradling protectively. 'But – if you've got *The Green Dragon* – then what on earth is this?' she demanded.

The others helped her pull the wrappings away – and then they all gasped at the sight of the twisting white dragon, against a background of blue and gold stars.

'It's the other stolen painting!' Connie exclaimed. 'It's *The White Dragon!*'

Sophie leaned back, panting against the garden wall. All around her was commotion – whistles shrilling, the dogs barking, running footsteps. She wanted to follow the others, to see what was happening, but she had to stop for a moment to recover her breath. Her hands were throbbing horribly.

'Quick, this way – we've got Lyle – he's trying to escape!' called out a voice.

A moment later, another voice, low and urgent this time.

'Detective Worth, sir – the press are here. I don't know how they did it but they've tracked us down somehow.'

'Good lord, they'll have a field day with this. Take me to them, Potts – we'll have to try and manage this somehow.'

The footsteps and voices disappeared, and Sophie found herself suddenly alone beside the garden wall. But she had to tell someone what she had seen, she realised. She had to let Lil and McDermott and the others know that the Baron was here. He was back – he had never gone away at all – and he was the leader of the *Fraternitas Draconum*.

But even as the thought crossed her mind, she saw something that made her stop still. There was a dark shape clambering over the garden wall. Someone was escaping – someone who had taken advantage of everyone's attention being fixed on the front of the mansion block. Sophie drew back into the shadows, watching, though she did not need the familiar silhouette to know exactly who it was that was even now stealing down the alley and away. She knew at once that it was the Baron.

She looked around for the others, but there was no one there. She knew what she had to do. Instinct took over, and all she could do was follow it. She ran down the alleyway, after the Baron.

'Two stolen paintings returned – and two dangerous criminals apprehended,' said Mr McDermott. 'Even with your track record, that's not bad for an afternoon's work. I have a feeling that Detective Worth is going to be extremely pleased with you – and Mr Sinclair too.'

'We weren't sure that you'd come,' said Lil, smiling up at the detective, who stood with them beside the Sinclair's van, in the yellow light of a street lamp. 'You told us that you couldn't have anything to do with this case – but we just couldn't do it without you.'

'I'm certainly glad I didn't miss this,' said McDermott, giving her one of his rare smiles. 'All the same, I should have known better. I ought to have realised that warning you and Miss Taylor off a dangerous mystery would be of no use whatsoever.'

Joe laughed. 'Once Lil and Sophie make their minds up to do something, there's no stopping them,' he said. He gave Lil a little smile, and squeezed her hand – which she knew was his way of saying that he was proud of her.

She smiled back at him – then frowned, glancing around her. 'But where's Sophie got to now? She seems to have disappeared.'

'Maybe she went to patch up her hands?' suggested Joe. 'She hurt them pretty badly.'

Lil looked thoughtful. 'You know, I still don't understand why she stayed behind in Lyle's apartment like that,' she whispered to him. 'It didn't make any sense. She was so careful about the plan – and then it was as though she just suddenly decided to ignore it.'

She looked around again, rather anxious now – but though she could see half a dozen policemen, Billy and PC Potts making a fuss of Daisy, and Jack and the other art students excitedly examining *The White Dragon*, Sophie was nowhere in sight.

Sophie was running down the dark alleyway. Her feet skidded in the wet leaves. The hubbub of voices had long since faded; her heart was bumping in her chest and her breaths were burning her throat, but she didn't care. She couldn't let the Baron get away again. She had to prove that he was behind this, prove who he really was. Her feet slammed against the cobbles. She had seen his shadowed figure go this way, into the mist – he must be just ahead of her – he *must* be . . .

She stopped, bent double, gasping for breath. He was gone. The alley was dark and empty. Ahead of her was only a bare brick wall – she had lost him.

She turned, and all at once, a dark figure was standing before her, blocking her way.

'Good evening, Miss Taylor,' said that familiar mocking, casual voice.

Sophie stared at him, speechless. After all these months thinking about him, here he was. She stood before him, cornered and alone.

'What do you plan to do exactly, now that you have run me to ground?' said the Baron. He sounded amused. 'You stole my painting. You followed me here. You found me. What next?'

Sophie darted forwards but he pushed her back at once. 'No, no. Don't try to run away. That would be no fun at all. And don't try and scream either. Your friends are much too far away to hear you. Besides, this is what you wanted, isn't it? To face me? That's why you're here.'

'What I *want* is to know the truth,' Sophie heard herself say. Her voice sounded like a stranger's.

'The truth?' For a moment, the Baron looked surprised. 'But you know the truth already, don't you? You know that I killed poor dear Papa.'

Sophie stared up at him. For a moment, it was as though her heart shuddered in her chest, and stopped still.

'I suppose you want me to tell you *why*,' he went on in his airy, dinner-party voice. 'Always trying to work it all out . . . you really do have a thirst for knowledge. Quite something for a mere shop girl. But will you like what you discover, Miss Taylor? That's the question.'

He took a step towards her and instinctively she stepped back. She could hear the uneven rasping of her own breaths.

'Very well. It was I who killed your father. We had been friends once, he and I. The very best of friends – or so I thought, but then he betrayed me. Yes, that's right.

He betrayed *me*. After that, he followed me for years, you know. He was determined to track me down and *have it out with me*. But when we faced each other at last, *I won*. He was so sure that he could best me – but when it came to it, I was the better man.' He smiled coolly at her. 'What's the matter? Not the answer you were looking for? Dear Papa not quite such a hero any more?'

All at once, she experienced a sudden, sharp shock of anger. It was like a bucket of cold water being flung over her. How dare he speak to her in this indifferent way, about murdering her own father?

'I don't believe a word you say,' she choked out.

The Baron laughed, and something glittered in the dark. 'It's the truth. Take it or leave it. Here's something else you don't know. I killed your mother too. Beautiful Alice,' he said, with a little sigh. 'You know, when she was by my side, she was the toast of Cairo. We could have gone anywhere together. But she gave all that up for a home and a husband – and *you*.' For a moment, his voice sounded sharp, but when he spoke again it was in his usual indifferent tone. 'It was unfortunate, really, but I had no choice. I had to kill her. I did it with this knife.' He stepped towards her and she could see it more clearly now – the long silver knife with the twisting dragon handle that she had seen before, on the docks of the East End. 'Just like I could kill you now.'

He stepped forwards again, and Sophie tried to scramble away, but he was faster. He gripped hold of her. He was fiercely strong: his fingers clamped her shoulder as though they were made of cold steel.

'Let go of me,' she tried to say, but her voice was hardly more than a whisper.

'I could have killed you any time I liked, you know,' he said, almost conversationally, in her ear. I could have killed you the first time I saw you – in that box at the theatre. I could have killed you a dozen times over since then. You keep getting in my way, Miss Taylor, but what you have to understand is that you will never be able to get the better of me. I will always have you exactly where I want you – *at my mercy.*'

At that moment, Sophie heard a yell from somewhere in the distance. Tears of relief sprang to her eyes. 'Sophie! *Sophie!* Where are you?'

The Baron gave a little surprised laugh. 'Right on cue – your right-hand woman has come to rescue you. Farewell, Miss Taylor. This time I *know* I'll see you again.'

With a single swift, fierce movement, he pushed her to the ground. She fell sharply; her head struck the wet cobbles; she saw stars. A moment later, the Baron had gone and there was only the dark shape of his coat, flying out as he disappeared down the alley and into the night.

Lil came pelting up to her. 'Sophie – Sophie – are you all

right?' she gasped out. 'What happened? Oh my goodness, you're bleeding.'

With Lil's help, Sophie struggled to her feet. The hand she put up to her face came away bright scarlet. 'It was the Baron –' she began incoherently.

'The *Baron*?'

'You have to believe me. It really was *him*. He was in there with Lyle – he was the one behind all this. *He's the Black Dragon*,' she babbled out. The blood on her face mixed with her tears. Lil was never going to believe her, she realised with sickly horror. The Baron had escaped again and no one but herself had the slightest idea that he had been there at all.

'Sophie, you have to come with me – you're hurt –'

'Say you believe me,' she begged desperately. 'He was really here – he said he killed Papa and my mother too . . . he . . .'

'Never mind the Baron now,' said Lil, flinging an arm around her friend's shoulder. 'Oh *of course* I believe you, but you must come away from here.'

At last she managed to lead Sophie away from the alley, and back towards Mr Lyle's apartment, bright with lights and teeming with policemen. Lil looked urgently around for McDermott and the others, but before she could see anyone, a little group of half a dozen men caught sight of them, and came racing towards them.

'Look – there they are! It's them – Miss Taylor and Miss Rose! The young lady detectives – the girls who found the paintings!'

Sophie and Lil looked up into the dazzling glare of a camera flash.

PART VII
Dragon Regardant

Little is known about the seventh and final painting in the Dragon Sequence. Contemporary accounts suggest the painting may have been left unfinished, or even been destroyed by the artist himself later in his lifetime. What is known is that the painting was the largest in the sequence, depicting a single black dragon in standing position, foreleg raised and head turned as if looking at something outside the frame . . .

Dr Septimus Beagle, *The Life & Work of Benedetto Casselli*, 1889 (from the Spencer Institute Library)

CHAPTER TWENTY-SIX

Leo surveyed her table with pleasure. She had never hosted a tea party before, but she thought she had set out rather a good spread. All right, so she had bought the cakes and buns: she wasn't sure she'd ever be able to bake like Mrs Lim. But she'd brewed the tea and made the toast, and arranged a vase of chrysanthemums in the centre of the table, and now she felt like a proper hostess.

'Thanks ever so much for having us, Leo,' said Billy, grinning at her as he helped himself to his fourth piece of toast.

Leo blushed. 'I wanted to do something to say thank you,' she said. 'Besides, I thought there was a lot to celebrate.'

It certainly had been an eventful fortnight. Since they had rescued the two paintings from Mr Lyle's apartment, life had been rather interesting. Leo had found herself something of a heroine – especially when Connie and Smitty had told everyone at the Spencer how she had stopped Mr Lyle escaping, with only a very small pug to help her. And to her amazement, Professor Jarvis had called her over at the end of the drawing lesson, and had told her that he was impressed by what she had done.

She was beginning to like Professor Jarvis more and more. He would never flatter her like Mr Lyle had done, but he had given a few curt words of praise to a new series of paintings she had begun working on, based on the drawings she had done in the East End. She felt that she no longer had any interest in copying famous paintings; Mr Lyle and *The Green Dragon* had ruined that for her. Instead, she suddenly found that she wanted to draw real places, real people – rather like the drawings she had done from her bed as a child, when she had been ill. Her fingers were feeling rather itchy now as she sat at the tea table, watching the faces of her new friends as they talked, and she wondered whether they would mind if she fetched her pencils and her sketchbook.

They certainly had plenty to talk about. The daring rescue of the stolen paintings had been plastered all over the newspapers – featuring the somewhat blurry photographs of the two young ladies who had been at the centre of it all. Sophie and Lil's names had been all over town, lauded as the intrepid young lady detectives that had solved the crime. It didn't hurt, of course, that Lil was also known as a glamorous young theatre star – and, never slow to take any opportunity for publicity, Mr Sinclair and his team had swung into action. A fashionable photographer had been commissioned to take pictures of Lil and Sophie posing with the rescued paintings, dressed in stylish new outfits carefully chosen from Sinclair's Ladies' Fashions Department. Lil had loved every second of it, while Sophie had felt a little embarrassed. The cut on her face from where she had fallen in the alley was still very visible, and she did not feel in the least like she wanted to have her photograph taken. It was whispered that a message of thanks was even going to be sent to them by His Majesty the King.

'But we didn't do this by ourselves,' Sophie protested to a young newspaper reporter who Mr Sinclair had insisted should be allowed to interview her. 'We had plenty of help.'

'Oh yes, of course, your intrepid team of *friends*. We've heard all about them. And even Mr Sinclair's darling little *doggie* had a role to play. Do tell me all about them!' squealed the reporter.

Now, Sophie sat back in one of Leo's comfortable chairs and sipped her tea, very relieved to be somewhere where she knew that no one was going to try and interview her, or put a camera in front of her face.

'What I want to hear about is the end of the mystery,' Billy was saying. He'd brought along his latest notebook, neatly inscribed with the title *The Case of the Stolen Dragon Painting* – and Sophie knew he was itching to finish adding all the final details to his report.

'Yes, do tell us absolutely *everything*, Mr McDermott,' said Lil to the private detective, who was sitting smoking his pipe and listening to them all. 'What have Scotland Yard discovered? Has Mr Lyle confessed?'

The detective smiled at her. 'I'm sorry to disappoint you, Miss Rose, but Mr Lyle is saying very little to anyone at present – except for his lawyers, of course. He claims to have no idea how the paintings came to be at his home, and that he had never even met Randall before the day of his arrest. He insists he is completely innocent, and that he is being framed for the crime.'

'But he won't get away with that!' exclaimed Lil. 'He was caught running away with one of the paintings!'

'What's more, the police found a set of keys to Sinclair's department store hidden in his apartment,' McDermott went on. 'We believe he used it to gain access to the Exhibition Hall after hours. Of course, he claims he has never seen them in his life before either.'

'But surely that proves without any doubt that he was behind all this?'

Mr McDermott shrugged. 'Mr Lyle is a rich and powerful man, with clever lawyers and the right kind of friends. I have no doubt there will be plenty of people on hand to help him. Nonetheless, Detective Worth and I now believe that we have a fairly clear picture of the crime.

'We believe that Mr Lyle is one of the senior members of a secret organisation calling themselves the *Fraternitas Draconum* – otherwise, the Dragon Brotherhood. This organisation is not entirely unknown to us. Indeed, there have been rumours of a group operating under this name dating back centuries – although they have been rather quiet over the past few years. Little is known about them, except that they were a group of powerful men who worked together to promote their own interest.'

They all listened as Mr McDermott went on. 'It appears that Mr Lyle was given the task of obtaining two rare paintings – *The White Dragon* and *The Green Dragon*. Given their names, the paintings may have had some kind of special significance for the brotherhood – but what Sophie overheard at their meeting indicates that what really mattered to them was some information that they believed was secretly hidden in the paintings.'

'But how could information be hidden in a painting?' asked Billy, screwing up his face in a confused frown.

'I think I might know,' said Leo. She turned to Mr McDermott. 'I've been thinking about it, and I remembered something I noticed about the painting. There was a patch in one corner, where a new layer of paint had been added – it looked as though it might be concealing something underneath. Mr Lyle said it was nothing when I showed it to him – but of course, that's because he didn't want me to know about the painting's secret.'

Mr McDermott nodded. 'Quite right, Miss Fitzgerald. Scotland Yard have been working closely with His Majesty's art conservators in order to remove that layer of paint and discover what it conceals.'

'And what does it conceal?' asked Billy eagerly. 'Can you tell us?'

Mr McDermott looked thoughtful for a moment. 'I don't see why not – though I don't suppose the message will make any sense to you. It's written in French and it says: *Green Lion. Black Sun. 155.*'

They looked at each other excitedly. 'What does it mean?' asked Lil.

'I'm afraid we don't know – not yet, anyway.'

'So Lyle did all this just so that they could find out that message?' demanded Billy, incredulously.

McDermott shrugged. 'It would seem so. The message – whatever it means – is evidently of enormous importance to them.'

'It was rather a risk for Lyle to ask Leo to paint a copy of *The Green Dragon* in the first place then, wasn't it?' asked Lil. 'Surely he should have guessed she'd notice the overpainted place?'

'I'm not so sure he did,' said Sophie. She had been

thinking back to those moments, clinging on to the drainpipe in the rain outside the window of Wyvern House, of the dismissive way Lyle had spoken about Leo. 'He underestimated her.'

'He jolly well did!' said Lil with a grin. 'I bet he regretted that when she came at him with her cane.'

'I think perhaps he had originally hoped Leo would paint a straight copy of the dragon painting, which he could swap for the original. He was angry when he realised that Leo's painting was different, but then decided to swap them anyway – the false painting would confuse everyone, and help to throw them off the scent.'

'He put on a very good act,' said Billy, sounding rather admiring in spite of himself. 'He was so angry and upset – you'd never have guessed in a thousand years that he took the painting himself.'

'On the night he stole the painting, he must have crept in through the side door after the store had closed,' mused Sophie. 'He went straight to the Exhibition Hall. He probably thought everyone had already left. But then he saw you, Leo – and he was worried that you had seen him. He hid out of sight until you and Sid had gone, and then he let himself in with his keys, switched the paintings and left again, locking the door behind him.'

'And then he brought Randall in to threaten you – and frighten you into staying quiet about anything you might have seen,' finished Lil.

'Happily for everyone, Mr Randall is now safely in a police cell,' said Mr McDermott. 'Scotland Yard are well pleased to get their hands on him, I can tell you. He's someone they have been interested in for a long time. Not that he's saying a great deal at the moment, of course – especially not about who was behind this.'

'But we know who that was now,' said Sophie, sitting up a little in her chair. 'It was the Black Dragon – the Baron.'

They all looked at each other gravely. At first they had been astonished by what Sophie had told them, but when she had poured out her story, and they saw the cut on her face, it had been impossible not to believe her.

'Besides, I saw him too,' Lil had said with a shiver. 'When I found Sophie in the alley I glimpsed a man running away – and he looked awfully familiar. There's something about the Baron – he's just so jolly difficult to forget.'

For no one was that more true than for Sophie. In the days since their encounter, she had replayed what he had said to her in the alleyway time and time again. The others had listened, shocked, when she told them that the Baron had said he was responsible for the deaths of her parents. After she had finished relating her tale, she had looked at Mr McDermott.

'Ought I to believe what he said?' she asked him.

McDermott's expression was often unreadable, but just then, his face was full of sympathy. 'I'm sorry, Sophie – but I just don't know,' was all he said.

The Baron was back; they were all agreed on that. But he had a new name for himself now, and a new identity – as the mysterious Black Dragon.

'He was the one who wanted Lyle to steal the painting,' said Sophie now. 'I suppose he and Lyle must have orchestrated the theft of *The White Dragon* too.'

McDermott nodded. 'His Majesty's team will be turning their attention to *The White Dragon* next, to see if the painting also conceals a secret message,' he explained. 'We believe that Lyle was keeping both paintings in his safe, so that the Baron could examine them together before they were deposited safely in the bank vault out of harm's way. It is likely there may be some important connection between the two paintings.'

Joe leaned forwards. 'What I want to know is what that Wyvern House place has to do with all this. Surely the people there must know something about the Baron – and about this secret society too?'

'I'm afraid that when we visited, there was little to suggest it was more than a perfectly ordinary gentlemen's club – albeit one with a long history and many important members. Of course, Mr Lyle was one of them. They showed us the meeting room you saw through the window,

Miss Taylor, and explained that any of the members are at liberty to use these at any time for meetings with their guests. But there were no records of a special gathering on the night in question and the gentlemen we spoke to there told us they had never heard of the *Fraternitas Draconum*, or anyone who went by the name of the Black Dragon. They remembered Beaucastle and that scandal, but they all said that they hadn't seen him since. To be honest with you, they behaved as though they were rather more interested in their port and newspapers than in talking to us. Scotland Yard will continue to investigate of course – but for now at least, Wyvern House appears to be a dead end.'

'So that's it?' asked Billy. 'The Baron has gone – *again?* And we don't know anything more about the Dragon Brotherhood?'

McDermott shook his head. 'That's all I know,' he said. 'It may be that Worth knows more – but as you know, Scotland Yard don't always tell me everything.'

'Mr McDermott?' asked Lil tentatively. 'Can you tell us why you said you couldn't help us with this case? We wondered – well, we wondered if it might be to do with what Lyle said about your history. And PC Potts told Billy that you used to work for Scotland Yard.'

Mr McDermott looked thoughtful for a moment. Sophie found herself watching his familiar face, drawn and lined, his cheeks hollowed. It was a while before he spoke. 'Some years ago, I was a detective sergeant, working for Scotland Yard in the Criminal Investigations Department. I had a partner there named Simmonds – John Simmonds. We worked together, but he had also become a dear friend. Together we began to rise through the ranks, but then something changed, and Simmonds became . . . different.'

'Different?' repeated Lil, drawn in by the story.

'He became withdrawn, distant. We had been close – now he drifted away. He missed appointments, and I found myself working on our investigations alone, covering for his absence with our superiors. When I did see him, he seemed jumpy and anxious – but I didn't then understand why.'

'What had happened to him?' asked Billy.

'He was in grave financial difficulty. I didn't know it, for he kept his secret well. But as his situation worsened, he became more and more desperate – and soon he took the only route he could think of to get more money.'

'He turned crooked?' asked Joe.

McDermott nodded gravely. 'He began to sell information. Sometimes he would destroy evidence, or look the other way during an investigation – all for a price, of course. It took me a long while to realise what he was doing – and by then it was too late. His corruption had already been discovered. There was an inquiry, and a trial.

Lyle was one of the members of the jury.'

'Mr Lyle?' repeated Sophie in surprise. 'So that was how he knew you?'

McDermott nodded gravely. 'Simmonds was sent to prison of course, but he became very ill there. He died soon after. The last time I saw him, the man that I had known – my partner – was almost unrecognisable.'

There was a silence in the room, and then Lil asked softly: 'And what happened to you?'

McDermott shrugged. 'Even though I had never been party to Simmonds' corruption, as his partner my reputation was tarnished by what had happened. I couldn't stay at Scotland Yard, so I left and after a time I became a private detective. Some of my colleagues there continued to work with me – they gave me a second chance. Detective Worth was one of them. Most people now have forgotten all about John Simmonds, though every now and again someone dredges up that old story. It certainly proved very convenient for Mr Lyle on this occasion, providing him with the perfect excuse to keep me away from the investigation, and from Sinclair's.'

McDermott paused for a moment, and then looked at Sophie. 'There is probably one other thing that I ought to tell you about poor Simmonds,' he said quietly. 'I did not understand it fully at the time, but now my investigations have led me to believe that what happened to him originated with a man who also exploited and manipulated many others. A man who I never saw and whose real name I still don't know, but who I very much hope will one day be punished for that as well as for his crimes.'

Sophie stared at him. 'The Baron . . .' she whispered.

McDermott gave a brief nod.

The conversation turned away from Mr McDermott's past after that. None of them liked to dwell too much on the grave story that the private detective had told them. Soon, they were all chattering between themselves again: Leo fetched more tea; Lil was making Joe laugh with a funny story from the theatre; Billy was talking to Mr McDermott about Daisy the guard dog, who would stay at Sinclair's after having played such an important part in their adventure.

Meanwhile, Jack turned to Sophie. Their rescue of the stolen paintings had had some unexpected consequences for him. Since all of their names had been published in the newspapers, he had faced some extremely uncomfortable conversations with his mother and father about what on earth he had been doing in London when he was supposed to be studying at Oxford – never mind why he had been described as a first-year student at the Spencer Institute of Fine Art.

'I say, Sophie – I wondered if you'd like to come out

with me tonight,' he said now, in a low voice, pushing the dark hair back out of his eyes in his habitual gesture. 'I thought we could go to the Café Royal – just the two of us. It'd be good to talk to you about all this.'

Sophie looked up at him, rather flattered that he had chosen her to confide in. Jack was just as handsome and charming as ever, and she still felt a kind of electric tingle when he smiled at her. All the same, she wasn't altogether sure whether she wanted to spend an evening with him alone at the Café Royal – or not yet, at any rate. Besides, tonight was out of the question.

'I'm sorry but I can't,' she explained. 'Lil and I are going with Mr McDermott to see Mr Sinclair. He said he wants to meet with us, and Mr McDermott is being rather mysterious about it.'

'All right. I'll let you off this time. But remember, you did promise you'd go there with me, the day that we first met – remember?' He gave her a quick grin. 'I'll persuade you to come out with me one of these days, Sophie Taylor – just you see if I don't.'

Two hours later, Sophie and Lil were staring at each other over the table at Lyons Corner House on Piccadilly. Mr McDermott had left them alone to take in all that Mr Sinclair had said to them.

'There's only one thing I could think to do after a

conversation like that – and that's have tea and cake,' gasped Lil. 'Golly – I can hardly believe it – can you?'

Sophie shook her head in disbelief. It had been extraordinary enough just to find themselves sitting inside Mr Sinclair's elegant office.

'Well, you two are quite the toast of the town,' he had said, smiling at them broadly from where he sat behind his huge mahogany desk, exquisitely dressed as always, Lucky curled on a silk cushion at his side. 'I've got to say, I'm proud to have a couple of young ladies like you on my staff. But we've got to be smart about this. I can't have you spending your days selling hats and taking part in dress parades any longer, can I?'

'Can't you?' Lil managed to say.

Sinclair grinned. 'I've got a plan for you. It's something a little different, but as McDermott here knows, I rather like to do things differently. What I'm envisioning is this – a detective agency, right here at Sinclair's department store.'

'A detective agency?' repeated Sophie in astonishment.

'Right. We've got everything else after all – the best hairdresser, the finest beautician, a fellow who can get you tickets to any show in town – why not the most fashionable detective agency too? I've got it all planned out. Your own office on the first floor – I'll have Claudine kit it out. And you two will be my detectives.'

'Us?' asked Lil, her eyes round.

'Oh I know you've got your theatre commitments, Miss Rose, but don't worry. We can work around that. And McDermott here will be on hand to help oversee things. Let's see now – we'll need a name. Something snappy. *The Young Ladies' Detective Agency?* No that's a little dry. I've got it – *Taylor & Rose*. It's perfect – just like the two of you.'

Sitting at the tea table in Lyons now, Sophie realised that her dream of just a few short weeks ago had become a reality. She would not have to go back to selling hats now. Instead, she would be doing what she loved best – solving mysteries. At last she would have the chance to really use her brain. Better still, she would have Lil at her side, and she felt quite certain that Billy and Joe – not to mention all of their other friends – would be there with them to help too.

Even as they sat there, one of the Sinclair's delivery boys came racing into the tea shop clutching a yellow envelope. 'Mr Sinclair's compliments, miss,' he said, holding it out to them. 'He said I was to bring this to you. He's had them make up the first advertisement for the new detective agency. It's going out in tomorrow morning's paper.'

The girls tore the envelope open eagerly, as the boy touched his cap and darted away again.

Sophie dropped the advertisement on the table. 'But –
this makes us sound ridiculous!' she exclaimed. 'Like we're
just there to fix people's love affairs!' She looked from Lil
to the newspaper advertisement and back to Lil again. 'Mr
Sinclair doesn't take us seriously at all, does he?' she said,

as realisation slowly dawned. 'This is just another one of his clever publicity stunts. He isn't really expecting us to be proper detectives. He just wants us to – to look decorative, and to be a *curiosity*. The young lady detectives – just another novelty to bring people into the store.'

Lil picked up the advertisement, and then set it on one side. 'Well maybe that's what he's expecting – but that doesn't mean that's what we have to *do*,' she said in a matter-of-fact voice.

Sophie frowned, not really understanding, but Lil went on: 'Look, Mr Sinclair is giving us an opportunity to do what we really want to do – to solve mysteries. To help people, just like we helped Leo. All right, it might be dressed up with this silliness – but it doesn't make it any less real, does it?' She paused. 'It's our own detective agency, Sophie. It's about the two of us – *Taylor & Rose*. We don't have to let Mr Sinclair – or anyone else for that matter – decide how we're going to do it. Or who we're going to be.'

Sophie stared at her for a long moment. Lil was exactly right, she realised. They didn't have to let anyone else make decisions for them any longer. With the two of them together at the helm, they could make their detective agency whatever they wanted it to be.

She put up a hand to her face and felt for the cut where she had fallen in the alleyway. What was more, she knew that now, she would be able to set out on the trail of the

Baron – and find out the truth about what had happened to her parents. This time, she was quite determined that he would not get away. She smiled slowly at her friend across the tea table. 'All right,' she said. 'So where do we begin?'

AUTHOR'S NOTE

The Spencer Institute in this story is partly inspired by one of London's most famous art schools, the Slade School of Fine Art which is part of University College London. In the years before the First World War, many celebrated artists studied there, including Stanley Spencer, Paul Nash, Mark Gertler, Dora Carrington and Richard Nevinson. Although all the characters in this story are fictional, Professor Jarvis in particular owes a small debt to the renowned Slade professor Henry Tonks.

The Café Royal was a real-life favourite haunt of the Slade students, and many others from London's artistic communities during the Edwardian era. In the late 19th and early 20th century, its customers included the likes of Oscar Wilde, Arthur Conan Doyle, Virginia Woolf, Augustus John and many more. Although it is very different from its Edwardian incarnation, you can still find the Café Royal on Regent Street in London today.

ACKNOWLEDGEMENTS

Thank you to all at Egmont UK, most especially wonderful editor Ali Dougal, Art Director Benjamin Hughes, and everyone who has been part of Team Painted Dragon. Huge thanks to Karl James Mountford for his absolutely magnificent illustrations and cover art.

Very big thanks, as always, to my brilliant agent and friend Louise Lamont.

Special thanks to Rosi Crawley, Ben O'Donnell and Hannah Davies for letting me borrow their names for this book. (Ben, I know that you'll appreciate that it's the one with the dragon in the title.)

Thank you to all the colleagues and friends who helped keep me sane when I was writing this - most especially Claire Shanahan, Nina Douglas, Katie Webber, the YALC Working Group, and of course the Down the Rabbit Hole gang. Particular thanks to my mum and dad for all of their support and to Duncan for ideas, Bloomsbury walks and restorative dinners.

There are lots of other things that helped enable this book to be written, including: wanderings in the National Gallery and the British Museum; *The Quantocks Quartet* by

Ruth Elwin Harris (now sadly out of print); the Gilmore Girls episode 'The Festival of Living Art'; listening to author Leigh Bardugo talking about writing a heist; and the film *Titanic*, which apparently looms larger in my subconscious mind than I had realised. Special thanks must also go to Ophelia in the Isle of Man who asked 'when will Sophie and Lil meet the Suffragettes?' and all the children who told me that the cover of Book 3 should definitely be green.

Biggest thanks go to all the booksellers, librarians, teachers, bloggers and readers who have been so enthusiastic about Sophie and Lil and their adventures.

The Sinclair's Mysteries

THE MIDNIGHT PEACOCK

Sophie and Lil will return in their next thrilling adventure

Coming October 2017

Christmas has come to Sinclair's and our heroines are spending the holidays at snowy Winter Hall. But it turns out that this is no ordinary country house party...

As **SINISTER SECRETS** come to light, our **INTREPID HEROINES** find themselves faced with a more **BAFFLING MYSTERY** than ever before!

With the help of their friends, can they uncover the truth in time to foil a truly **DIABOLICAL PLOT**? Or will Mr Sinclair's New Year's Eve Ball spell **DISASTER** for the dauntless young detectives?

www.egmont.co.uk

EGMONT

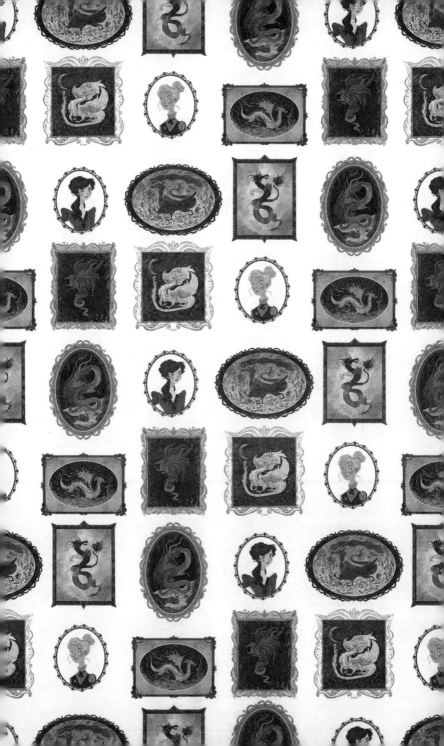

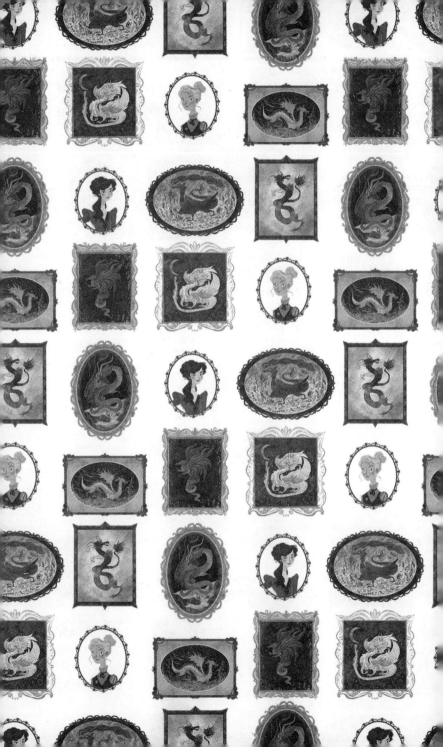